Down Red Creek

Book One of the Red Creek Series

Rachael Llewellyn

An Imprint of Sulis International Press
Los Angeles | London

Library of Congress Control Number: 2019906298
ISBN (print): 978-1-946849-50-2
ISBN (eBook): ISBN: 978-1-946849-51-9

Published by Riversong Books
An Imprint of Sulis International
Los Angeles | London

www.sulisinternational.com

Contents

For Mum

Please don't read too much into it that I've dedicated this book to you

PROLOGUE

Sylvia didn't have many positive memories of school. As far as the day to day was concerned, she could recall shuffling from desk to desk, classroom to classroom, stuffed into cramped corridors like sardines, crumpled notebooks, and cigarettes behind the bike sheds. Her classmates were the same variant of a faceless boy or girl. Her teachers wavered uncertainly through her memory.

She did recall one music teacher, a recent divorcee who smoked in class and wore brightly-coloured shawls, going on a rant about "the beauty and power within the female form and the majesty it contained", to her bored eighth-grade class.

"Women are the closest thing to God", she had said. "Their bodies have the power to hold and create life. What could be more godlike than that?"

Sylvia remembered, at fourteen, thinking that this was *incredibly* pretentious, but probably a very important thing to believe if you were, you know, recently divorced, lonely with grown-up children who never called home, whose only solace was in shawls and making profound Berkeley-grown declarations to a horde of apathetic teenagers.

However, fifteen years later, she couldn't help but think about that as she watched her daughter play. Fiona – she had called her Fiona after her grandmother – was eighteen months old. She was sat in front of her on the lawn, big brown eyes deep in concentration as she fumbled around with her colourful shapes.

I made you, Sylvia thought. I made you practically alone, and here you are. I can't believe someone like me managed to make someone like you.

Apparently sensing her mother's gaze, Fiona looked up at her and shrieked with delight, waving the blue triangle at her with a pudgy brown arm. Sylvia smiled and bent down to take the blue triangle from her.

"What are we making, Fiona?"

Another shriek. She was drooling over her pretty pink dress, delighted and happy. She wriggled away from Sylvia's cloth when she went to wipe her chin. Laughing and batting her hands at the shapes sending them tumbling down, thrilled at the destruction in her wake.

"I see we are making a mess."

Baby nonsense and then her daughter stuffed a round fist into her own smiling mouth, rattling it against her teething gums. Resisting as much as she could when Sylvia went to remove it. Tears and then, as she held her in her arms, soft breathing and silence. Her daughter was asleep and her lawn covered in brightly coloured triangles, circles, and squares.

I learn something new about you every day, Sylvia thought, glancing down at her fuzzy sprouting head of hair and sulky sleeping face. You like to sleep, you like to put everything in your mouth, and you like making a mess.

Fiona didn't stir. She stayed sleeping, still and trusting in her arms.

It was so strange – despite her fears, despite her initial concerns – the odd moments waking up pregnant and panicked in the night, despite all of those little doubts that what she was doing wasn't a good idea; Sylvia found her relationship with her daughter was easy. She actually understood herself in relation to Fiona much easier than she had for any of the other people in her life. There were no mind games, no little non-verbal signals she didn't understand, no probing questions or nosy stares.

Fiona was a baby, and she needed her for food, warmth, shelter, protection. In fact, she needed Sylvia for just about everything. She'd never manage on her own. She depended on her. She had to trust her to do those things.

So, if, for example, Sylvia was going to pour rat poison into the gunky baby food that smelled so bad, Fiona would not think twice about eating it. Sylvia could just pile it onto a spoon, make aeroplane noises, and that would be that.

Fiona would eat it and just die.

And if, maybe, Sylvia got sick and tired of her incessant crying, and maybe, smashed her tiny head against a wall. Fiona wouldn't be able to stop her.

She would just die.

Or if one morning she couldn't be bothered, Fiona would just stay in her cot and wait. And say Sylvia didn't fancy dealing with her that day, say she wanted to go to the shops without the pram, without the baby, without the judgmental stares and the baby changing rooms and the extra nappies – Fiona would just stay in her cot and cry and starve. Maybe Sylvia wouldn't bother going in her room for a while.

Fiona would die.

Her hand faltered as she stroked her daughter's fuzzy head of hair. Sylvia shivered and held her a little tighter.

No, she would not let any of that happen. She kissed her hair and tried to stop herself from shaking.

Things will be different now. They can't be like they were before. They have to be different. I have an example to set for her now.

Fiona opened her eyes and started to wail loudly. Sylvia rocked her gently, shushing her softly and humming some tune she had heard at the Mommy and Baby class she had been badgered along to. Fiona cried louder, twisting her tiny body in discomfort.

"It's alright," Sylvia said. "Mommy's here. I wouldn't let anything happen to you. Just you wait and see.

CHAPTER ONE

Beth complains that her mother is embarrassing. She tells me all about the times her mom has presented friends and family members with photos of her with her underwear on her head or wearing her spaghetti dinner. Beth goes bright red when her mom joins us in the living room, offering snacks. She tries to make jokes about music and pronounces all the names wrong. She asks us 'what's happening in our lives' and winks when she asks about boys.

It embarrassed all of us, so we never give Beth a lot of grief for it.

Our group doesn't share these kinds of things often. Talking about the past is stupid. Whinging about your parents is a waste of time. However, when the two of us were alone, Beth always liked to tell me these things. I'd listen and laugh along with her.

"You're so lucky, Fiona," Beth always said at the end of her rant. "I bet your Mom never does anything embarrassing like that."

On this matter, Beth is one hundred percent correct. My friends have never been issued photographs of me drenched in spaghetti or toddling around on feeble baby legs, naked and drooling up at the camera. I know my mother has photos, but she keeps them to herself. I have never seen them. My image of infancy is for her eyes alone. I'm fine with that.

My mother would never come downstairs and start chatting with my friends about their lives. She would never try to joke about music or TV or join in like she was one of the gang. My mother can't even remember my friends' names. She couldn't tell you the boy/girl ratio in our group, she's never gotten ratty about me having boys over. She has absolutely no interest in things that she perceives as tedious. Our insipid chatter bores her, and she smiles a cold, crocodile smile when my friends talk to her. They have no idea that she is repulsed by

4

them. Beth isn't the only one to comment on how down to earth she is, how cool she seems like a mom.

I never tell them that we don't get along.

Don't get me wrong, I'm glad she's not fussy or demanding or like Beth or Matt or Sukhy's mothers. But that doesn't mean I like things the way they are.

Oh no.

They have no idea what she's like.

. . . .

There's no reason really to stay out late, but we'd do it anyway. It's all about pointless rebellion right now. So, we stay out all night. We smoke and drink, we talk shit about the people we know. Then, when the sun begins to rise, we just go home.

It is four forty-nine in the morning. I watch Beth sneak into her house from my front porch. She scrambles up a tree and into her bedroom window like an incredibly wobbly ninja. I watch her stumble around her room, edging towards the bed, trying not to make a sound.

Her parents are strict. Her father is on the town council. Her mom has a false and insipid smile. They have complained to my mother that I am a bad influence on their daughter. Beth lives in constant fear of disappointing them. I have no such restrictions. I can go back into my house without disturbance, walk right through the front door without the fear of parental judgment.

The house is cold and quiet. Mother isn't home, her shoes are missing. I walk upstairs, change, and go to sleep, all without having to explain where I have been.

. . . .

Close my eyes, open them up, and it's seven forty-six. Mother is home now. She puts a cup of coffee at my bedside and reminds me that I have school. From my window as I dress, I spot Beth's mother coming into her room to switch off the alarm that Beth was sleeping through. She's about to notice the smell of smoke and Beth awaken to a war zone of the domestic kind.

I turn up the radio and wait for her to bang on the floor with the broom. Glancing out the window, I can see Beth and her pinch-faced mother screaming at each other to the beat of my music. Mrs Green seems to have found Beth's cigarettes. Beth is crying.

My mother bangs on the floor again.

As I glance down, I notice that guy again. He's always running laps around here. I see him staring up at the house. Right now, he's taking a breather outside Beth's. I see him looking and smile and wave. He pretends that he hasn't seen me, or maybe I'm just not on his radar, and he resumes his running.

Look at him, still pretending that he's not a cop.

The coffee goes cold as I get ready, and I leave the cup upstairs.

She is on her laptop, half paying attention, ignoring her breakfast of a piece of fruit. She nods at me as I enter the room, and I nod back. I stub my toe on her stupid cello case that she's left against the wall by the fridge. She makes no word of apology or attempts to have a go at me for swearing. I give it a kick for good measure, which she also doesn't deign to register. So, I eat cereal in front of the TV and turned up the volume to irritate her.

"Have you recently gone deaf, Fiona?"

Her parenting style is mostly about shaming and sarcasm. It used to be successful, but these days, I tend to ignore her.

She disappears downstairs to the basement before I'm finished eating.

Good.

I leave the bowl and spoon on the coffee table for her to pick up and slam the front door behind me.

I know Beth won't be ready yet. Beth will probably be getting the lecture of the century right now. Her parents never let things go. I suppose they do it out of love, or at least that is always what they tell her.

To be honest, I don't think I'd ever want to be loved that much.

I sit down on the porch and light a cigarette while I wait for him to come around the corner again, still on his pretend jog round and round the block. The policeman incognito. Hovering outside the garden gates. I've seen him a few times before. He kind of stood out.

Tall with good posture and built—like really built. He wears glasses and a baseball cap that help conceal his face, a bit. The first time I saw him, I remember thinking, yeah, ten years ago, he'd be the type that the girls in my class go gaga for.

He's always here. Sometimes in his car, just opposite our house, sometimes walking around on his phone. Always pretending that he's not with the police, though.

"What are you doing outside my house?"

He looked startled, moving away from the gate.

"Oh, is this your house?"

"Yes."

He smiled at me.

"I'm sorry, I didn't mean to intrude. I was just admiring the building."

"Hmm, right."

"Do you live with your parents?"

"What kind of question is that?"

He laughed. "Right, ok, smart girl. It is always best to never answer these kinds of questions."

"That's what they teach us in school." I folded my arms. "I've seen you hanging around here a lot. Are you a stalker? A pervert for houses?"

"No, no, nothing like that. Do those kinds of people even exist?"

"Yeah, I saw a documentary about it. I'd recommend it, but I can't remember what it was called."

"I'm sure I'll be fine without seeing it," he said.

"So, I should be going, this is my house, after all."

"Of course. You have a nice day now." He steps aside, letting me through the gate. "There's just...one thing?"

I turned to face him.

"Yeah?"

"I'm actually a detective." The badge in his jacket came out. I've never seen a real police badge before. And there was his name, Detective Peter Brankowski. "You can call me Pete. I'm kind of working on a case here."

"A case that involves my house directly?"

"Well, not exactly. I'm in the area looking for leads."

"And you want me to do what exactly?"

He has kind eyes, that's the most striking feature, even despite the hench-ness and the Clark Kent glasses and his obvious cop-ness. And I wonder how someone like that ended up in the police. How long has he been doing the job? Must be awhile to be a detective, but not long enough to lose that kind, non-threatening stare.

"This is my card, it has my contact number on it. If you see any-thing weird, or you need to talk to someone about anything. Please call, I'll be available any time."

The card smells like cigarettes and has sharp edges. His name spelled out in clean navy-blue font. I examine it and then slide it into my coat pocket.

"Thanks," I say, offering my hand. "I'm Fiona by the way. Fiona Taylor."

If my surname meant anything to him, he didn't show it. And I watched him walk to his car from the front gates.

Beth appeared in his place, red-eyed and pale. Hungover, unhappy and shaken up from all the yelling. I guess nobody likes to wake up to an attack.

"Who was that guy?" she asked. She wants to pretend that she hasn't been crying.

"Some guy asking for directions, I don't know."

"Oh, cool, that's weird."

"Not especially. How are you feeling?"

"Shitty." She brushed back her hair. "I'll actually be pleased to go to school."

I notice Beth's pinch-faced mother staring at me through the win-dow and offer her a patronising smile. Yes, I do see you, bitch.

My mother used to drive me to school when I was very little. It was back when she had her crappy mini-van. My elementary school was only a few blocks away, so the drive took all of ten minutes even in traffic, but she always drove me anyway. It was part of our rou-tine. I remember sitting in the front seat and having her bat my hand away when I tried to switch on the radio. She still drives in silence, she has always hated music. It's why I have always thought the cello case to be an incredibly poor choice for her.

She stopped driving me to school when I was seven. I told her that I wanted to walk to school with Beth, whose parents make her walk even in thick snow. To 'build character' apparently. An expression that always jumps out to you when adults are trying to make you do something bullshit or unfair.

I remember practicing the right way to tell her that I didn't want her to drive me anymore. I was so nervous she'd take it badly. But when I told her, she just sort of shrugged and said 'Yeah, that's fine'. I mean, it can't have offended her. It wasn't like we talked on those rides or bonded or anything. It was just routine.

I know when she's going through the motions with me.

Beth mumbles on the walk to school, mostly about how much trouble she is going home to. Her parents have always been strict parents. I've seen her going home with her report card in tears over a B minus. Grades and clubs are what matters to her folks, not the fact that they are terrifying their daughter to the point of a nervous breakdown every single time we have a pop quiz.

Her mumbling isn't exactly something that enhances our conversation, so I just let her go on, adding the occasional sympathetic nod. Sometimes I say, 'Oh seriously? Your mom is such a bitch', and I think that helps. Usually, I leave this kind of thing to Sukhy.

Sukhy Khan, my best friend since pre-school. I think we bonded over being the only non-white kids in the area at the time. Which is important, you know, when you're like five and you catch an old lady openly just staring at you while you're trying to get some mashed potatoes for lunch. But that's not the only reason why we're friends. I honestly don't know what I'd do without her. She keeps me here, stable, safe, present. I'd be all kinds of screwed if her folks ever made good on that threat to move her to the more expensive...better school on the other side of town.

"How's the head?" Sukhy asked as she spotted us outside the school gates

"Fine."

"Lousy," Beth mumbled.

"But you did wake up to World War III, so that can't have helped," I add, scooping an arm around her shoulders. "Beth's mom was so loud I could hear her across the street."

"Oh, stop it, Fiona!" Beth groaned, pulling away, "I feel bad enough about it!"

She stomps off ahead, leaving the two of us smirking.

"Don't wind her up," she whispers, grinning.

"Hey, hey, hey, I'm not doing anything."

Our high school used to be an old hospital from the civil war, so essentially it looks a lot grander than it is. They built an extension for a computer lab a few years ago, the brickwork clashes horribly with the old regimented style and it sort of lurches towards the school gates unceremoniously. I couldn't have an uglier place to spend the next four years.

They made a huge fuss when we started, going over and over how difficult we'd find navigating the maze-like corridors, how we shouldn't be scared of asking the quite frankly sociopathic seniors for directions. I mean, do teachers live in the real world? Have they met their students? I mean, we have a limited number of classes, once you know the way to those, that's it, no need for directions, no need for unnecessary conversation. We are three months into our freshman year, and I'm not overly impressed with the concept of the four-year wait for college credit and the right to leave town.

I spot Matt, hiding out, checking through a dog-eared novel that I suspect just took a little trash break. He smiles when he sees us, wiping the book on his jacket one last time for good measure before coming over.

"Good morning, ladies."

"No, Matt, this morning is just the worst, you won't believe my mother..." Beth grumbles, brushing past him and tugging him along by the sleeve. He shoots me a bemused look before trudging along after her.

It was through Sukhy we met Matt, his mom works in the same office as Sukhy's. He's quiet and shy and clever and too good for this place. Ever since elementary school he's been branded as 'the wrong sort'. I do my best to help him, but since high school, that has gotten harder. Sure, in elementary school, me and Suhky could yank ponytails or cover people in paste. But now, in high school, I weight 110 lbs. What damage could I do against four football player victims of toxic masculinity? More than Beth, whose major and only concern is her mean mother and not the bruise on Matt's wrist that he thinks he's covered properly.

"Has anyone seen Jase this morning?" Sukhy asks as we walk through the rickety doors near homeroom.

"Oh, he got in trouble earlier. He's with Mr Greenberg," Matt said.

"Shit, what for?"

"He put Riley Sanders in the trash-can out there," he mumbled.

We met Jason Danvers in First Grade. His family lives on the outskirts of town, he has three brothers, and his dad sells crappy used cars to broke teens and loser adults. Beth wasn't allowed to play with Jason when we were little, her mother found out which part of town he lived at and actually forced Beth to un-invite him from her sixth birthday party.

I mean, yes, he did used to bite people for no reason when we were in the first grade. In fact, he originally joined our group as a punishment. He'd bitten Matt on the hand, and our teacher made him sit with us to finish some dumb art project as a way of saying sorry. After that, we just kind of let him stick with us.

I know that's how Sukhy likes it anyway.

The five of us have always been together ever since we were little, despite the differing hobbies, like Sukhy having to play two different instruments and head the debate team, we keep together. We cheer Sukhy on at nationals, we clap politely at her piano recitals, we watch Matt in plays even though there is this one girl who always gets to sing who sounds like she's practically on the verge of climaxing? Mostly, we head off into the woods late at night, light up a campfire, drink and talk shit until real late. This late-night tradition of ours has become ever so more essential ever since she joined our happy troop.

"Guys! Hellooooo!"

That was Lisa Jones, she's Beth's cousin from England. And I swear to God, she didn't sound like she'd swanned in off the set of Downton fucking Abbey when she first moved here. The elevated accent is a new feature.

"Oh, Lisa, hey," Sukhy says.

"I called your house last night," she said, "Couldn't get through to any of you."

"Why not just text us?" I can hear the irritation in my voice and then Sukhy elbows me very slightly in the ribs. I guess she has a point, I know full well there's barely any signal in our camping spot.

"Erm, I had better things to do," Lisa said, shaking her head. "I wanted to know if Sukhy wanted to see a movie this weekend." She'd made a massive thing recently of wanting to be Sukhy's best friend. She keeps pairing off with her in class and showing up at her house uninvited.

"Oh yeah, cool, when would suit you?" Sukhy said.

"Maybe on Thursday? They have a special offer on."

"That could be good, yeah, what would you like to see?"

"Pitch Perfect is out."

"Are we not invited?" Jason said, draping a heavy arm over Sukhy's shoulder. "I, for one, am a massive Pitch Perfect fan."

"Oh, be serious," Lisa said. "I was thinking this would be more of a girl's thing. But like, I know my cousin is grounded at the moment, and Fiona hates musicals and, although I'm sure Matt would love to come."

Matt frowned and raised his eyebrows.

"I just thought this would be the best way not to exclude you," she finishes, raising her eyebrows and smiling at him. "Get it?"

Jason gasps, "Fiona, I didn't know you hated musicals."

"You know," I say, grinning, "I'm not sure I do."

"And like I said, I love Pitch Perfect, big fan of Anna Kendrick. I'd love to check it out. And I guess if I'm going, it would be a shame to leave Matt out, right?"

Lisa frowns. "Beth's still grounded."

"And yet, we live in America, it's a free country. I'm sure Mr and Mrs Green wouldn't deprive her of some time with her dear cousin all the way from sunny old England," Jason said, beaming at her. "That settles it, this Thursday, guys."

Lisa scowls and links arms with Beth as they make their way through the crowded corridor to homeroom. Sukhy smiles and elbows Jason playfully

"So since when are you such a big Pitch Perfect fan?" she whispers.

"Never seen it," he said. "But I can't let you date Lisa, pal."

"Oh, stop it."

Matt groans and whispers to me, "But, Fiona, I genuinely don't like those movies!"

. . . .

The school day never changes. Three weeks into high school, and I am pretty sure I have the basics down. We go to homeroom; our teacher calls our names, and we mostly answer. We head off to first period English. On the way, Dave MacDonald and Trevor Cormac try to bash into Matt. He has started walking the long way around, which takes longer and makes him late to class. Naturally, the rest of us have joined him in this, all except for Lisa, who tries to talk to Heather Drake and Carmen Sallenger on the way to English. She is desperate to get in with them, and I'd rather be late for class to get that smell on me.

English is bland. I think the only person more bored by Great Expectations is our over-worked, miserable looking teacher, Miss Miller. You can tell when she's had a date—she is very much overly enthused—and you can tell when the date's gone bad—she barely gets out of her chair, has red-rimmed eyes and keeps her voice scarcely above a whisper.

If she was dressed a bit more old-timey instead of you know, I'm thirty-four, but I still wear teenage Miller's wardrobe—she would be a dead ringer for Miss Havisham.

I don't really have anyone to share this with. Beth is sat next to me, aggressively tearing through her copy of the book. Last year she couldn't pick her grades up past a C for English, so she got moved into class with Jason and I.

Unlike our friends who are either really good or really bad at school, the two of us are consistent middle achievers. We never fail, but we never excel. His dad doesn't care, and my mother's attitude on the matter is pretty much impassive. So, aside from homeroom and lunch, I spend the whole day with Jason as we have every class together. The most grief I ever get in class is people saying that me and Jason are screwing each other.

That's the world we live in, where a guy and a girl can't hang out without people talking like that.

"Hey, Beth, what's happening with our boy Pip?" Jason whispers from the seat behind us.

"Do your own work," she grumbles. "I'm trying to concentrate."

"Is he getting told off by that cow again?"

"That was just in the movie," she hisses. "Jason, really, leave me alone."

He chuckles and leans forward to whisper to me, "What's up her butt?"

When Beth spins around and knocks his copy of Great Expectations onto the floor, it lands with a sizable thump. Our sleepy Monday morning class all jump up awake, eyes on the two of them.

"Beth Green, what is this commotion?" Miss Miller said in a somewhat pitchy whisper.

"She's crazy, M'am," Jason said, laughing. "She's messing with my learning materials."

"He's being stupid," Beth protests.

The class laugh louder as Jason shrugs.

"Please, can you all just be quiet?" Miss Miller says, rubbing her head in irritation. "I am really not in the mood this morning for your childish antics, Mr Danvers."

"She's assaulting my textbooks," he said. "I'm the victim."

The class burst out laughing again.

"Mr. Danvers, I am not in the mood for any idiocy today!"

"No need to be nasty," Jason said, "I didn't dump you."

The class is laughing hysterically now. I'm not in the mood to participate, so I start to think of ways I can get out of the house later. If I get home before seven, I get to see the hot policeman doing his laps again. But then I'll be in for the night. On nights like that, it feels like a basement with my room on top. I can't leave my room, open the door and the hallway won't be there. It'll just be another door, the red door that leads right down to the basement.

"Fiona! Oh, my God!"

I look up, over the house, Beth is nudging me and laughing, her face red from amusement. I glance around, startled and notice Miss Miller frantically trying to fix her skirt which has ripped at the seam, exposing her well-worn underpants. It appears she angrily got up from her desk to yell at Jason and her skirt snagged on a loose nail on her desk and tore right in front of everyone.

I start laughing with the others. It seems to be the easiest thing, to laugh along with the others while our teacher tries to compose herself and adjust her damaged clothing.

Beth shakes her head in disbelief.

"Delayed reaction, much?"

"I didn't see."

"Erm, you were looking right at her."

The shame starts to pool in my stomach then. I try to calm down before it goes to my face. I hate being caught out, it makes me feel stupid for laughing, like a big faker. How dare she call me out on that? She just thinks about herself. She doesn't know how hard it is to act like everyone else all the time. She doesn't fucking know anything.

"I was kind of zoned out."

I don't need to explain myself to you!

"So spacey," she says and laughs, shaking her head. "Oh my God, I wish I'd had a camera!"

"I know, right? Oh God, did you see her hairy legs?"

I fucking hate Beth sometimes.

· · · ·

The school day pushes on like that. Miss Miller's fashion accident is a hot topic. I get to listen to the same story over and over and over again. Beth doesn't get distracted from my lack of reaction when it first happened—even though I was 'looking right at her'!! Until I get annoyed and remind her subtly of her furious pinch-faced mother and that soon shuts her up.

At lunch, we all like to sit in the courtyard. None of us get lunch at the cafeteria except Lisa, who is desperate to assimilate us into that. The football team eats in the cafeteria, so that counts us out. We meet as a group under the big clock that doesn't actually work and go and sit under the dead oak tree in the far corner.

It's out of sight and nice and private. It can be a good place to smoke, depending on who's on lunch duty. Today it's Miss Jefferson, so that's definitely out. She teaches PE and is sort of angry beyond all reason. So, smoking benefits aside, this also means no trouble from the football team.

This means Matt can enjoy his lunch in peace.

"So what happened this morning?" Sukhy asks.

"Riley Sanders was up to the same shit," Jason says. "He dumped Matt's stuff in the bin, so I grabbed his legs and kind of tipped him forwards."

Matt chuckles. "He screamed. Had no idea you were behind him."

"And he was alone?" I ask.

"No, no, three of his meathead friends tackled me, and then Mr. Davis intervened and took us all to see the Principal."

"You need to cut this shit out," Sukhy says, "You can't keep getting in trouble."

Jason shrugs his shoulders and leans back. "I gotta have Matt's back. We all look out for each other."

"To be fair, I'd have done the same if I could lift Riley Sanders," I add.

"He thought it was me grabbing his legs," Matt said.

"Oh, shit, yeah!" Jason gasps, laughing, "He was like, don't grab my ass, right before he ended up face-first in garbage."

"Priorities much?" Beth said, smirking.

I wish it could be like this all the time. Just the five of us. I wish we could just live in the woods, away from prying eyes and questions and the basement. I hate that so much stuff always gets in the way. School, parents, stupid Lisa, and all the others. They are all just distractions from the happy times.

· · · ·

Beth has a yearbook committee after school. Jason has to go and work for his dad, and we fortunately managed to ditch Lisa before she clocked that we were all leaving together. My house feels less like my room and a basement when I have the others with me.

Matt and Sukhy hanging out on the sofa, while I make tea and find some snacks from the cupboard, is the best way to finish a shitty Monday.

"Fiona, you want to watch a movie?"

"Yeah, let's watch something totally shit."

Sukhy is scrolling through the channels. Matt is humming loudly and tunelessly. I think it's some original piece from one of those awful plays he's in. Thankfully this one isn't sung by the breathy orgasm princess.

"We could watch something Christmas-ish, something super cheesy? I know it's early, but…"

"No, we are too early," I say. "But maybe that ball-park."

"Or you know, we could watch something good?" Matt suggested, before all three of us laughed. "Nah, didn't think so."

And like always, just when I'm about to completely relax, there are footsteps from downstairs, a creek of the steps and the basement door opens. Mother comes out, blank-faced.

"Fiona, I didn't realise we had company."

"Not sure how, we aren't exactly being quiet," I say.

Sukhy shushes me and smiles. "Nice to see you, Ms Taylor. Fiona said it was cool for us to crash here?"

"Of course." She never uses names, she honestly doesn't know them even though she's met Sukhy and Matt a hundred times before. "Movie night, is it?" She smiles that unsettling crocodile smile of hers, and I just want her to fucking leave.

"Yeah, we're finding something bad to watch."

"Or good," Matt says. "I'm trying to steer them towards good."

"Well, good luck with that," she says. "Fiona, I'll be back late."

"Yeah, I figured. Bye."

She scoops up her stupid cello case with her and heads out the front door. It's empty, so it's not a struggle. I watch her leave while Sukhy and Matt argue over the movie. She's loading it into her car, and Mr. Not-A-Cop is jogging past. He looks at her, but she doesn't notice. I wonder how many laps he's done to try to get a glimpse of her today.

I should be jealous.

I think about waiting for her to drive away and running out after him, grabbing at his strong arms and saying 'Help me, help me, help me' over and over until he takes me away from here for good.

I think about finding the spare house keys and sticking them in all the doors and keeping her locked outside when she tries to come back tonight.

Also, I think about leaving Sukhy and Matt in the living room, putting on my sneakers and walking out of this house and just never, ever coming back.

Chapter Two

Newspaper article reporting the missing person's case of A.H.

MISSING GIRL

Police are requesting any persons who may have information on the recent disappearance of Miss Abigail Henderson, age 17. Abigail was last seen leaving her part-time job at Philbert's Record Store on Blue Street on Monday 31st October at 6.45 PM. Abigail is pale skinned with blonde hair and brown eyes, at approximately 5'5. She is a senior at Franberg High School and is described by her friends and teachers as kind and fun-loving. Mr. and Mrs. Henderson have offered a reward for anyone who can provide information to bring their daughter home.

Transcript of public plea from Mr. and Mrs. Henderson

"Our daughter is a kind person, she's (sob) sweet and t-trusting. To the person who is holding our Abbie, please, talk to her, you'll see that for yourself. She wouldn't hurt anyone. We just want her to come home. Please, you have the power to do that. Please bring our baby home. Please. We will do our best to offer you all the help we can, we just want our Abbie back."

Transcript of news broadcast reporting on the A.H case

"And the search goes on for missing teen, Abigail Henderson, age 17, who was last seen leaving her part-time job on Monday 31st October. Police have ruled out kidnapping as a motive and it was announced this morning that they believe they are searching for a body."

Newspaper article, Franberg Gazette

HORROR AT READ CREEK

Late last night officers and volunteers searching for the body of young Abigail Henderson, missing since 31st October, came across a shocking and vile display at Read Creek in the Black-wood Forest. Detective Phillip Morgan had suggested to the press that the police had ruled out the possibility of the teen being found alive. The creek was being searched for a body throughout the evening and into the late hours of last night. There was an accident where a young volunteer, later identified as Gretchen Reinstein, 22, damaged a rock formation which dislodged an enormous number of body parts that floated to the surface of the water.

Police have confirmed that these are the remains of several different people. However, the young victim, Abigail Henderson was identified from the distinctive emerald ring her parents bought her for her sixteenth birthday. Mr. and Mrs. Henderson could not be reached for comment.

Due to the heavily-decomposed nature of the body parts due to water damage, the police have not yet been able to identify the victims. Detective Morgan could not be reached for comment; however, the police have made it clear that this appears to be the work of a serial killer.

Transcript of news broadcast reporting on Red Creek murders

"Police are still identifying all of the victims round at Read Creek, now becoming known as 'Red Creek' due to the gruesome nature of the killings. We are asking anyone to come forward who may have had a missing relative or friend over the last several years."

Interview with coroner Dr Michelle Anderson

"To speak perfectly frankly, I've not seen anything like this. This is a nice town. The worst I see is…well, it just doesn't compare. The bodies parts were swollen and aged from water damage. Some bones were included, these bodies were decomposing quick-ly. There were black victims, white victims. It's hard to tell their ages to begin with, I identified one very elderly man. I found the bones of a small child, just the jaw, which seems to be from a long *time ago. I just can't... I'm sorry. This has been hard...(pauses) It appears that the bodies were cut with a very sharp and long object, the bodies were then cut into small pieces, completely deformed. And with all the damage, it's hard to tell what belongs to whom. I can't believe someone could do damage like this on this kind of scale. I just... I'm sorry. I need some air."*

Red Creek Memorial Service
Sunday 3rd April 1985

We stand together today to commemorate those who lost their lives in the Red Creek Murders. You are loved and you are remembered, always.

Abigail Henderson, age 17
Thomas Anderson, age 45
Richard Edwards, age 14
Cassandra 'Cassie' Furey, age 27
Amiee Levenski, age 39
Jonathon Harris, age 52
Joshua Ruff, age 16
Miriam Keogh, age 44
Colonel Rolf Grey, age 78
Kelly-May Matthews, age 23
Alex Roberts, age 31
Crystal Daye, age 33
Lacey Thompson, 22
Yuri Makowski, age 29
Anna-Lynn Beau, age 22
Sarah Morris, age 30
Tony Costelli, age 39
Dominic Costelli, age 33
Alyssa Gibson-Granger, age 28
Luke Eardley, age 32
Levi Aster, age 28
Danielle Morgan-Jones, age 43
Harry York, age 48
Harriet Kent, age 53
Robert 'Bobbie' White, age 7

Interview with Detective Morgan

"The awful thing is, we don't even know if we identified all the victims. Lot of missing person cases in this state. The water was running so fast that day, we don't know if some parts and pieces

got away. God, the way that bastard cut them up turned them into something that couldn't even be seen as human anymore. I told the Hendersons I'd bring their daughter home. And I believed that as well. I believed it. I just…I didn't think this sort of thing could happen. Not here."

Extract of W. Gail's book on the Red Creek murders

I first became acquainted with the Red Creek murders as a humble volunteer in downtown Franberg. After graduating at the top of my class and Valedictorian, I chose to stick to my roots and work as an intern at the local paper, the Franberg Gazette. Usually restricted to grabbing coffees instead of hot stories, I did everything I could to stand out.

I never thought I'd find my big break as a journalist in the wake of a tragedy. I knew the Henderson family pretty well, I actually used to babysit Abbie when I was still in high school. She was a sweet girl, very shy and artistic. The two of us used to gossip about boys and do each other's nails.

So, of course, having such a personal connection to this tragedy, I volunteered to search for Abbie. We all worked tirelessly with the police, exploring the woods and towns for something, anything to indicate Mr. and Mrs. Henderson might get their little girl home safe and sound. I was there that day all those body parts came out of the creek. I liked to stick around Detective Morgan to try and get his insight into the case, what did he think was happening next. I was chatting to him when Gretchen Reinstein fell into the creek and dislodged some of the rocks. There was a huge splash and as Gretchen surfaced, reassuring the rest of us that she was alright, I noticed a long pale leg float to the surface beside her. The crowd of volunteers all started crying out in alarm. Miss Reinstein, a quiet and respectable local librarian, started screaming and had to be pulled out of the water by a few of the volunteers.

The creek was, and is still, fast running, I close my eyes and can still visualise the arms and legs and chunks of torso rushing down the river. The dismembered face of whom I later came to know as Levi Aster, who was believed to have left town in the summer, was caught up on some of the weeds running by the river, clumped amongst the rocks like a Halloween mask. Detective Morgan and the police were attempting to create a blockade where the creek met the river further down to prevent the limbs going too far.

Fortunately, in the panic, I was able to collect myself. Using my personal video camera, I roped another volunteer, Cindy Hayward (photographed left) into recording my report on the incident.

This was how my relationship with the Red Creek killings began but dear readers, I assure you, the story only starts there.

Personal notes – Detective P Brankowski

06:45AM – Returns to residence, parks car. Removes cello case from backseat and carries into house. Subject appears to be struggling to carry it.

07:30AM – Subject's daughter can be seen smoking outside the garden.

08:00AM – Subject's daughter leaves for school with kid from across the street.

08:30AM – Upon closer inspection of front garden, drilling noise can be heard faintly from lower level of the house.

10:45AM – Subject leaves the residence and goes for a run. Route follows through the nearby woods and back through the town.

11:30AM – Subject stops off at All Hours grocery store and picks up household supplies—pink rubber gloves, 6 pack of bottled water and anti-perspirant, before running back to her home.

13:00PM – 16:00PM – Subject leaves house and drives to the residence of Mr. Andrew Matterson. The two of them talk in the garden for 20 minutes before the subject is left alone with supplies and begins planting and digging up the front of the Matterson lawn. Four rose bushes are planted and a gazebo in the back garden is painted. Mr. and Mrs. Matterson and the subject have tea in the garden. Following this, the subject returns to her residence. Observed from upstairs corridor window.

17:00PM – Subject's daughter returns to residence with two friends.

17:15PM – Subject is seen leaving the house. Drives to PTA meeting at the high school.

18:30PM – Subject witnessed talking to three other women in the staff parking lot after the meeting.

18:35PM – 19:45PM Subject goes for a drive through the town centre, through the countryside and into the next town over. She stops off at a gas station and buys cigarettes and fuel. She sits on the hood of her car and watches the woods before driving home.

20:00PM – Subject's daughter leaves residence with a very reluctant seeming girl from across the street. The two of them go into the woods and do not return. Subject goes into her garden and smokes a cigarette before returning indoors. Drilling noise can be heard from the lower level of the house.

Observation concluded for today.

Final comments:

Subject seems stable, fixed routine. Unusual amount of time driving around at night. Whereabouts unknown the night before, pattern seeming to always match my shifts, i.e., she seems to stay out all night when I specifically can't be there to observe her. Unlikely but will speak to the Chief about changing shift patterns.

Can be noted that the subject is well regarded and requested in her profession as gardener/landscaper, but her own garden is unmaintained and poorly managed.

CHAPTER THREE

The woods are dark and thick. There's a footpath, but we know our way so well that we don't need to rely on it. We can take short cuts— through the trees, past the pond in the clearing, up the hill with all the blackberries and finally, into our dark clearing with all the big grey rocks. Our little haven. Beth always clings too tightly to my arm, nearly tripping me as we use our phones to navigate in the faded light.

"If my mom finds out I disobeyed her—" Beth mumbles.

"Oh, can you just shut up about your mom for five seconds?" I say. "She is tucked in for the night, and she would never suspect you'd be out again after the blow-out this morning. Can we please just relax and have a good time?"

Beth sighs and slid her arm in through mine. "Fine, God, I don't know why I let you talk me into this."

As we approach, we can see that the fire is already lit and I spot Matt's head poking out amongst the rocks.

"Hey," I call.

"You guys made it," he said. "I was worried Beth's folks would have locked her up in a tower and thrown away the key."

"Oh Matt, please don't," Beth begs. "I'm nervous enough about sneaking out." She takes her seat beside him and rests her head on his shoulder. "I'm sorry about Lisa this morning. She's seen too much Sex and the City and is obsessed with having a gay BFF."

"Really? I hadn't noticed," he said, rolling his eyes.

"I can't believe her sometimes," Beth says. "It really makes me cringe. I don't know what's going to come out of her mouth."

"I still blame you for her," I say, opening a beer and passing it to Matt.

"Yeah, how dare you pick her to be your cousin," Matt teases, taking a sip. "God, Beth."

Beth laughs and rests back against the rocks. "None for me tonight, I want to have a clear head when my mom bulldozes into my bedroom at fucking 7AM."

A rustle in the bushes and Jason and Sukhy appear, carrying more bags of booze. Sukhy looks flustered and Jason looks nervous. I don't think they want us to notice.

"Nice supply," I say, leaning over and taking one from him. "Please help me distract Beth from her mom. I'm so sick of hearing about her."

And boom, that's it, the five of us, here until the late hours. I'm not my mother's daughter or some other faceless high school kid. I'm part of a unit, part of something that's mine. My happy place in a town that makes me so bored I want to roll over and die sometimes.

"So when is your date with Lisa?"

"Never," Sukhy says, laughing and shaking her head. "I don't know why she's suddenly so obsessed with me."

"I just want her to stop doing that thing with me," Jason says, "You know the constant rudeness and then flirting? Like some 'that little boy is mean to you because he likes you' bullshit."

"Well, at least you're not her gay BFF who will just die if he doesn't make it to see Pitch Perfect. Thanks for that by the way, dickhead."

We all laugh and Beth groans, covering her face.

"Alright, guys, I've said it before and I'll say it again, I'm sorry I got us landed with my cousin. Now can we please talk about something else?"

"Like what?"

"She's excellent source material," Sukhy says with a shrug.

"Well, what did the three of you do earlier?"

"Went to my place," I say, "We watched a bad movie."

"We also watched Fiona being as charming as ever to her mom," Sukhy adds. She is a model of politeness to everyone's parents, even Jason's shitty dad. If my mother was capable of acknowledging other people, she'd probably want Sukhy to be her daughter instead.

"Oh, come on, she's just the worst ever."

Jason sighs, "Your mom is so chilled out though. She never gets on your ass about anything."

"She's so creepy though, like a robot. I could go to school naked and she'd be like 'Have a nice day' before I left the house. Surprised she didn't forget to feed me when I was a baby, she's such a space cadet."

I hate when they bring up my Mother. I always have to go for a different tactic than the truth, so usually I end up saying she's robotic or switched off or dazed. I'm glad when Beth switches to the story about Miss Miller again. It's easier. I can relax I switch up the music on my phone and lean back with a beer. Beth and Jason are arguing over Great Expectations again, Sukhy interrupts to let them know they are both wrong. Matt keeps checking his phone.

I wonder who he's texting.

"Matt, is there anything we should know?" I whisper.

He smiles and shakes his head. "No, it's nothing really." He stuffs his phone back into his pocket. "You do know we live in a backwards town in the Midwest, right?"

"Hey, I'm an optimist!" I nudge him. "I want to live in a world where you can find someone nice."

He grins and nudges me back. "Cut it out, you."

I always try to smile because she never does, not properly. She's flat, dead-eyed, with only that cruel crocodile grin. I watch the others, I know to frown when they frown, I smirk when they smirk. I can look obnoxious, angry, scared, humble, excited, I can do them all. I learned from these guys and I hardly ever slip up.

I don't want to look at my face and see her face staring back at me. I guess I really am just another dumb fifteen-year-old who hates her mother. It's such a cliché.

I honestly don't remember a time where just looking at her face didn't fill me with contempt. I used to glare at her from the school gates when I was in pre-school. She used to tell the staff that it was some weird, cute thing I did.

As if.

I remember getting told off for rolling my eyes when Beth's mother kept making a big deal about how alike me and my Mother look. How we have the same hair, the same eyes, the same face.

"You'll grow up to be a looker, just like your Mom."

Thanks, I can't wait to grow up to look like that friendless weirdo. Also, what a creepy thing to say to a child. Unfortunately, she wasn't wrong, and now the resemblance is more obvious than ever. Mr Cooke, the creepy Religious Studies teacher, said that we looked like sisters last year at Parent's Night. Mother didn't react at all. He must have thought she was the type of woman to laugh and smile. Idiot.

"What kind of family do you think we are?" I asked him.

Yeah, that didn't go down particularly well.

"Fiona, what are we listening too?" Beth asks.

"It's something weird I downloaded."

"I like it," Jason says, jumping to his feet. "May I have this dance?"

"Oh, you stop it!" She shrieks as he bends down and picks her up by the waist, spinning her around. "Jason! Jason! Jason, you're going to drop me!" He spins her anyway, breathless and laughing.

We all went to our middle school prom together as a group, too young for dates, though I know Beth got asked. We went as a troop and danced as a group no matter how awkward that made it for other people there.

"Jase, watch it!" Sukhy laughs as Beth's foot narrowly misses her face.

Jason sets Beth down, delirious and laughing.

"You're such a bastard!" she says, but she's smiling from ear to ear.

He pats her on the head. "You're so easy to wave around, though." He offers Sukhy a hand, and she takes it. They dance back and forth, laughing and awkward on their feet. The colour starts to come to her face, so she grabs my hand and jerks me up to dance with the two of them.

Matt switches up the music on my phone, and the three of us are spinning around, doing the robot, tapping our feet and waving our arms. Sukhy and Jason are laughing, so I start laughing along with them. It's fun, and my head is spinning.

"Well, well, what do we have here?"

I see Riley Sanders stood in the clearing. Beside him is Freddie Hankerson and Butch Smith. They look drunk. Butch is using a tree to prop himself up. I glance behind me and see Matt inching slowly towards the rocks to try to get out of sight.

"Just a late-night gathering," Jason says.

"Y'all don't have homes to go too?" Riley asks. The others sort of laugh along with him.

"We come here for the views," Sukhy says.

"Oh yeah?" He smirks at her.

"So, what brings you out here?" Jason says, "You fella's been drinking?"

"Yeah, we just ran out," Riley says, "Care to share?"

"Sure, whatever," I say before Jason can say anything else. "We've got plenty. Help yourself."

Riley grins at me and reaches down to take one. He notices Matt in the corner and steps back. "Can I have one Her Majesty hasn't touched?"

"Oh no, we might be out of luck," Jason says. "A lot of these have been getting passed around tonight."

"Don't be smart with me, freshman bitch," Riley snaps. "You got a lucky shot in this morning, but Mr Davis ain't here to save your ass now, is he?"

"Funny, I don't see him here to save yours neither," Jason says.

"Jason, it's fine, stop it," Matt says. "It's all good."

"Am I talking to you, Queenie?" Riley says, leaning around Jason to leer down at Matt. "No, I'm talking to your little white-trash boyfriend here, so why don't you wait there until I feel like a chat, huh?"

I step bodily in front of Jason at that point and push some beer into Riley's arms. "Look, wow, you have beer. Isn't that great? Come on, Riley, can't we just get along? We've got no problem with you. We're just being drunk and stupid." I smile at him the way Beth does when she wants something from a guy.

He looks drunk and stupid and angry, then he smiles.

"Gee, thanks," he says. "Now why can't you teach your friend there some manners?"

"Well, we're trying," I say. "He's kind of slow on the uptake."

Riley is smirking as he turns to the others, "Come on, fellas, let's leave them to it. Thanks for the beer." They disappear back into the woods, I can't help but notice Freddie Hankerson turn and smile at Matt before he vanishes into the undergrowth.

Mystery Texter, perhaps?

"Fiona, what the fuck?" Jason snaps, shoving me.

"There were three of them, idiot," I snap back. "It'd be a lot harder to send them away with some beer once you'd started getting your ass kicked by them."

"There are more of us than there are of them," he protests.

"They're seniors," Beth says. She looks pale and frightened. "And boys. Matt's not going to fight them, and neither would we."

"I'm sorry," Matt mumbles. "I'm sorry, guys."

"Matt, don't, it's fine. They are idiots, they'll be gas station attendants next year after they graduate. We just need to get through this year," Sukhy says.

Jason kicks the empty cans over, letting out a grunt of frustration. "For fuck's sake!"

Sukhy puts a hand on his shoulder. "Jase, come on."

He stuffs his hands into his pockets. "I'm just so sick of this. I get my old man giving it to me in the neck all the time and having to listen to fucking Riley Sander's bullshit at school. I just want them to all just fuck off."

"It's not forever," I say. "It's just high school. Fighting them just gets you in trouble or worse. Really hurt."

He looks so fed up. "I know. I'm sorry, guys."

Beth gets up and hugs him. Sukhy hooks an arm around Matt and I rest my head on her shoulder.

We stay like that for a little while and then it starts to rain. First lightly, then heavily. The fire starts to die down, and Beth is, of course, the only one who came in a raincoat. We disperse, letting the fire die and taking off in different directions. Jason towards the north, leather jacket pulled over his head like a bizarre umbrella. Sukhy and Matt down to the east and me and Beth towards the west. I watch her from my porch, climbing up into her room like a somewhat less wobbly ninja.

I wait for her to go inside and wave from her window before closing the blinds.

I walk slowly back into the woods, and I wait in the clearing until I spot a cat, trying to get itself out of the rain. I bend down and make kissy noises, holding out a hand and whispering until she comes close. She's sweet, trusting. Perhaps hoping that I'll have food, or can take her somewhere dry and warm. She brushes her face against my hand. She purrs, and that is the last sound she makes before I twist my knife up against her throat. There's blood and then she goes still.

I sit there in the dark, cutting away at her. I remove her fur, her flesh, I take out her tiny organs and look at how they fit together. I find her little trusting heart and feel sad for a moment.

I'm digging a grave for her when Mother finds me.

She's standing a few feet away from me in the clearing, holding an umbrella. She's just watching with that cold crocodile smile on her face.

"Are you pleased with yourself?" she asks.

I wish that I could go away and never ever come back.

CHAPTER FOUR

I am in no kind of mood for Lisa this morning. No kind of fucking mood. We sit huddled together on the playground, keeping warm through the rain, all stuffed under Sukhy's umbrella. Lisa appears with her own, loud and bright and cheerful and I just wish that that cat was alive instead of her.

"What are you guys doing Friday?"

We all meet each other's eyes.

"This Friday?"

"Yes, Jason," she says, rolling her eyes. "This Friday."

She thinks that being rude to guys is flirty and cute. She goes out of her way to act like any contributions from either Jason or Matt were the dumbest thing she's ever heard. She never seems to realise that her weird style of flirting is wasted here. Jason hates her, and Matt is gay and probably also hates her.

"Nothing."

"Yeah, probably nothing."

"We could go to the arcade?" Sukhy's suggestion—knowing that Lisa hates going to the arcade. It's too noisy, and you can't even talk!

"No, no, we're going to a party."

When she doesn't get the reaction she wants, Lisa always gets louder.

"Riley Sanders invited me to Rob Dawson's party, he said to bring friends. Guys, we're going to a proper high school party."

"Rob Dawson, on the football team?" Matt mumbles, nervous.

"Of course."

"You guys can go without me." That is always Matt's line when he's nervous. If we go to someone's house with a dog, or near his

33

mother's church friends, or past the football fields, he always claimed to have somewhere else to be.

Don't worry though, guys, you can go on without me.

"No way," Lisa said. "I can't go without my sassy gay friend! Come on, we'll have such a good time."

Matt raises his eyebrows to dramatic new heights.

In Lisa's world, there were men she wants to date, men she's grossed out by, and gay men, who seem to exist to gossip with, compliment her clothes and act like some sort of engaged fan of hers.

"Calm down, Carrie Bradshaw," I say. "We won't have 'such a good time', it'll be a dumb high school party. It'll be crowded and loud and full of people we get to see at school every day, anyway."

"Yeah, Riley Sanders is a bitch," Jason says. "We can do something else."

"Well, I don't know, it could be fun," Beth said. "I mean, Matt, if we all go, Riley won't give you a tough time. And you know, if you hang out outside of school, he might realise you're, you know, fine? He might stop being such a jerk."

You. Fucking. Traitor.

"Well, I guess if we all go?" Matt said.

This is how it always goes. You guys can go without me, he says. So the rest of us bargain and twist things around, and Matt changes his mind as long as we're all together.

It really bugs me still that this is the only part of the group dynamic that Lisa has caught on to.

"Hey, I didn't want to go anyway," Jason counters.

"Whatever, Jason," Lisa says with an exaggerated sigh. "We can go without you."

"Oh no, I'll just die!" he says, clutching a hand over his mouth in shock.

As we head inside, bells ringing and people shoving, I notice Matt looking dejected. I scoop an arm through his and lean over to whisper, "It'll be fine, I'll be there too."

"It's different," he says. "You're a girl. If you want Riley Sanders to fuck off, you can smile and bat your eyelashes and send him on his merry way. If I tried that, he'd put me through the nearest wall." He sighs. "And I'm sick of Jason getting his butt kicked and getting into trouble with the teachers."

"Don't let him hear you say that, he thinks he's a badass."

"You know what I mean, Fiona."

"I won't let anything happen, I promise."

He smiles at me. "Thanks."

I'm not like her.

I do care.

I care about Matt and Sukhy and Beth and Jason. I like my life with them in it. I wouldn't ever let someone change that or take even one of them away.

It's why I stop inviting them over when she's in a bad mood.

Matt's phone goes off again, and he's shielding the screen as he checks his messages.

"Plus," I add, "Mystery Texter might be there."

He goes bright red and shoves me.

"Oh, shut up!"

· · · ·

Math class, no Beth, just Jason, who actually knows the answers, but it's easier to pretend that he doesn't. He yawns and draws a pirate on the textbook in between us. I add a shark in the water. He sets the mast on fire. I shade in half the pirate's face.

He beams delightedly.

"Can you go suck each other's cocks somewhere else?" Laurie DelMonte mutters from the seat behind us.

I imagine poking holes in her eyeballs.

"Why? We interrupting you being horny for math?" Jason says, leering at her.

"Freak," she mutters.

He rolls his eyes and turns back to illustrating pirates along the margins of the book. I roll my eyes at her and turn back to my desk. I hate dealing with people like that. Self-important little bitches who can't just mind their own business and feel the need to comment on others.

Mr. Rhyerson groans on for another half an hour, and when we get up to leave, Laurie starts sneering to her friends about the two of us, two little fucking weirdoes probably too high to be in school.

They are in our next class, Chemistry 1, so we have to walk down the corridor with them behind us. I let it roll over me, I just keep thinking about how Laurie would look with pinprick holes in her eyes. But Jason is twitching, his hands stuffed in his pockets, angry.

"They're probably on crack."

It doesn't matter.

"Such a cliché."

"Fiona Taylor is a ghetto bitch."

Jason spins around at that point and lurches back towards Laurie and her friends. I manage to grab his arm and hold him back in time, but the force nearly pulls me off my feet.

"Jason—!"

"Fuck you," he snaps. "You're a fucking little skank asshole."

The girls start laughing.

"Jason, come on, I don't care."

"You should listen to your friend, Jas-on," Laurie sneers.

"Jason, really, they're not worth it."

He stops pulling against me and straightens up.

"You watch your fucking mouth," he tells her.

"Oh, like I'm scared," she says.

He shakes himself free, and we turn and head to science, followed by their catty laughter all the way to class.

· · · ·

"I'm so done with this place," Jason says.

"Tuesday, worst day of the week," Sukhy says.

"Laurie DelMonte is a fucking axe wound," he says. "She started shit with me and Fiona in Math and was a total bitch in Chem 1 as well." He groans and brushes back his hair. "I don't know why we bother coming here."

"How often are we going to get to spend time together like this in the future?" Beth says. "We'll be off in college or whatever, so these four years need to count."

Jason throws his can at the bin, it misses and sprays soda all over the grass. He flops back on the ground. "Does it count when every other person at this school is a total brain-washed piece of shit?"

I sigh and shrug at Sukhy, who leans down to put grass on his head. "Come on, Jase. It's just a shit Tuesday."

"I've managed to get through the day without anyone starting something," Matt says brightly. "I mean, that never happens. I even made it to Chem 1 without the football team flunkies calling me 'Her Majesty' when I enter the room."

"That still shouldn't have taken fucking 3 months to happen," Jason snaps. "Matt, come on. I don't know how you just take it. I'm like...up here?" He gestures around his temples furiously. "Why do they have to be such dicks?"

"Because we know you prefer us that way," Laurie DelMonte calls as she and her friends walk through the courtyard to sit on one of the benches.

"Yeah, good one, Laurie, always a pleasure," Sukhy says, waving a hand dismissively.

"Erm, sorry, could you try that in English, Border Control?" Casey Beckard sneers back.

I don't see Jason move until he's too close to them and too far from us. His hand swings out, there's a clap like thunder and Casey Beckard is off the bench and onto the ground howling.

Her mouth is bleeding, there's blood spotted on the grass. Jason is red-faced, he bends down to jerk her upright by her collar.

"You apologise—!"

Laurie is up off her feet, grabbing at his jacket. The other girls are all screaming and trying to break the space between Jason and Casey, who's crying, breath ragged, hiccupping. She wails when he grabs her clothes and brings her hands in front of her face in terror. Our group is stunned, Sukhy is there, trying to pull Jason away from Casey, she's yelling. Matt and Beth are yelling.

"Mrs Harris—!" Laurie screams. "Miss!"

There's the screech of a whistle and Miss Harris and Mr Goldstein are there, pulling the two of them apart. Mr. Goldstein's arms are around Jason's middle, Jason is struggling, legs strained as he's pulled off his feet and forced down onto the ground. Jason is yelling 'Fucking say you're sorry!' at Casey, whose bleeding and crying. I can see the swollen red welt on her cheek from here.

The girls are all crying. Jason is face down in the dirt, snarling and swearing. The others are all talking, yelling, frantic and I realise, that

I'm just sat here, frozen to the spot, looking at Casey and her injured face and that blood all over the ground.

What a wonderful thing.

. . . .

Jason is suspended, whether Casey made a racial comment or not. The school does not condone violence, and it is certainly, not ok for a man to ever raise his hand in anger to a young lady.

Unacceptable.

Jason's dad comes and picks him up from school, I spot him, red-faced and angry in the parking lot before the two of them drive away. Sukhy is in the girl's bathroom, crying and angry, red-faced with frustration. I go to art class later to stay with her for a while.

"He's such a fucking idiot."

"He has a short fuse, this was always going to happen."

"He's going to get kicked out of school."

"We won't let that happen," I say, squeezing her hand.

"I don't want to be the reason for that. Every time someone says something…I can stand up for myself. He knows I can."

"He's an idiot."

"Yeah, he is." She hugs me tight, and we stay like that for a while.

. . . .

After school, we avoid Lisa, who wants to know what the hell happened with Jason in the lunchroom. Apparently, everyone is talking about it!! I tell her to buzz off, and the two of us go back to my house.

Mother is in the basement, she's left an ugly red stain on the floor in the kitchen. I stick a box over it, so Sukhy doesn't notice.

This afternoon isn't about her. So Sukhy and I climb out of the attic window and sit out on the roof. We've done this ever since we were eight, the age we became brave enough to face climbing out onto the roof. We'd sit and look out at the woods at the back of my garden.

It's our way to unwind, just the two of us.

I want to distract her from Jason, so I don't protest when she finds this stupid photo album she'd found in the attic before we climbed out the top window.

"Look at you," she says, delighted.

"Hey, do you really think that I was born in a time that included black and white photos?"

She smirks and lifts it up. "You can't deny that there's a resemblance."

"You know I hate it when people say that."

"Yeah, I know, I'm sorry. But look, your mom was such a gloomy little kid."

It's a family photo. My grandparents I've never met, what looks like an aunt she's never mentioned and an uncle I know died young. Of course, these are things I can't admit, even to Sukhy. It'd sound too weird. And in the centre of this photo is my mother sat on her mother's lap.

She looks about two years old, her hair is tied up on top of her head. She's well dressed, clearly well loved, but her expression is flat while the others all smile.

"Well, at least we know it's a lifelong habit."

"How's she been lately?"

"Same as ever," I mutter. "I can't wait to get out of this place."

"Well, maybe start studying and we can make it to the same college."

"Sukhy..."

"Come on," she says. "We could share a room, wear stupid college jackets, go to smoky French cafes, burn our bras." She nudges me. "Or, I guess I can do that stuff and you can stay here and go into the landscaping business and get a face like this." She frowns deeply, I laugh and lean back.

"Hey, I've got four years to pick my grades up."

"I know you can do it, Fiona. I'm starting to think you just love slumming it with Jason in middle set. You two not telling me something?"

"Gross, no," I say.

"Gross yourself," she says, then, colour coming to her face, she adds, "Jason's not...that bad, you know? I reckon he could get a girlfriend if he managed to cut the One Angry Man shit out."

"No way," I say. "If Jason got a girlfriend, she'd have to come along to everything. And he'd be all over her. And we'd sit out in the woods with them being all PDA and the rest of us being super awkward."

"You're probably right."

"I think Matt is more likely to get a girlfriend than Jason, he's got the worst personality. Like, only we can put up with his attitude."

"Oh my God, right?" She laughs and hugs her knees to her chest. "I'd feel sad, you know? If things changed like that. I know it's not always ideal. Matt is getting all this shit at school for no reason, and Jason is like eight days from expulsion, but... I'm pretty happy."

"Yeah, me too," I said.

"And I was serious, you know, about us going to college together," she says. "I would love that. I know studying isn't your thing, but that's in school. Imagine only studying one thing you're really passionate about. School is just a really horrible character-building step to get you there."

I groan. "Character-building again."

"I know. Only props up right before we have something shit to do."

We laugh, and I sigh heavily, leaning into my knees.

"I guess that could be fun."

I can see it now. The two of us going to go to the same college. We'll room together, re-invent ourselves, and never have to come back to this shitty town. I'll become a vegetarian, get a cat, cut my hair really short and sexy.

I'll never carry a knife with me when I go out.

This will be the past and none of it will matter.

I'll never speak to my Mother again and we'll both be happier for it.

"I'll be happy when I'm away from here," I said.

I flick my cigarette off the roof and watch it shrivel up on the concrete below.

. . . .

We don't meet in the woods that night. Jason texts to say that his dad has basically got him under house arrest after his antics at school. Beth's mom has decided on hosting movie night where she's basically under surveillance for not leaving the house. Matt says he has to stay in and study but tells me to clear off when I private message him to ask if he has a hot date.

Me and Sukhy walk around the woods for a while before even she turns in too. I have our whisky and go and sit by the grave I made for the little cat and drink it. I know I'm missing the hot policeman, but I don't want him to see me like this.

I look at the mound of earth, slightly higher than the rest. I wish she hadn't sniffed me before she died. I wish she'd known I was bad news and stayed away. And suddenly I'm crying like an idiot.

I'm not like her.

I'm not.

And yet...

• • • •

She is just arriving at the house when I got home that night. She struggles with the cello case, trying to find her key. I watch her and wait at the gate until she was inside before breezing in behind her.

She rolls her eyes when she notices me.

"Should you be drinking spirits when you're not even mature enough to open the door for your mother?"

"Shouldn't a woman of a certain age be home at a respectable hour?"

"Fiona."

I kick the door closed behind me and take off my boots.

"You're not going to ask me to help you haul that thing down to the basement, are you?"

"Oh, no, I know much better than that, dear," she said.

The case creaks along the floorboards, grinding against the wood. I hate that stupid thing. I want to burn it and throw it in the trash. I want to stamp on it until it's flat. I wish I was strong enough to pick it up and just throw it at her.

But I do want to talk to her. I've wanted to talk to her since last night, but I got too scared. It was something I've carried around with me. Whether I like her or not, I suppose there are times you just need your mom. Whether she's any good or not in those situations, is up to her, I suppose.

"Mother," I said.

She turns and glances back at me.

"When...did you...first have a cello lesson?"

There is amusement in her face.

"A cello lesson? Is that what the kids are calling it now?" She must have seen my face because the entertained expression on hers vanishes and she folds her arms. "I was thirteen."

"And...was it to help someone?"

"To a degree. It was very helpful to me."

Like a crocodile. Always like a crocodile.

"Yeah, who was there?"

"Just me, and my...audience, I suppose. It was a supply teacher I wasn't particularly fond of."

"Right, but why did you do it? Was he mean to you? Or abusive or...?"

"She, actually. No, she always had lipstick on her teeth, and she always made me go and take the registers to the front office for her. And as to why? Well, it was sort of like an itch," she said, frowning now as she spoke. "It was something that I just had to do. If it hadn't been her, I would have...debuted with someone else."

She smiles again like she'd told a joke.

"Well, good talk," I said, frowning as I went to pass her and go upstairs.

"Oh, Fiona," she calls after me. "Have you had any extra...cello lessons I should know about?"

No.

Slam the door, lock the door, under the covers and sleep.

CHAPTER FIVE

(Newspaper article on the Red Creek Killer)

A NIGHTMARE TOWN

Citizens of Franberg are in shock following the recent spiral of tragic events that have shaken the community over the last several weeks. This safe and friendly community was drawn to the depraved acts of the serial murderer now known as the Red Creek Killer, after the disappearance of young Abigail Henderson. Since then twenty-three victims have been identified from Read Creek, though police believe there may be further victims we have not yet discovered at this scene.

Since the discovery of the bodies in the creek, the Red Creek murderer has taken the lives of two more citizens in Franberg. On Tuesday night, emergency services received a 911 call from a distressed young woman who identified herself as Lacey Thompson, 22, who had run away from home following a dispute with her father. She believed there to be a man following her in a truck and had stopped inside the Riverside Diner for safety. Officers were dispatched to the Riverside Diner, advising Lacey to stay inside and not leave. Upon arrival at the diner, staff advised that Lacey had gone outside for a cigarette after making the call and not returned. Officers searched the woods nearby, and the wrist of a young woman was found in the shrubbery.

The rest of young Miss Thompson's body was not uncovered until Thursday morning, it was in six separate pieces and buried in the Blackwood forest. Officers also uncovered body parts of a middle-aged male, believed to be between the ages of thirty-five and fifty. We are requesting that anyone with information in regards to this come forward and speak to the police.

(Transcript of interview with Detective Morgan)

Morgan: I know why I was kicked off the case. It was because I started drinking. You know how it starts, everyone drinks, but suddenly your work starts suffering, and they need something to blame so they leech onto that and suddenly you're a shitty detective who can't do his job. You can't know what it was like. The town was terrified, everyone was scared and wanted answers, and I didn't know where to find them. It was like uncovering the bodies just gave that maniac an audience to really give his all to.

Yeah, that made me a little fucking frantic. I mean, imagine if it was you? You're trying to understand that kind of person that could chop up actual human beings into blobs of flesh and bone, everyone screaming in your ear and the whole time that, that bastard is out there, chopping up more people and feeding on that fear...

No, I wasn't the one who collared Randall Kayne. No, I'd been long kicked off the case at that point. I wish I could say I contributed at all, but all I did was help feed that wild goose chase.

I got hung up on a weird witness and that was it.

Brankowski: What do you mean a weird witness?

Morgan: It was the sister of the youngest victim. I met her at the funeral. She was just...wrong.

Brankowski: That would be Robert White, wouldn't it? The seven-year-old boy?

Morgan: The very same. His sister, Sarah, would have been four, maybe five when he was killed.

Brankowski: Well, you know how it sounds, a five-year-old kid?

Morgan: Hey, you asked why I was taken off the case. I'm telling you. You don't like what I have to say, go and interview my former partner or Winnie Gail or some other hack.

Brankowski: Sorry, I didn't mean it like that. So, what drew your attention to the sister?

Morgan: There was just something wrong about her. The rest of the White family, mother, and father and another sister, the three of them were distraught, quiet, frozen in grief. Sarah White was just numb. And at one point at the service, I saw her smile. It was just for a second, just as I happened to be looking at her older sister, who was really crying, I notice this girl, Sarah White, couldn't be older than fifteen and she's smiling, full-on smiling, like this is the greatest day of her life.

Brankowski: Could have been a nervous reaction.

Morgan: Could have been a lot of things, but it freaked me out. So, I start digging around, asking questions. What sort of kid was Bobbie when he was alive, did he get on with his little sister, that kind of stuff. And Mrs White tells this story about little Sarah taking trinkets from her siblings when she was little, hiding them around the house. How it drove Bobbie crazy when he was alive.

And the whole time her mother is talking, Sarah is just staring at me, and it was chilling. It was like there was just nothing there at all. Right up until her mother says, 'These last few years have been hard, we couldn't even grieve for him, could we, Sarah?' And her face transforms, she's nearly in tears, her hands are shaking, and she says, 'I've missed him so much'. It was like she'd put on a mask.

Brankowski: I don't see how that got you kicked off the investigation though.

Morgan: It was years later. The killings kept happening, the feds got involved, the whole operation, and we couldn't find anything. Killings would go dark, or they'd spread out. This lunatic just seemed to pull us from one place to another. And every now and then, I'd check back in with Miss Sarah White, check what she was up to, where she goes, who she talks to.

I mention her to my partner, and he doesn't see it. Says she's just a quiet teenage girl. Says I'm reading into things because I'm frustrated. And to be honest, yeah, I see it. It doesn't seem likely that a teenager would be doing something like that, cutting folks up like that. But my gut just told me I was right.

Brankowski: Did you ever approach her?

Morgan: Just once (mumbles)

Brankowski: Sorry, could you just repeat...?

Morgan: I don't want to talk about this. I need a cigarette. I'm going outside!

Highlighted extracts from Winifred Gail's book on the Red Creek murders

(pg. 32)

I met the Red Creek Killer many times. We went to high school together. We went to the same diners, walked the same streets, saw the same movies. That's the scary thing about a murder in a small town. We all know each other, and we all knew that there was a wolf among this pack of sheep. For me, a single woman living alone at the time, it was scary going home, leaving the safety of my car and exposing myself to the dangers between my car and my apartment, knowing that there could be someone lurking around the corner, knife in hand, ready to make sure I never saw the light of day.

(pg. 151)

After two long years Detective Morgan had made it abundantly clear that he was never going to crack this case. The handsome young detective was looking paler and more drawn as each day passed and our killer was still out on the loose, ready to take out victim after victim. The townsfolk were getting frustrated and scared. People were leaving town for fear of their lives.

But I love this town, I wasn't going to be chased out by a cold-hearted killer. Since my debut broadcast, where I showed this country the horrors I had experienced at Red Creek first hand, I moved from strength to strength, reporting on the case, sharing my insight and interviewing witnesses for the Franberg Daily News. I felt like I had come to know this monster all too well.

(pg. 78)

This was a person with a complete disdain for other people, someone who was perhaps distanced from their peers, socially awkward, unable to connect with the real world. That was why they cut up the bodies so small, to make people something bite-sized that they could understand. I, of course, do not mean to im-

ply that the Red Creek killer was a cannibal. However, the way in which he dismantled his victims completely showed his hatred for the human race and the people of this town. This could also explain the wide range of victims, as you can see from page 3, Red Creek had victims of all ages, all walks of life, there were black victims, white victims, Hispanic victims, old, young, even going as far as to kill a little boy no more than seven years old. This was someone who wanted desperately to understand other people but couldn't.

(pg. 208)

I said it before, and I'll say it again, the police needed to be looking for a loner, someone without friends or family, who kept themselves in a bubble. Someone who couldn't relate to other people even if they wanted to.

I suggested this often in my broadcasts and received little to no support from Detective Morgan or his colleagues. In fact, it was their lack of focus on this case, which cost many of the later victims their lives*.

*Ms Gails did not mean above to suggest that the Franberg police department was responsible for the deaths of the remaining four victims.

(pg. 213)

It was a brave young woman named Sylvia Hardey (pictured left) who brought the murderous pattern of Red Creek to a sudden and impressive halt.

Young Sylvia, only seventeen at the time, was the last intended victim of the Red Creek Killer, who we now know as Randall Kayne. He followed her home from a high school pep rally. Sylvia became suspicious that she was being followed and sensibly stuck to the main roads that were well lit and in plain sight. Red Creek didn't approach her until she took the path under the St John tunnel to get back to her home on the outskirts of town. Kayne had parked his van on the other side of the tunnel and tried to chase Sylvia towards it, intending to trap her inside it and move her to a remote location.

He gave chase to her towards the end of the tunnel, there was a struggle, and he cut her arm at the shoulder and stabbed her in *the stomach. This incredibly brave young girl was able to pull herself free and run into the road at the end of the tunnel to try to alert passing drivers.*

As those of you who are familiar with the story of how Randall Kayne was captured know, I happened to be driving nearby that night. I was returning from a gal pal's baby shower and spotted this frightened, curly haired teenage girl, waving frantically from the road outside the St John tunnel like her life depended on someone, anyone to rescue her.

I pulled over, and Sylvia jumped into the front seat, hysterical and crying. I saw the figure of a man coming out of the woods towards his truck and took off at full speed to the hospital where poor young Sylvia's wounds were tended to, and her life saved.

Personal notes – Detective P Brankowski

08:35AM – Overslept this morning, request to change shift pattern rejected. The Chief does not approve of what I'm doing. Received pep talk trying to dissuade me from my investigation. Subject's daughter, Miss F. Taylor, has now made a habit of speaking to me when she sees me outside the house. Family resemblance is very clear. F.T is friendly, forthright, and seems curious about me. Seems cautious of giving away too much. From brief inspection, F.T appears unharmed, no signs of self-abuse or fearful. This morning we spoke about the weather and where to buy good sneakers.

09:00 – Subject has no work this morning. Spotted her doing her daughter's laundry in the back garden.

10:45 – Mrs P. Green from across the road, the mother of the very reluctant seeming girl F.T. takes with her on her late-night woodland walks, arrives at subject's home. Subject speaks to her on the front porch. Mrs Green is naturally loud, and the conversation could be heard from my car. Conversation concerns the incident at high school yesterday regarding Jason Danvers. Mrs Green wants the subject to dissuade her daughter from continuing association with Mr Danvers. Noted that the subject throughout the conversation begins to raise her voice and reflect Mrs Green's anger, tone, and opinions. Common characteristic of sociopathic behaviour.

13:15 – Subject has gone to the supermarket for her weekly shop. Note Subject always does the bulk of her grocery shopping on Wednesday while topping off at other places in the week. Her shopping list is typical, non-suspicious. She buys alcohol but doesn't appear to drink. Suspect that this is being consumed by F.T. when she goes off with her friends into the woods. Three of the PTA mothers approach the subject in the cereal aisle. Conversation recorded below:

K: Sylvia, you're looking well!

S: And you, Karen. Nicole, Amber, we have to stop meeting like this.

N: We were just saying that you simply have to join us, we've just come from yoga.

A: It's a scream, Sylvia, honestly!

S: Is this the class at the town hall? Free Blossom yoga, isn't it?

N: Oh, I knew you'd have heard of it!

A: We need a bit of relaxation in our lives with everything going on? My Tina came home last night, obsessing over the incident with that boy.

N: Jason Something, isn't it?

S: I think I've heard about this.

K: Danvers, Jason Danvers, his father owns that tacky little used cars place on the outskirts of town?

S: I don't think I've seen the place.

A: Well, you wouldn't be sorting out the patio around there, hon. Not a nice family from what I've heard. Five sons, all headcases and this Jason—!

N: Hitting a girl, can you imagine?

K: My Lucille is friends with Casey, Casey Beckard, the girl who was hit.

S: Dreadful, I'm almost afraid to send my Fiona into that school sometimes with someone like that around.

N: Well, it makes you wonder what those teachers are even doing to protect our kids.

A: I've heard they've suspended the boy, but who knows how long that will last.

S: It's frightening, isn't it?

A: I'm raising it at the next PTA meeting.

K: Well, we have to do something.

N: Sylvia, Carmen mentioned to me that Fiona is sometimes seen hanging around with this Jason character

S: That daughter of mine, I honestly don't know what to do with her sometimes.

K: Oh, I know what you mean, I'm at my wits' end with my girls too.

A: Still, you might want to watch a character like that. Family has no morals, I'd be worried about him stealing something if he comes over. I hear his father is a crook.

S: Not to worry, ladies, I run a very tight ship.

N: Oh, I wouldn't doubt it. If your home is anything like that wonderful job you did at the Matterson house, I can't imagine one single thing being out of place.

(All laugh)

S: Well, I must dash. I actually have to pop over to the Mattersons' after this, last minute paint job on the gazebo. Oh, the work never ends!

N: Well take care, Sylvia, dear!

A: Yes, so nice to see you, hon!

K: And the offer is still open for Free Blossoms next week!

Notes: Observed subject's face during interaction, she copied the three women she spoke with completely in their mannerisms and expressions. The second they were turned away from her, she resumed a mask-like, blank expression. It was disconcerting to witness.

15:00PM – F.T. approaches me on my run along the block. She made a joke about me hanging around the neighbourhood to try to get a date with her mother. We were interrupted by the subject, who returned from her meeting at the Matterson house. She questioned me for talking to her teenage daughter—I can imagine how it may have looked. Subject seemed to show genuine concern, seems protective of F.T. In contrast, F.T seems to show real dislike towards the subject. Hard to tell if this is just typical teenage lashing out or something more. F.T told her I was a neighbour asking for jogging advice and info about the woods. I am curious as to why she felt the need to lie to her mother about me being a policeman. The subject was quiet on the subject and dismissive. Encounter was unnerving, she maintained eye contact. Felt unusual to talk face to face after just observing and researching for so long.

Comments conclude for the day.

· · · ·

The hot policeman, or rather, Detective Pete, is outside my house when I get home from school. The others have to stay late, so I have the afternoon at my house. Mother is off at her fake job, I hope. I don't want to see her

"Ah, it's young Fiona, out of school early today," he says.

He's wearing a really ugly polka dot baseball cap. Seeing my expression, he takes it off. I wonder who it was a present from? His mother, maybe?

"Yeah, I have sixth period free today," I say. "Pretty lucky, huh?"

"That's the one to have."

"So, is there a dangerous crime by my fence?"

He laughs and doesn't let on how much he wants to go in and check out the basement.

"No, no, just on patrol again."

"You could probably ask my mother if she's seen anything in the area. She usually jogs in the day, you know, when decent people are all at work."

He looks more alert when I mentioned her. Of course, he does. She's the reason he spends taxpayer dollars wandering up and down my street, isn't she?

"I should do. I've seen her a couple of times. But she kind of strikes me as difficult to start up a conversation with."

I smile at him like I don't know that he comes here just to see her. "Oh yeah, she can't do small talk or anything like that. Hey, Detective, is this just your weird way of trying to get a date with my mother?"

Jesus, he goes bright red at that.

"Kids these days," he says, shaking your head. "So cheeky. No, Fiona, I wouldn't use police time to try and get a date."

I laugh as well, leaning against the fence. "Never? But you get the chance to look all heroic and stuff? Lots of women like that, men too."

"I'll keep that in mind," he said, shaking his head. "Right, I don't want to get in the way of free sixth period. I'll wish you a good evening, young Fiona."

"Fiona." She appears from the car, dragging her stupid cello case with her. "Who is your friend?"

Was that the first time they'd ever spoken? The last time she was brought in for questioning, I doubt he'd have been old enough to be a detective. It must be exciting for him, after all that time.

"This is Pete," I said. "He lives in the area. I see him jogging. Fired up a conversation. You know, social like."

She glares at me like I was the biggest idiot alive before fixing him with one of her cold, long stares. "So, Pete, do you make a habit of talking to teenage girls?"

Where is this weird protectiveness suddenly coming from? Between this and the other thing, I'm starting to think that she had maternal instincts after all.

But he laughs and shakes his head. "Not usually, no. I'm actually new to the area, Fiona here, offered to give me some directions. I'm starting a running club and want to try a route through the woods. You two must know them pretty well." He offers her that big Disney prince smile. "It's nice to meet you, ma'am."

She folds her arms and surveys him carefully.

I don't know why he told that ridiculous lie about a running club. I mean, what? Is that what they teach you in Detective Academy? It was hard for me to keep a straight face. Well, it's me, so not really, but in my mind, I was looking at him like, what??

"Right," she said, without introducing herself. "Well, don't listen too carefully to what Fiona says. She's often straying from the path. Not the best go-to for a run in the woods."

I scowl at her.

That crocodile smile and then she goes to walk to the house.

"Here, let me help you with that," he said, reaching for the cello.

"I'm quite fine, thank you," she said.

So that was your first encounter with her, I think. How did you find it?

CHAPTER SIX

Lisa insisted and now somehow, I'm here, sat on Lisa's bed while we spend hours getting ready for some shit party I don't even want to go to.

Lisa is holding court by the mirror where she's short of making love to Sukhy's hair as she straightens it.

"Wow, you have great volume! Is all Indian hair like this?"

"Yes it is actually," Sukhy said, tone ripe with sarcasm that definitely went over Lisa's head.

Beth is drinking to hide her embarrassment. Matt is here in spirit only—he's texting from his house where we're going to meet him after this. Lisa's 'Getting Ready Pre-Party-Party' is a very exclusive, high-profile event. No boys allowed, of course.

I only really agreed to go along because Beth wouldn't be allowed out at all without Lisa.

Lisa's house is extravagantly large, she has a pool despite the fact that it's usually not warm enough here to warrant really using it. She has a counter-top in her kitchen that she aggressively refers to as the breakfast bar. I feel like my house is too big for me and my mother, so I can't even imagine what this place is like with it being only the two of them.

Ms Green, formally Mrs Jones, Lisa's mother looks a lot like Beth and her pinch-faced mother, so Lisa, I guess must take after her father, whose photo they keep on the mantelpiece. All three of them smile too wide, they're like a family in a toothpaste commercial. It's unsettling.

Her mother lounges around 'the den' which seems to be a somewhat less comfortable upstairs living room, or 'the gym'—it's a room with a treadmill in it and a large cardboard box. She keeps popping her head in to give us unsolicited fashion advice.

She dresses exactly how you might imagine a middle-aged out of work actress might dress and talks in an accent that ricochets from being English to American with every other word.

Though, as grating as she is, Lisa's mom has supplied us with tweenage booze that mostly tastes of sugar. She pronounces Sukhy's name as 'Sucky' and frowns a little every time before she says it.

It's just a name, get over yourself, you old hag.

And she has told me that I have nice skin three times in a way that has kind of made me wish that I don't actually have skin in the first place.

"Fiona, why don't you let me do your face?" Lisa asks.

"No, thanks, I prefer what I've done with it."

She rolls her eyes and smiles at me before going back to fussing Sukhy, who is smirking at me in the mirror.

"Touchy," she mutters.

My phone buzzes, one from Mother, who never texts and one from Matt.

Matt, reminding me that he's bored on his own, and when the fuck are we going to be ready?

And Mother is reminding me to have my key with me. She must be out at her pretend job or driving around for hours on end.

"I think I'm ready," Beth says. "We don't want to be too late."

"Nah," Lisa says, "Only losers show up early."

Who died and made her the party queen?

"Yeah that's true," Sukhy says.

"Do you know if Jason is turning up?" Lisa asks, interested.

"His dad has him under house arrest," Sukhy says with a sigh. "I don't think we'll be seeing him."

"Probs for the best," Lisa said. "Casey Beckard is going to be there."

"I hope he shows up," I say.

"I have no problem with Casey as long as she keeps her mouth shut," Beth says.

Lisa doesn't seem to hear and starts ranting about how dangerous Jason is and broadcasts all the opinions she heard across the lunch-room.

Gee, did I ask any of those people?

"To be honest," Sukhy says loudly, cutting her off. "I don't really want to talk about this."

"Oh, I'm sorry," Lisa gasps. "I didn't mean it like that. It's just…"

"No, it's fine, just he's a good friend, and I'm kind of sick of everyone giving their five cents."

I smile at her over the top of Lisa's shoulder.

"People have always done it, ever since he was little just because of where his family lives. It's bullshit."

"To be fair, he did hit a girl in the face," Lisa says.

"He has a temper, but so do you," Beth says. "You threw your hockey stick at the wall last week because you got frustrated with your shoes."

Lisa glares at her. "Ok, never mind! Let's just have a good time. Is Matt meeting us there?"

"No, again, he is not. We are getting him from his house."

She tugs up her jacket, adjusts her bra for the hundredth time and beams cheerfully at me. "Shall we go then?"

Lisa's mother tells us to 'not do anything she wouldn't' and then winks really exaggeratedly. Sukhy laughs so I do as well. But I really want to cringe.

We get guys beeping their horns in approval as we walk from Lisa's to Matt's place. It's gross, and when they slow down to get a good look, Sukhy says 'Yeah, we're fifteen,' and one of the guys tells her that she's forgotten her burka.

She throws her can of beer at his car as he speeds off laughing like he's just been declared funniest man alive.

I slide an arm through hers and say horrible things about that guy until she smiles again. Lisa keeps finding new ways to say that she finds being honked at by strangers on the street really liberating. I switch off. I'm buzzed and don't want to start feeling bad.

Relief as we approach Matt's house and spot him talking to Freddie Hankerson, at his drive underneath the oak tree. Freddie is carrying a crate of beer, he looks almost nice without his douche friends with him. He's wearing a letterman jacket, and I notice him tuck a strand of Matt's messy hair behind his ear before Lisa calls out to Matt, and the hand is swiftly retracted.

"Fred (which she pronounces as Fre-er-edddd)! I didn't know you were out tonight!" Lisa says excitedly, rushing up and forcibly linking her arm through Matt's.

"Oh yeah, all the guys from the team are going," he said with a shrug. "No getting out of it."

"Hey, shall we all go in together?" Beth asks with a little too much enthusiasm.

"Sure, I guess, we're all going the same way."

Yeah, they are definitely cousins, possessed by a hereditary desire to be seen walking into a bullshit high school party with a football player. I see them, either side of Fred, smirking and laughing and batting their lashes, while he glances right over the top of Lisa's head to shoot shy smiles at Matt.

. . . .

I don't like parties.

That probably makes me sound boring. Or like one of those people who are needlessly alternative for no reason? Like people who say their favourite number is 13, or that Christmas is overrated.

But no, I hate crowds at school, so being bundled together in a stranger's house with all my classmates, isn't really my idea of fun. It's like school, but I'm expected to be enjoying myself.

Me and Sukhy are cramped up on a counter-top, legs outstretched, sharing a beer. Beth is in the bathroom behind us, throwing up. It's nerves. It was always nerves with her like she expects her mom to appear in a puff of smoke. I can see Matt outside smoking with a couple of gloomy looking guys. Lisa is chatting with Riley and a gaggle of his stupid, slack-jawed friends.

Lisa keeps leaning forwards to give the guys a look at the goods, and she's doing this weird, cutesy laugh.

Do guys really like that sort of thing? Do men like it a well, or is it just a high school thing?

"Do you reckon Riley will just keep Lisa after this?" Sukhy asks.

I found myself smirking, despite myself. "Well, let's just hope this goes well."

"I did think that was the point," she hands me another beer. "Do you think we should be having more fun?"

"I mean, we could join in with Sing Star?"

Kath Kaine and Lucy Hart have taken over the living room with their dumb karaoke game. As if that made any of it more tolerable, this party. Just add music and poor singing. Voila. Hell.

"Fuck no."

Then suddenly shouts from the front of the house, lots of offended yelling. Sukhy jumps down from the counter and slides straight onto her knees. She starts laughing, and I stumble as I go and help her.

"What's going on?" I ask one of the girls rushing past, whatshername.

"Jason Danvers just showed up," she says, "Rob is gonna tell him to leave."

"Oh shit," Sukhy says. "What's he doing here?"

We edge through the crowd to find Jason stood there smiling in the entrance, opposite Rob Dawson, who seems to be way too drunk to be kicking anyone out any time soon.

"Hitting girls isn't cool, bro, s'not," Rob slurs.

"Man, I know," Jason says. "I got confused cos Casey is kind of mannish."

Rob hiccups and laughs.

"Not funny," Laurie Dellmonte snaps from her seat on the sofa. "Go home, freak."

A few people echo her, and the crowd around them narrows.

"Hey, Casey was being racist to my gal pal," he says, "Hitting girls isn't nice, but neither is being a racist."

"It was a joke, God," Casey mutters. She glances briefly at Sukhy before looking away. I see her face is still swollen, despite the make-up.

"Come on, Rob, let me come in," Jason says. "I'll be good as gold."

"Man, nah, you should go," Rob says, he stumbles and has to lean against one of his friends. "It's not happening."

Jason shrugs and sighs heavily.

The girls playing Sing Star look pleased and nudge each other enthusiastically. I hear Laurie mutter something possibly homophobic under her breath. Then the crowd gasps as Jason produces a bright green bottle from his jacket pocket.

"The only thing is, I brought you some absinthe and since I'm not a guest, I guess I'll have to keep it."

Rob gets elbowed out of the way by Tommy Rhodes, who's beaming.

"Is that the stuff that makes you trip out?"

"Oh yeah, trip out, trip in, it's all in here," Jason says, holding it up. "You guys can have it if I can maybe, I don't know, stay and have a beer or two?"

The guys start laughing and patting him on the back, the green bottle vanishes into the crowd, and Jason slides in, past the disapproving stares towards me and Sukhy. He laughs and picks her up and spins her around.

"Made it!"

"What about your dad?" she asks, still laughing as he sets her down.

"He's got the guys 'round playing poker. He's probably drunker than those guys."

"Jase, didn't we drink your dad's absinthe?" I ask.

He grins. "Yeah, I had filled it with water. But now it's part... everything Dad had in the liquor cabinet, I guess. Bit of vodka, bit of whisky, bit of this really gross coffee liqueur. Those assholes won't know the difference. Come on, let's find Matt."

· · · ·

I guess parties aren't that bad. My throat hurts from yelling over the music and smoking too much. Most of my classmates have started to leave. Lisa is trying to flirt with Riley and Matt is actually having a good time outside, him and the group of guys are goofing around, throwing pizza boxes across the garden like shit un-aerodynamic Frisbees.

Plus, we have free beer, so yeah, we stay.

Riley and Rob and the rest of their clowns eventually shift out into the garden too. Lisa cheers them all on with Beth and some dopey faced girl from the grade above. Sukhy and Jason are fumbling around with a guitar they seem to have found.

Riley picks me up and spins me around on his shoulders, telling the others excitedly that I gave him beer the other day.

And, for once, this is fine, they actually weren't giving Matt a hard time. They aren't giving anyone a hard time. They are just stupid kids like us.

I lie on the grass and stare up at the stars. Sukhy is smoking next to me, lying on her front, babbling about her piano teacher being a douche. Rob and Jason are on the floor, wheezing with laughter about some joke I haven't heard.

When we are like this, at this level, nobody cares if I don't react, if I don't hear the joke, if I can't be bothered to be like them. It's ok, being blank doesn't mean being like her.

I'm glad I'm here.

I mean, yeah, my idea of fun isn't really watching a loud of drunk guys chase each other around over a half-deflated basketball or a pizza box, but it isn't actually that far off tonight.

Riley plonks himself down on the grass in front of us.

"Hey, beer girl."

"Hello yourself, Riley."

Lisa is passed out drunk on the garden furniture, and Beth is humming tunelessly on the ground beside her. Jason lay next to the guys who tackled him on the playground the other day, wearing the deflated basketball as a crown.

"So, how're ya guys liking this party?" Riley slurs.

"It's in the top five," Sukhy said.

"Top five? Like you guys go to any other kind," he said, his words jumbled over themselves. "You just hang out in t' woods like river people."

"River people?"

"Yah."

"Hey, you caught us out."

"Yeah I did," he said, hiccupping. "How are you?"

"We're good. We have beer. Want one?"

"Noooo," he says, bashing the ground with his fist.

"You should get some sleep, Sleeping Beauty," Sukhy said, smirking at him.

"Nah, I just need a casual five. Real casual. Real casual. Hey, where's Hank?"

"Who?"

"Hank. Hank, where's Hank?"

He means Freddie Hankerson, I realise. And since I can't see Matt, I'm guessing Freddie probably doesn't want Riley rushing around looking for him.

"He's probably somewhere, leave him."

"No way, he's my ride home."

"Erm, yeah, neither of you can drive like this."

"Nooo, we're walking home together," he says. "We all buddy up on party nights. Gotta get home safe. Gotta get to the game, get to the game." He repeats this phrase a few times before leaning back and yelling, 'HANK!!!!'

"Don't know where he is, man."

He staggers up and trips over Beth, who jolts awake. He laughs, and suddenly Beth is crying about how angry her parents might potentially be. And it's tedious, so I didn't listen. Sukhy is walking off to the bathroom, so I guess she's not interested either.

I'm thinking about heading home when Riley and Beth say that they were going to look for Hank together. He is walking off into the woods with Beth following him—I remember hearing a rumour about Riley and Becca Phillips, and Riley and Caitlin O'Learey and Riley and Lucille Mornstein—and suddenly letting Beth wander off, drunk, into the woods with him, alone, seems like a good way to continue the Riley saga with 'Riley and Beth Green'.

So, I follow them, I keep enough distance, I don't want to walk with them, talk with them, I just want to make sure she's ok. I don't think I could do much damage, I mean, the guy is built like Captain freaking America. The two of them are talking, he's sobering up, grumbling about Hank being unreliable.

I have to be careful not to be heard, I realise as it strikes me how quiet it is out here compared to the blaring noise of the party. I can hear it faintly in the background, but Riley's shouts for Hank become clearer and clearer. I lose sight of him and Beth and start to worry.

Stupid Beth.

I trip and stumble and nearly land in a clearing in the woods. Steadying myself upright and still concealed by hanging branches, I see two figures on the ground a few feet away from me. I recognise Matt straight away, with his stupid floppy hair. He's sat facing someone bigger and broader, his hand moving frantically between the other man's legs. The two of them are kissing hurriedly.

And it's Freddie Hankerson, of course.

He wasn't exactly subtle. I decide to leave them to it, stolen moments and the like, and turn to make my way back to find Beth, when across the clearing, someone charges through the bushes, shouting angrily.

"What the fuck, man?"

Riley is red-faced, lip twisted upright into a sneer. Freddie leaps to his feet, trying and failing to zip up his trousers.

"Riley, Riley, man, it's not what it looks like!"

Matt is still on the floor, inching back. He looks completely terrified. This isn't like at school, this isn't like where we force him to come somewhere that he doesn't want to go. This is a real terror.

"Well, it looks like you're messing around with that fucking faggot."

"I—I'm not!"

"Yeah? So, is he's forcing himself on you then?" Riley steps forward, closing the remaining distance between them in one step. He shoves Freddie hard, nearly knocking him to the ground. "Well?"

"I—I'm drunk," Freddie says, his tone is defeated and weak. "Look, I'm just drunk."

"Is this what you do? You perv out on the rest of us after practice and then come here and gets your rocks off with this freak?"

Matt looks up at Freddie the Mystery Texter, and his face seems to fall as he realises that Freddie isn't going to help him.

Freddie manages to do his jeans up and keeps shaking his head, his face red and flustered.

"No, no, it's not like that. I was drunk, I'm drunk! He said that he'd jerk me off and I just…"

"Does your dad know you like this gay shit?"

"Riley, come on," Freddie said, tears in his eyes. "He confused me, I thought…"

Riley stops shoving him then. His expression softened.

"No? I get it. You were drunk, man. Her fucking Highness there just likes waiting around at these kinds of things, for guys like us to lose our standards." He claps Freddie on the back. "You're lucky I was here, right?"

"Y—yeah, I'm lucky. Y-You're a pal, man."

Riley shoves him again, this time away from Matt and back towards the party. "Yeah, I know. Sooo, why don't you fuck off back to the house?"

"Yeah, let's go."

"No, I'm staying. I want to have a chat with Little Miss Man here. Gonna teach him a few life lessons, show him what we do to perverts 'round here."

Matt, who had been going to stand up, freezes.

"Come on, leave him," Freddie said. "He's drunk and stupid."

"He's fucking sick in the head. This time it's you, next time he could be coming for my fucking ass," Riley says.

"Riley, I'm not—!" Matt tries.

"Hank, I just told you, right, fuck off back to the house. Or would you rather stay and hold your boyfriend's hand while I teach him a lesson?"

Freddie doesn't look back at Matt as he runs back through the woods. He passes me but doesn't spot me crouched there, watching.

We wait like this, the three of us, Matt on the floor, Riley stood over him and me in the shrubbery, until Freddie's footsteps start to get really far away and then we can't hear them at all.

"Riley," Matt starts to say.

Riley's arm jerks out, and he pulls Matt to his feet by his collar. His fist swings back, and there's a rush of air as he smashes it into Matt's stomach. Matt grunts and the sound rings out through the clearing like a gun. Matt's legs give out from under him, but Riley, still holding him upright, backhands him, sending him sprawling and as he lets go, Matt falls on his side on the floor.

"Hey! No! No! Stop!" Beth dashes out of the woods and rushes at Riley. She grabs his arm and tries to drag him back. I feel a twinge of love for her as I see her struggling to hold Riley back as she yells, "Leave him alone! Matt, run! Run away!"

Riley snarls like an animal. He grabs her by her face and throws her bodily to the ground. She lands with a loud thump, her head smacking against the floor. Riley spins around in a flash and grabs Matt by his hair before his knee comes up and collides with Matt's chest knocking the air out of him. He lets him fall to the ground again, leaning down to sneer, "Where are you going, princess?"

He goes to kick him again, but Beth has dived forwards and grabs his leg.

"Get off me, bitch!" Riley kicks her in the back twice until she lets go.

Beth lies on the ground, crying loudly now.

"HELP!" she wheezes. "Someone! Help!"

Riley snorts as he walks past her and bends down over Matt. He sits down on his chest with a thump.

"You don't think about this happening when you try and get with guys, do you, faggot?"

Matt starts to scream, but the noise he makes is a squashed shout as Riley's fists come down on him.

What occurred next seemed to happen in slow motion.

Riley is bent over Matt, hands clasped together as he bashes his palms down at his face and chest like a sick CPR.

Beth is on the ground, bloody, screaming for him to stop.

I step over her and with medical precession, cut Riley where his neck meets muscular shoulder.

His body goes stiff, his bashing fists stop smashing into Matt, up and down, up and down.

He looks at me.

And there's fear.

There's confusion.

There is a lot of blood.

More than Casey Beckard in the courtyard.

More than the cat.

Riley goes to speak, it sounds like he's saying "What".

My foot collides with his stomach.

He falls backwards and hits the ground with a thud.

I kick him again, this time in the side.

He rolls onto his back, a hand clasping the wounds in his neck.

He can't form words, just wheezes that might have been words before.

My boot slams into his stomach, winding him.

He arches up, his hand comes away from the wound.

He's bleeding faster now.

I sit down on his chest.

He brings his hands up to protect himself as the knife comes down.

Again.

Again.

Again.

I slash his wrists, I stab at his chest. I cut his cheek nice and deep.

He wails, undignified and incomprehensible babbling, tears running down his cheeks.

Eventually, he stops.

His bleeding arms come down to his sides, and he is quiet.

All is quiet now.

I get up and look at the others. Matt hasn't moved from where he was. He stares up at me through his bruised eyes, mouth open, soundless. He looks frightened. I want to tell him that he doesn't need to be now.

Beth is vomiting.

I wipe my knife on my jeans and stuff it in my jacket, before bending down and offering Matt a hand.

"Can you stand up?"

He doesn't answer. Looking down, I realise that my hand is dark with blood.

"Matt."

He takes my hand then, legs shaking as he stood.

"Is he dead?" His voice catches in his throat.

"Yes. I'm going to need you to help me get rid of this."

"Fiona, I don't think I can. Why would you—!" He covers his bruised face with his hands and cried weakly.

"Do you think he wouldn't have done the same to you?"

"I don't…"

"He would have beaten you to death. He would have gone and called his pal fucking Hank to help him get rid of your body. We would think you ran away. Your parents would think you ran away. But you'd be dead."

"You don't know that, Fiona, you don't—!" He starts to sob loudly.

I couldn't stop myself from rolling my eyes. "Help me get rid of him."

"You can't—!" Beth gasps. "Fiona, he has a family, friends. We can't just throw him away. We will get caught."

"We won't," I said.

"Fiona—!" Matt croaks. "Fiona, what can we do?"

"Go and get Sukhy and Jason," I whisper.

"What?"

"Sukhy, go and get Sukhy and Jason, Beth," I yell at her. "I can hardly go, can I? So, GO! Fucking GO, Beth!"

CHAPTER SEVEN

I think Matt was talking to me, but I can't hear him. I can't hear the others when they come back through the woods. I sit on the ground by Riley's body and notice that I've cut off his wrist. I've cut his chest into chunks. His face has been sectioned up, and he doesn't look like himself anymore.

I know Matt is talking to me, but I can't make sense of what he's saying.

Hands are on my face.

"Fiona."

Someone is whispering in the background. I hold on tight to my legs, I dig in my nails until they draw blood.

"Fiona."

Sukhy makes me look up at her, I stare, wide-eyed into her face.

I want to answer, but it's like she's talking to me through a tunnel.

"Fiona, can you stand up?"

I stand up and shake my head.

"I think she's in shock," she says to Jason.

I'm not though.

"She was laughing," Beth whimpers. "She was laughing."

"Stop it," Jason says. "Shut up, Beth." He reaches past Sukhy and grabs hold of my shoulders. "Hey, Fiona. Hey." He shakes me hard, and suddenly I can hear them all. I'm not down that tunnel anymore. "You ok?"

"Yeah," I say. "Sorry. I got…a bit side-tracked."

"He was going to kill me," Matt says. "Riley…He was beating me up." His face is swollen already, his eye blackened, he limps as he walks over. "Fiona was protecting me."

"We know," Sukhy says. "Fiona, we should call the police."

69

"No," I say.

"This was self-defence, Riley is four times the size of you and Matt."

"No," I say.

"Sukhy," Jason says, "I don't think we can call this self-defence. The guy is in four pieces."

Beth starts coughing again and vomits on the ground.

"Fuck," Sukhy groans, covering her face. "Oh, fuck."

"And she has a knife," Beth says, "Fiona, why do you even carry a knife?"

"I always carry one," I say and then regret doing it.

"What?" Beth gasps.

"Beth," Sukhy interrupts. "It doesn't matter now. So just stop it. Let me think."

Jason bends down and prods Riley's face, he laughs out in shock when Riley's left cheek comes away from the rest of his face.

"Fuck, gross!"

"Jason, stop that!" Matt says. "Stop it!"

"You've pulled a Red Creek," he says, shaking his hands clean. "You know that, right? You've cut him up like he's Abigail freaking Henderson."

"No, I haven't," I snap.

No, I don't want that to be true.

But look, there he is, half in pieces.

"We have to get rid of him," I say. "Alright? We have to get rid of the body."

"What?" Matt says.

"He's in pieces already, I'll cut them down a bit more," I say. "If we clean up here, and hide the bits of his body all over the place, we can cover this up."

"What do you mean, we? I'm not hulking body parts around," Beth says. "No! We should have called the police already!"

"We can't call the police," I snarl at her.

"We have to—!" Beth says.

"No, what we have to do is cover this up. People will think he ran off or fell in a river drunk somewhere. If you let me finish cutting him up, we can put him in plastic bags and hide him."

"My dad has an incinerator at the hospital," Sukhy says. "I'm pretty sure I can get access to it in the week."

"We can put a bit in Lake Rhine," Jason said. "He's coming apart already. If we can get him into five pieces and work together, we can do this."

"He has a family," Beth said.

"So do I," Matt said. "Do you think he wouldn't have done the same to me?"

"I don't know why you had a knife," Beth says and starts crying again.

We leave her to it. Sukhy and Matt go and get vodka from the party to pour around the clearing, clean up the ground. Beth sits on a log and weeps.

"I found this, in the tool shed at the party," Jason said, staggering back through the woods. "Might be easier to cut through bone."

I wipe my knife on my clothes and put it in my pocket and go and sit down by Riley's side. Jason goes to swing it, but I grab his arm, feeling myself shaking.

"It's cool, I got this," I say, "Give me the axe."

"No," he said, "It's fine. My dad has me do it all the time. It's like chopping wood. Very red wood."

So, between the two of us, we separate his torso, we detach his legs, we remove his wrists and hands. I clean his nails and wash his hands to remove any trace of Matt that he had on them. Riley was wearing a woven bracelet around his wrist, it is worn and speckled and done up way too tight. Jason passes me the axe, and like an executioner, I take off his head. Then with my knife, I remove his ears and his feet. I take out his organs.

Jason whistles.

"Didn't realise you were another Red Creek fan," he says.

"Don't be fucked up," I say.

"Oh, come on, you've got his style down cold," he says. "It's pretty much the creepiest story I've ever heard. Bite-sized chunks."

"Stop it," Beth groans.

I get up and wipe my hands on my jeans.

It smells more than I expected it to.

Jason grins and starts folding them up in plastic. He makes quick work of it, putting the pieces of Riley into five plastic bags. They look like they could be someone's shopping, not someone. Sukhy and Matt re-emerge with vodka and sweeping brushes. They dowse the clearing, getting rid of most of the blood, at least on a superficial level. And for reasons I can't explain to anyone, I have a bottle of hydrogen peroxide in my jacket pocket. I sprinkle it all over the ground and brush it in with the sweeping brush. Nobody asks why I've carried it with me. I put some on a rag and clean the axe thoroughly, and Jason puts on Sukhy's gloves to take it back to the tool shed.

"Will this be enough?" Sukhy says, "The police have black lights and stuff, I don't think this will be enough to clean up…all of him."

"The hydrogen peroxide should cover it to a degree," I say, "But the police…they will be looking for a missing person at first. Even if they do find something, they won't be looking for a body straight away. It'll rain. It'll be fine."

She doesn't look convinced. So, we kick up the dust and spill more of the vodka.

I change into Sukhy's spare clothes, and Jason burns my clothes in the campfire. It's a shame, I really liked those jeans.

We all take a bag. Even Beth, even as she cries. The five of us walk through the woods. Sukhy's jumper itches the back of my neck, and I scratch until my neck starts to bleed a little. Jason hums loudly, and Matt doesn't dare make a sound. Sukhy and Beth are just ahead of us.

"I can't believe we're doing this," Beth hisses.

"Stop thinking about it," Sukhy says.

"I can't stop thinking about it! Why did she have a knife?"

"That's not the point."

"It is! Sukhy, why does she carry a knife?"

"I don't know, alright. But it's a good thing she did. I know this is scary, but she was just protecting Matt. And you, he hit you, babe."

"She was laughing," Beth hisses. "She was laughing her ass off."

It goes quiet between them. Or maybe it doesn't. I feel like the ground has opened up under me, and the others are leaving the woods without me. I want to vomit. I want to scratch my eyes off. I was laughing? No, it was quiet. There was just Riley and the knife and those wordless whimpers. I couldn't have been…

It wasn't…

I feel sickness pool in my stomach. I want to throw this bag away, far away, and never come back out here again.

"No."

"What?" Jason asks.

"Nothing," I say. "Let's just go home."

· · · ·

We discuss how this will go. I reassure them I know a place for mine, where it can be gotten rid of and untraceable. Sukhy will burn hers at the hospital using her father's key. Matt will bury his in a landfill site on the outskirts of town. Jason will feed his to his three dogs while his dad and brothers are sleeping when he gets home. Beth will hide hers in the woods by a creek. She mumbles something about leaving a marker for a grave. I think I dissuade her.

We part ways as the sun begins to rise. The others all hug me, all except Beth.

Beth walks two paces ahead as we walk back down our street. She won't look at me. Beth just cries and cries.

She slumps into her house through the front door and doesn't care when her parents wake up and angrily demand to know where she's been all night. I stumble into my house, kick off Sukhy's trainers and walk like a zombie through the hall, towards the kitchen. I open up the basement door and toss the bag down the stairs into the darkness.

I close the front door and lie down on my bed.

And for once, I fall asleep easier than I ever have in my life.

· · · ·

She doesn't bring it up with me in the morning even though I know she wants to. I see her watching me while I eat my toast. I see her open her mouth and then close it again when we cook together that evening.

I won't bring it up until she does.

That's on her.

I don't really talk to the others over the weekend. We'd usually go and hang out in the arcade or meet in the woods. Sukhy snapchats about watching something lousy on TV but other than that, we are quiet. We are all quiet. On Saturday night, I see Lisa go over to Beth's house. The two of them sit around her front porch watching something on their phones and talking quietly, excitedly. Beth's eyes seem red.

I want to ask her how she's doing, but I can't seem to bring myself to talk to her. She said I was laughing. And if we talk about it, just the two of us, face to face, I'll know for sure that I was. I want to talk to them, but I feel slimy and wrong inside. Like there are hands pressed tightly around my throat, and no matter what I do, I'll never be able to pull myself free. I find my neck itches more and more, and I keep scratching.

But no matter what I do, the itch doesn't seem to go away.

Then all of a sudden, it's Sunday night. Me and Mother are chopping up vegetables for a curry. It's pretty much the one thing we do as a pair. We have the radio on, I've managed to persuade her to let me have the radio on rather . It's a local station, nothing great, the DJ is always the same guy, DJ Mike who gets a really obvious sore throat towards the end of the day.

But then the music stops and DJ Mike introduces an emergency broadcast from the sheriff's office and the county police.

"This morning, we have been made aware that local teenager, Riley Sanders, has gone missing. Riley is 18 years old, six foot three, with blonde hair and blue eyes. He's the linebacker for the Greystation High School football team. His parents have reported that Riley has not been seen since he went to a friend's party on Friday night. Police are asking if anyone with any information regarding Riley's whereabouts on Friday night, can come forward as a matter of urgency. Ain't that sad, ladies and gentlemen? Can I repeat, anyone with information regarding 18 yr old Riley Sanders on last Friday night, please report it to Sheriff O'Leary right away."

A sting of pain.

Ow.

"Look what you've done," she says and pulls my wrist upright. I realise as pain blossoms in my arm that I've somehow cut myself. I wince and pull away from her.

"Don't touch me."

She rolls her eyes and inspects my wrist from afar as I go and put it under the cold water. "You should be more careful."

"My hand slipped. I am careful."

"You look pale, Fiona."

"I said I'm ok. God, stop fussing me."

She smirks and goes back to her preparation.

My wrist aches. I've cut it just where the hand meets the bone. Blood oozes from it, and I squeeze it harder despite myself.

"That little present you left downstairs for me," she says after a moment. "If I was to hazard a guess, I'd say that leg might have once belonged to...a 6-foot 3-inch, eighteen-year-old linebacker with blonde hair and blue eyes."

My hands are shaking violently now. I look up and see her face, blank, nothing at all, just blank and staring at me like this doesn't matter, like none of these things matters at all.

"I'm not hungry," I snarl at her. "I'm going to my room."

I feel those cold dead eyes on me as I storm past, as I run up the stairs. As I shut my door and pull the covers over my head. It's like those eyes are on the other side of the blankets, staring down at me.

. . . .

Beth doesn't wait for me on Monday morning. She's long gone when I call outside her house. I spot her on her own when I reach the playground. She's huddled with Lisa and two other girls, talking in hushed whispers. My heart sinks.

"Morning, Fiona," Matt says.

He has two black eyes, a bust lip and is still walking with a limp. I reach around and hug him very gently.

"You look awful," I say.

"Flattering," he says. "But yeah, I know. Sorry I was quiet this weekend. My mom wanted to call the police. She wouldn't stop hounding me all weekend. I told her I fell over drunk, but..." Fist-sized bruises on his face, both eyes. Fingerprint bruises all over his body. I'm not surprised that she doesn't believe him.

"But you're ok?"

"Yeah."

"And you hear from your Mystery Texter at all?"

He looks sad. "Yeah, he's been in touch. I've told him never to contact me again."

"Do you think he'll report that he left Riley with you?"

"I don't think he'd want anyone to know that he went off for a walk in the wood with me," he says bitterly. "He'll keep his mouth shut."

"I'm sorry, Matt."

He shrugs his shoulders, defeated. "I was stupid to think otherwise."

"What did he say? About the whole Riley thing?"

"I told him that Riley hit me and left me and wandered off drunk," Matt said. "He asked if he could come over, so I doubt that he thinks I've done him in or anything." His eyes water a little, and he runs a hand through his hair. "I feel sick thinking about it."

"Then don't."

. . . .

In homeroom, Mr. Skallenger repeats the message about Riley from the radio. He sounds bored, I know he doesn't much care for the football team. Our class is shocked, scandalised. Some of the guys snort in apparent disinterest, some of the girls gasp and look shocked. People talk about how he's probably just run off, someone mutters about him maybe shacking up with some girl. Someone leers at Becca Phillips and asks if she's seen him recently.

I notice how her hands tremble.

Lisa is nudging Sukhy, I hear her say 'Oh my Gawwwd' in that irritating way she does. Matt doesn't look up from his book. I try to focus on looking concerned when I notice Beth sitting there with a hand over her mouth. She looks frightened, worried, like she's going to be sick. The colour has vanished from her cheeks, and it's like I can see the veins in her face, like her skin is translucent and fragile like a jellyfish, like I could pop her with a pin.

I squeeze my hands together and panic that people are staring at her, thinking she knows something.

"Fiona, oh my God, you're bleeding!" Lizzie Ryan says from beside me.

I look down, and I realise that I've dug my nails hard into the wound on my wrist. Blood sticks to my nails and drips down my arm. I cry out in alarm and wince, holding it to me.

"Miss Taylor, what's the matter there?"

"Sorry, sir, I cut my arm the other day. Can I go to the nurse's office? I think I caught it on my bag."

"Yes, yes, of course, go right ahead."

I spot Sukhy staring at me as I head out of the classroom. I pass the nurse's office and instead just go to the bathrooms. My wrist goes under the cold tap, and I watch the blood circle the drain for a few seconds until the water runs clear, and I'm left with only a throbbing pain in my arm.

Everything's going to be ok, I say to myself. It's going to be fine. Just calm down. It's all ok now. Everyone's fine.

I return before everyone leaves for first period English. Sukhy asks if I'm ok and I say yes but can't seem to smile. My face just doesn't want to do what I want it to. Beth won't look at me. I wish she would. I wish she could see how cruel she's being.

"Fiona Taylor cuts herself," Daisy Jones hisses as she walks past.

"No, she doesn't. Why don't you start though?" Sukhy sneers at her. "Buzz off."

"Ignore her," Matt says.

Daisy sneers and turns the corner toward English.

"Come on, let's get to class."

I wish I'd done better in the middle school exams so me and Sukhy could be in class together. Without Jason, I'm left alone with Beth, who won't turn and look at me no matter what I do. She's sat right next to me, but her hair conceals her face like a hood. She twists her body away from me, and for a second when our hands touch as I go to turn a page in the book, Beth flinches.

"Beth, it's just me," I say.

She ignores me and aggressively stares out of the window.

Class ends, and she takes off like someone's stuffed dynamite in her bag. I don't rush to catch up. I just feel like there's a big hole in my heart. It's opened wide, and I can't feel anything. And I want someone to grab hold of me and shake me until I wake up and I'm fine again. But Beth won't look at me. And the others feel so far away.

I keep digging my nails into the wound on my wrist just so I can feel something other than blank.

. . . .

My mother isn't home when I get in. Pete, the hot policeman, isn't going for a lap. I wonder if they are somewhere alone together. I re-bandage my wrist and go and lie on the sofa. I close my eyes and try not to think.

My phone is buzzing. It's Jason, I barely register before I toss it onto the coffee table and clench my eyes shut. And for a moment, just a moment, it's so quiet. It's so quiet that I can almost believe that nothing happened at the weekend. That Riley Sanders is going to swagger back into my high school and everything will be fine. Everything will be ok. It's going to be fine. Just keep calm. Everyone is ok. Even fucking Riley Sanders. But then that moment ends, and I hear someone moving around in the basement. It's slow first, like someone crawling along, but then it gets louder, a dragging sound, a low moaning.

I get up and storm over to the basement door and yell, *"Shut up!* Shut the fuck up!" through the thick redwood. I kick it so hard that my foot bursts with pain.

But the groaning stops. The scraping stops, and it's just me in the house with that big red door.

Then she comes home. She sees me there, standing in front of the basement, shaking.

She smirks at me.

"There something you want back down there, Fiona?"

If I could run away, to another city, change my name, change my face, burn down this life and everything it was. I know she'd still be able to find me. If I could run to the sea or the sky, she'd find me.

She's always there.

She is my mother, after all.

CHAPTER EIGHT

A week passes, and Riley doesn't come home. His mom comes onto the news and begs him to come back. She cries, and her eye make-up rushes down her face and makes her look like a raccoon. I watch it back a few times.

Missing posters go up, his picture seems to creep out and stare at me from every lamppost and every corner. Jason comes back to school and whispers to me that he's got one of Riley's Missing posters in his chemistry book and doesn't look offended when Sukhy tells him that it's morbid and really sick.

One Thursday morning, Mr. Skallenger tells us that a few of us are going to be interviewed by the police. It's all people who were at the party. I sit and wait throughout the day to see when I'll be called upon. Beth is pale-faced and frightened. Sukhy tells her that everything is going to be fine, and she smiles nervously.

She gets called away from our fourth period English class to go and speak to the police. And I spot Pete, the handsome detective welcoming her into one of the empty classrooms. He smiles at her, and I can see colour returning to Beth's cheeks. She's smiling when he closes the door behind them.

"Everything ok?" I ask her when she joins the rest of us at lunch.

"Yeah," she said. "They didn't ask much, just about the party. How did Riley seem...that sort of thing."

"They spoke to me this morning," Matt said. "I think they are going to ask to see me again."

"What? What happened?" Sukhy asked.

"Hank spoke to them, he told them that me and him went on a walk and Riley came and found us and hit me in the face."

"What did you say?" Jason whispers.

79

"I told them that was true. What, Jason? Mr. Davis vouched that Riley gives me a hard time. The whole school has seen me covered in bruises, I couldn't not say that it was true," Matt snaps. "I told them that Riley hit me a few times. They asked if I retaliated, I said no. They asked if anyone witnessed it, and I said no. I told them that I pretended to be unconscious and Riley stumbled off drunk into the woods."

"And they believed you?"

"Yeah. The younger guy asked why I didn't report the attack. And Mr. Davis pointed out all the times he has escalated the whole bullying thing to the principal. I'm really glad he was there."

I touch his hand and squeeze.

"I'm glad he was there with you."

"Me too. I was shitting myself."

"Miss Taylor?"

I look up and see Miss Kein, the principal's assistant staring at me from the courtyard door. I get up and notice the others looking at me nervously, and I itch my bandages as I start walking towards her.

I find myself imagining that Beth and Matt were lying. That they told the police everything. I imagine the others sat back there, knowing that I'm going into the little classroom to be arrested. I look back at them before the doors close, and I see the tension in their faces.

Jason offers me a thumbs up.

The door closes behind me.

· · · ·

"Young Fiona," Pete says and offers me that winning smile. "So, you do go to school sometimes."

"And it's nice to see that you're really a cop," I say.

His partner is fat and middle-aged, who balances his folded arms on his stomach. I smile at him, but he doesn't return it. Mr. Davis pulls a chair out for me and pats my shoulder encouragingly.

"Now nobody thinks you've done anything wrong, Fiona," Mr. Davis says. "We just want to know about the party at Mr. Dawson's house last week. It's just to see if you might have seen something to help us find Riley."

"Ok," I say.

"Alright, so this is Detective Gary Albright, and I believe you already know his partner, Detective Peter Brankowski."

"Nice to meet you, I guess."

"Hm," the partner says before jumping straight in with, "Miss Taylor, you're the daughter of Sylvia Taylor, aren't you?"

"Erm, yes," I say.

"Your mother was previously known as Sarah White?"

"Yeah. My mother wasn't at Rob's party, by the way."

I see Pete smirk behind his coffee.

"What's your relationship with your mom like?"

"She can be a pain."

"Has your mother ever spoken to you about your uncle Robert?"

"No, unsurprisingly she doesn't like to chat about her dead brother."

I can see that bothers him because he grunts and leans forward.

"Did you get on well with Riley Sanders?"

"He was fine, I guess."

"See, that surprises me," he says, "I know he isn't too fond of your friend Matthew Hale, was he?"

"Ok, well, I didn't want to say bad stuff about him while he's missing, I don't really know Riley, but he seems like a jerk. He picks on my friend every day for no reason, and nothing happens because Riley chases a ball around the field for the school."

"Sounds like you've got a chip on your shoulder about him," Detective Fatso says.

"Not really, I don't know him. I'd just like Matt to make it through the day without someone trying to hurt him."

"Are you and Mr. Hale close?"

"Yes."

"Are you dating?"

"Matt's gay, that's the reason Riley likes to knock him around. So, no, we're not dating."

"When was the last time you saw Riley?"

"About two AM at the party."

"Two AM, exactly? You know that, exactly?"

"Two AM-ish," I try.

"We don't need an exact time," Pete says, leaning forward. "Did Riley talk to you?"

"He was goofing around in the garden playing frisbee with some old pizza boxes. I was sitting outside with my friends."

"And was Mr. Hale there?"

"Yes. I was pleased because they usually give him such a hard time."

"You kids drinking?"

I give him a flat stare.

"It was a party. Everyone was drinking."

"Was Mr. Sanders drinking a lot? In your estimation?"

"I mean, yeah, he was swaying around, yelling a lot of rubbish. He seemed pretty wasted."

"And, when was the last time you saw Riley?"

"I saw him walk off into the woods, he was looking for Fred Hankerson, I think they had plans to walk home together."

"So that would be around two AM-ish?" Pete said, smiling at me.

"I think so, yeah, it was pretty late."

"And how did you go home, Miss Taylor?"

"Me and my friends all walked home at around four. We walked home slowly, we were all trying to sober up before we go back to our houses. Beth's parents are kind of strict."

"This would be Beth...?"

"Green."

"Did Matt Hale go with you?"

"He came and met us before we left the party, yeah."

"And can you comment on his appearance?"

"He'd been beaten up pretty bad. He had a black eye and his mouth was all bloody."

"Did he tell you what happened?"

"He told me that Riley Sanders had beaten him up. That wasn't exactly new behaviour for Riley. We were all pretty mad. Jason wanted to go and find Riley and hit him."

"This would be Jason..."

"Danvers," Mr. Davis adds. "He's a bit of a hot head. He had an altercation with Riley last week."

"Jason tries to protect Matt from the football players," I snap.

"But you didn't go after Riley, did you?"

82

"No. Matt was just frightened and upset. So, we patched him up best we could and started taking a long walk home. He was frightened about what his mom would say about his face."

"And you didn't go off on your own?"

"No, I just told you, I went home with my friends."

"And would you be comfortable showing us the contents of your bag there, Miss Taylor?" Detective Fatso asks.

"Erm, a bit, why?"

"The other students weren't asked," Mr. Davis interrupts.

"It's standard procedure if I feel there is cause," Detective Fatso says firmly. "So, you wouldn't be comfortable doing that, Miss Taylor?"

"I don't see why I should have to," I say.

"Gary," Pete whispers, "I don't think—"

I open my bag and toss it out over the table. My books and tampons splash out over the surface and onto the floor. But my knife stays stashed in my underpants.

"Would you like to do a cavity search as well?" I snap. "Fucks sake."

Detective Fatso looks flustered but doesn't stop scowling at me.

"I'm sorry, Fiona," Pete says. He starts helping me pack up my things, and I realise my hands are shaking. They are shaking really bad, and I tug my bag over my shoulder and pretend to wipe my eyes even though I'm not crying.

"There could be lots of reasons for someone to change their name," I hear Mr. Davis say to the police. "I don't care what you might think or some prior investigation, I told you not to upset my students."

"I'm fine, sir," I say. "I'm fine. Can I just go back to class?"

. . . .

The corridor seems too long, and my head spins as I walk past the others and drift into the biology classroom. I'm suddenly sat next to my lab partner, Kelly Binkley, who smells very strongly of some expensive perfume.

I'm half with it as Mrs. McKenzie says that we'll be dissecting a cow's heart today. Kelly is complaining about how gross this is, and

I roll my eyes and agree. Jason is joking around about taking his home for dinner, and the girls are all screeching in horror. We have gloves and scalpels, and Kelly starts making the initial incision.

We work slowly, we are chatting. Only I can't seem to follow what she's saying. I keep thinking about how red the cow's heart is. It's so red, and the blood is red, and it's so distracting that when it's my turn, I slash it wrong and blood splatters over our lab coats, over the table.

Kelly says something that isn't really that funny, but I laugh anyway. I laugh and laugh, but then she starts looking at me like, 'What?'. And I realise that I shouldn't still be laughing. So, I put my hand on the table to get up from the lab stool, only my gloves were covered in blood, so I left this huge red handprint on the wood.

Kelly shouts, 'Oh my God! What are you doing?' I think.

I don't remember the rest, but Jason told me that I fell on the ground and started breathing really erratically. Mrs. McKenzie couldn't get me to calm down or look at her or speak. So she called for a first aider. Jason and the first aid woman from reception walked me to this little office by the front of the school. Apparently, I was crying my eyes out, but I wouldn't talk or make a noise. All I did was breathe really hard.

Pete and Detective Fatso were leaving, and they saw me sitting on the floor with my head between my legs. I remember him asking me some questions, I think he was trying to get me to focus. He took my bloody lab gloves off my hands, they felt boneless, I didn't realise they could move again until he touched them.

That must have been super gross, I kept trying to say that I was sorry. But I don't really remember if I responded to anything he said. I don't really remember anything between trying to stand up from the lab stool and being driven home by the good Detective.

"Am I under arrest?"

"Oh, she speaks," Detective Fatso says.

"How are you feeling, Fiona? No, you aren't under arrest. We're going to your house."

"My mouth feels dry."

"Here," Detective Fatso passes me a bottle of water.

"How do you feel now?"

"I was in class and I think I got upset. My head hurts."

"I think you were having an anxiety attack. Have you had anything like that before?"

I say no.

That isn't true.

"I'm sorry if we scared you," Pete said. "I know it must be horrible to have a classmate vanish like that."

"No, I'm fine. I just need to lie down."

"Is your mother home?"

"No. She's working. But I have my key."

"That's good. It's going to be alright, Fiona. You just rest your eyes until we get to your place."

We arrive at my house, and he walks me to my door. It almost feels like a date. I wonder if he goes on many dates. Probably not if this is how he spends his days off.

He probably wants to come in to have a look around without that search warrant, huh? I probably should let him and just get it over with.

"Will you be alright?" he asks.

"Yes, I'll be fine. Thanks again, Pete."

He leaves me at my door like a gentleman, and I'm left all alone with myself. It's better this way. What could I even say in my own defence?

What would I say to him if he knew? If they find out that he isn't coming home because I cut him up into something unrecognisable. If they lock me up and maybe Detective Pete comes to see me like always, and he asks if I got anxious today because I feel guilty for hurting Riley. Maybe he starts to think I'm upset about what I've done? That I don't want to hurt anyone. That deep down, I'm a nice girl who made a sincere mistake trying to protect her friend.

What would he say to me, if he knew how badly I'd hurt Riley Sanders? How scared I made him before he died?

What could I say?

Something like, yeah I'm so sorry to disappoint you, Detective. I freaked out because talking it through with you and Detective Fatso, going into class to hack up a heart…it made me freak out because I hadn't been able to stop thinking about how good it felt to cut him.

It was why I cut him so many times.

It was why I chopped him into little pieces.

And when there was nothing left, even when you guys were literally coming in and practically accusing me of doing it, all I could think about was how much I wanted to cut something again.

I freaked out because this was something I'd been fighting for a long time. Something that I wasn't ready to deal with.

. . . .

"Your principal called me," she says as she comes back. "You got upset at school?"

"I'm fine."

"Your science teacher said you were hysterical."

I don't look up from the TV screen. "She exaggerated."

She sighs and goes into the kitchen and starts getting things out of the fridge. "In case you're curious I got rid of that thing in the basement."

"I didn't ask."

"Well it was yours, wasn't it? Your little passion project."

"I know you're getting old and all, but have you already gone deaf?"

She looks up at me. "Did you get a lift home from your friend the policeman?"

"He's not my friend, and he's not a policeman. I told you, he's part of a running club."

She snorts, and the noise is strange and alien from her mouth.

"Whatever, you're so paranoid," I sneer.

"He may be part of a running club, but he's still a cop. If you aren't smart enough to see that then maybe you should avoid making a mess."

"Mind your own business."

"Did they ask about me today?" She asks.

I don't want to answer that. I don't want to feed her fucking vanity. I've seen those true crime books on the bookcase beside her bed. I've sat in the car when she drives back to Franberg once a year for the candlelight memorial service. I've seen the expression she makes when she notices Detective Pete staring at the house.

"You didn't come up."

"Really? Not at all?"

"They didn't ask about me?"

"Why? Are you important?" I sneer at her.

She raises an eyebrow, and I turn back towards the television.

"Do you want pasta? I was going to make pasta?"

. . . .

"Soooo, you get to miss school?"

"Well, I don't 'get' to, but Mr. King said to my mom that I might want to take some time to get my head together."

"Aw, the fuck, man," Jason said. "I'm going to be alone."

"You'll be fine," Sukhy said, elbowing him. "Don't cry about it."

We are out in the woods, eating chips and star gazing. Yeah, sometimes we even star gaze. Never constructively, mostly we pretend that we can see the shape of genitalia in the sky. Come on, we're fifteen.

"Are you ok, though?" Matt said quietly. His face is healing nicely. His eye can open all the way now, and the cut on his lip is healing. Maybe when he's back to normal, when he's all healed up, maybe then I can feel better and like the whole thing with Riley is done and dusted.

"Yeah, I'm fine."

"You seemed so upset."

It was the first time Beth had spoken all night. She sat the furthest from me, curled into her big green coat.

"What? About Riley?" I snort.

The horror on her face briefly features on all of them.

"I mean, even I was spooked when the police came by, asking about the party," Jason said. "And everyone knew he had it out for Matt."

"I was scared," Matt said. "When they asked about the bruises, I felt like I was going to piss blood."

We all laugh, except Beth.

"Riley was a bad guy. We have Matt with us, and someone truly vile is gone," I said. "It was just a weird moment, and it gets me out of school for a bit, so all good things."

Jason hands me a beer, and he smiles with all his teeth.

"How did he look when you cut him?"

"Like he was going to shit his pants."

Our laughter is interrupted by Beth. She bolts up, hands shaking, tears in her eyes.

"How can you all do that? Laugh like it's some kind of joke? Well, it's not! He's dead!"

I manage to keep the irritation out of my voice and said as flatly as I can. "Yeah, and?"

Sukhy shrugs her shoulders. "Beth, we've been over this, Fiona was protecting Matt."

"I'm not sorry he's gone," Matt said, his voice shakes as he says it. "I know I should care, but I don't."

"There's no reason to care," Jason snaps. "Don't be stupid, Beth."

"But...the police are going to find something," she said. I can see her legs trembling behind that thick coat.

"They won't," I said. "Not for a long time, and none of this will even matter. Don't worry. Have a drink."

"No, thanks," she said. "My mom chewed me out last time."

She sits there shaking like a little kid while the rest of us drank. The others think she'll forget about this eventually, but I know she won't. I know she will remember this forever. Maybe if we get away with it, in ten years' time, she'll call from a payphone with an anonymous tip-off. Or in sixty years when she's had her children and her grandchildren and maybe a great-grandchild, she'll go and hand herself in. I can see how she's holding this tightly to herself, gripping it in her hand. I know she won't ever let this go.

I want to shout over Sukhy and Matt and Jason all joking around. I want to grab Beth by her hair and yell at her.

What could I have done? I want to scream in her face. What on earth could I have done? He was big and strong and wanted to hurt my friend. You tried to fight him and look what happened. He hurt you and stepped over your body to keep hurting Matt. What else was there to do but to just get rid of him?

I want to shake her and make her believe it.

But I don't.

Because I know that this is just an excuse.

I was a time bomb, waiting to go off. It's built into me like hard code.

••••

My mother has this little red box. She used to keep it in her bedroom, but after she started getting really pretentious about clutter, she moved it down into the basement. Detective Pete would probably kill to get his hands on it. I used to really like going through it when I was a little girl.

It's a box full of red things. A ruby red earring, a little red purse, a red book of poems, a red hair scrunchie, a red charm bracelet, a spongy red thumb tac. I used to love laying them out in order of height or how much I liked them. Apparently when I was really little, if I spotted something someone was wearing, something I thought would be suitable for the little red box, I'd shout, 'That's mine!'.

It is a really cute story. She doesn't really have anyone to tell it to. My really early childhood memories are hers, unless she decides to go through them with me.

Well, it was a really cute story. With context, everything is more fucked up.

••••

Once Beth's pinch-faced mother said that if she didn't work, she would be bored out of her mind. That she wanted to do all this extra stuff when she retires, to keep busy. She's always saying stuff like that 'keep busy' or calling us 'the gang', like we wear sweaters around our shoulders and white sneakers.

But I think that's horseshit. I haven't been in school for like three days, and they have been fucking amazing. Mother has had more stupid gardening fake job bullshit to do, so I have had the place to myself. I live on the sofa, I watch everything on My List, I go through Mother's and move all of her episodes two ahead.

I send out snapchats of me drinking in the day to make Jason and the others jealous. I watch Detective Pete on all his house checks. He waves to me from outside my window when he notices me watching him.

'Lucky you being traumatised and all,' Jason sends back.

But he's wrong, I am not traumatised, I just don't go back to school because I'm bored. I am so bored with it. I don't want to hear people moaning about how sad it is that Riley is missing. I don't want to pretend I gave a shit about anything Lisa says.

And I don't want to be anywhere that could be greatly improved by stabbing something. I feel like a time bomb. I can't imagine going back to class and risking that urge coming up again. Like I'm sat there minding my own business, and Daisy Jones comes past and hisses something about me cutting myself. So then, after school, I follow her home later, and I cut her. I start with her neck so she can't scream just like Riley. And I cut her all over until eventually there's nothing left of her and that's just for the best.

Or Laurie Delmonte and her friends call me a ghetto bitch, so I damage her tyres so she gets into an accident.

Or I get tired of Lisa talking and yapping away, so I invite her to the woods one night, and I decide to just get her out of my hair.

I can't be in school right now.

I wake up cold and wince as my head burns. It's late, nearly ten AM, and I can hear my mother wandering around downstairs. I crawl over to the window and lean out to light an early morning cigarette. I am fumbling with my lighter when I notice Detective Pete pretending that he's just taking a walk like it's nobody's business. I wave, and he smiles at me and waves cheerfully before turning the corner.

Did you worry about me? I think as I watch him vanish out of sight. Would I be massively flattering myself to think that he does? I mean, even in a basic way that relates to his job, he must worry a bit, he thinks I'm living with a mass murderer. I lie back on my bed to smoke and wonder about the kinds of girls he likes. I wonder when he last went on a date. Must have been a while ago as he tends to spend his time here, pretending to be vigorously exercising across the same few streets.

If I was older, I wonder if he'd consider dating me.

After I manage to muster my way out of bed, I text Sukhy my usual 'haha guess who's not in chem 1?' before going for a shower. Mother is gone by the time I get out, giving me a second's peace from her and her judging. After that, I mostly just watch TV and read some of my books from Christmas. I go online. And mostly that holds off all the...rest. I mean, as good as it is to stay away from a place like school that could potentially set me off, I still feel like I'm losing my mind.

I guess, if I was going to describe it, I'd say it would be like withdrawal?

After three days, the compulsion to cut got worse and worse. There'd be some irritating person on the TV, and I'd find myself scratching my own skin out of desperation. And suddenly I'd realise that I'm watching that stuff on purpose. I'm switching on Real Housewives or some dumb telemarketing show or Toddler's and Tiaras, and I'd dig my nails into the leather of the sofa. I'd find myself thinking about the basement, heading down there to pick up where she left off. I'd scratch my throat, my arms, my legs, leaving raw red and white train tracks in my skin. I'd writhe around on the sofa, itching all over like I was going to die.

I feel like I'm going to die.

I kick over the coffee table and actually hurt my foot badly. Mother comes home for her lunch and puts one of my textbooks underneath the leg I broke to keep it standing steady.

I try to put my energy into other things. I cut up loads of meat and made a ridiculous amount of food for me and her to eat when she gets home from her fake pretend job. I'd tell her to go and buy steak so I could take my time slicing into something. It was cold and bloody, but it was small and.... and just not enough.

I want to change. I do.

I don't want to want to hurt people.

But in the end, like fucking Daisy Jones said, the compulsion to cut got so bad that I ended up...You know, I think it's fucked up how people are dismissive of kids who cut themselves. Like, we're all indoctrinated to say that kids who cut are just attention seeking wastes of time, and yet adults act all baffled by the high suicide rate?

So when she's out pretending that she gives a shit about the right soil for fucking rose bushes, I cut my thighs up with a razor, keep reopening the cut again and again and again and again and again.

And it hurts so bad it always makes me stop.

She is frowning as she tries to work out how she's suddenly on Season 2 of the weird crime drama she's watching. I sit beside her to fully enjoy the expression on her face when the cut on my right thigh re-opens and drips through my shorts onto the sofa. Our eyes meet, and she tuts.

"You're being stupid," she said. "You think cutting up your dinner or making those little paper cuts on your legs, will make it all go away?"

"Well, what do you suggest?"

She smiles that awful smile again.

"You could always go down to the basement."

"I thought I wasn't allowed down there," I said snootily.

"Well, you never take my rules very seriously."

"I'll pass, thanks."

She shrugs her shoulders. "Suit yourself, of course, Fiona. But you're going to run out of skin, eventually." She chuckles to herself and glances back at me from the entrance to the basement. "Let me know if you change your mind."

I'm not like you.

I repeat it to myself, over and over and over again.

Hoping that it might come true.

CHAPTER NINE

Transcript of interview with Detective Morgan

Morgan: I'm sorry, Pete. I just find this stuff difficult to talk about.

Brankowski: It's alright. We are gonna do this at your pace.

Morgan: You've been great, really. I just don't get why you want to drag all of this up.

Brankowski: I mean, come on, you were the head detective for the duration of the case; you got to work directly with the feds. And you had your suspicions about Randall Kayne just being in a bad place at a bad time.

Albright: Kayne was a lot of things, but not what that Gail's woman said he was.

Morgan: I honestly don't know what I think anymore.

Brankowski: You were saying that you had a strong hunch about one of the victim's family members. A girl called Sarah White.

Morgan: Yeah, Sarah White. She was fourteen when we became aware of what Red Creek was doing. She was in middle school, came from a nice enough family. Sweet parents, Mr. and Mrs. White were both regular churchgoers, the kind of people who were always helping out their neighbours. There was an older sister too, Cee-Cee White, who was a real looker. She was a fashion model in Franberg when she was in high school. Did a few clothing catalogues. I remember Mrs. White telling me that they encouraged her to focus on school instead.

Albright: Whole White family is gone now.

Morgan: Yeah, Mr. and Mrs. White had a car accident in 95 and Cee-Cee died young of cancer.

Brankowski: That would just leave Sarah.

Albright: Changed her name to Taylor in 97 before she left Franberg.

Morgan: I didn't know that.

Brankowski: So you said before you became suspicious of Sarah White at the memorial service?

Morgan: Yeah, I thought that there was something off about her, something creepy. So, I kept tabs on her. It didn't lead to anything. She seemed like an ordinary school kid. A bit of a loner, but there's nothing weird about that. It was just a hunch.

Albright: A hunch you kept for the whole investigation though.

Morgan: She just kept turning up. A body would be discovered and I'd see Sarah White in the crowd. Like she'd booked herself a freaking front-row seat. So, I start looking into it, like, the case with Lacey, the girl who alerted the police with a 911. And who was eating in the diner at the time she made the call, but Sarah White. Franberg was a predominantly white area, so someone like Sarah White stood out. It became easy to identify her at a number of occasions where the victims were last seen.

Brankowski: Were you ever able to identify a motive?

Morgan: Not one. She went to the same high school as some of the victims, but it was never someone in her classes, never anyone she associated with. As you boys know, there was so much variety between the victims, Red Creek's pattern seemed sporadic and random. It was like it didn't matter who was killed as long as somebody died.

Albright: Apart from Robert White.

Morgan: Yeah, but even then, it was hard to see if there was a motive. It was so long ago that all anyone seemed to remember about

Robert White was how much everyone loved him, what a sweet big brother he was etc. Nobody's going to remember a squabble between two siblings ten years after the boy goes missing. Especially when his mother and father are burying his bones.

Brankowski: But you were convinced Sarah White had something to do with it?

Morgan: I brought her in for an interview once. It was after Joshua Ruff had died. He'd made some pretty nasty racist remarks to her older sister that got him in trouble at school. Red Creek got him on his way home from detention. Again, Sarah White had been seen leaving her track team exercises around the same time. So, I pull her in, under the guise of asking if she's seen something.

Albright: And what did she say?

Morgan: She was forthright, helpful. Described what he'd been wearing, commented on where she saw him walking. That sort of thing. I asked about his argument in the high school with her sister and she was just blank. It was like she hadn't prepped for that question in a pop quiz. So, I asked how that sort of remark made her feel personally. And she just stared at me and said that it made her real mad. That was the wording she used, she said it made her 'real mad'. And you could see it in her eyes that she didn't care.

Brankowski: That she didn't care?

Morgan: If that was my sister, some boy had said that sort of shit to, I'd have been furious. But she didn't care. She just said the words. And you know, say what you will about Winnie Gails, she got one thing absolutely right on the fucking money—Red Creek can't connect to people, this is someone so detached, they just can't pass off as one of us.

Brankowski: Yeah, I remember when she said that on TV. So what happened next?

Morgan: She asks me why I bothered calling her in, she already gave a statement. And I say that I'm just following up on all our leads because my partner thinks I'm barking up the wrong tree for even considering a skinny little girl could be our deranged psychopath. So the interview just sort of ends and she smirks at me and shakes my hand and tells me good luck catching Red Creek. That's when I thought, this is her. This is fucking her. She's smirk-

*ing because she knows that I know and I can do jack shit about it.
And I think, you smug little bitch.*

Brankowski: And after that?

Morgan: After that, Sylvia Hardey happened.

Extract for W. Gails novel 'Mad Minds: A Year After Red Creek'

*There was a lot of tragedy in the Red Creek killings, families with
husbands, wives, sons and daughters never coming home. A community ravaged by the depraved actions of one sick individual
with a taste for murder.*

*But it also resulted in the tragic end of a talented young man's
career. As I've mentioned in prior books, I worked quite closely
with Detective Morgan, who took on the case at the young age of
26. He was determined to catch the killer and make the town a
safe place again. He was friendly, forth-right and did all he could
to try to bring Red Creek to justice. Blonde and striking looking,
he made a compelling figure in the game of cat and mouse that
made our streets run red. However, Detective Morgan would not
see the killer he so despised caught, as he was removed from the
case just two months before Randall Kayne was arrested.*

*Despite his noble intentions, young Phillip Morgan was just a
young man like any other, in fact some criticised Sheriff Bill
MacDonald for not giving this case to a more experienced officer,
someone less likely to crack under the pressure of all those dead.
As a matter of fact, Detective Morgan became unnaturally fixated
on a young suspect. Nobody outside the investigative team knows
the identity of Phillip Morgan's Red Creek killer, so I am unable to
reveal that information to you, dear readers. However, Detective
Harvey Anderson, has spoken to me about his former and dis-
graced partner—informing me that there was absolutely nothing
to suggest the guilt of this person, who was in fact, a teenager
barely into their high school career, that Morgan had just become
desperate to point the finger at someone, at anyone. He convinced
himself of this person's guilt that no matter what his colleagues
said or did, he would not be convinced otherwise. He wasted police time and taxpayer money having this innocent individual
cross-checked and examined and even brought in for questioning
on a number of occasions.*

Sheriff MacDonald worried about the health of his officer and suggested that Morgan take some time off, have some time to get his mind away from the case. But Morgan was young and stubborn and wouldn't leave Franberg without his protection. For better, he believed.

I have shared many times the details of the night young Sylvia Hardey escaped from the clutches of the Red Creek killer. I was on my way home from my gal pal, Nancy's baby shower, coming towards the now infamous Killer Kayne tunnel, when I spotted Sylvia in the middle of the road. She jumped out in front of my car. I was shocked and scared out of my wits, but this brave young girl was even more terrified beyond belief. Though only seventeen, Sylvia Hardey was different from the others, she was stronger than she looked and she got away from the killer. Randall Kayne, a notorious loner didn't know that young Sylvia was the star of the Franberg High track team. And it was her strong, long legs and trained instinct to run that saved her from Red Creek's knife with only a few light stab wounds.

The scene still haunts me to this day. My stiletto covered foot on the brake, the screech of tyres. Sylvia Hardey, covered in blood and crying in front of my car screaming for help. In the distance, a man stood at the edge of the woods. A thick and imposing figure in the darkness. Quick as a flash, I opened the passenger seat and this brave, terrified girl climbed in.

"Please help me, I've been stabbed—" she wept. "He's going to kill me—!"

The man staggered towards my car, and like Hell was I going to give him the chance to get at myself or Sylvia. In fact, I'm proud to say that I very nearly hit him with my car.

The disaster for Detective Morgan happened after. I had stuck around the hospital to check on how poor brave Sylvia was. She had been left alone with her distraught mother and I was thanked profusely by Mr. Hardey, who wept into his hand's that his daughter was spared from the same violent end as the others.

The police were allowed to see her after she got out of danger and Sylvia agreed to speak with them right away, despite her parents' wishes to let her rest and recover.

"I want to get him caught," she said bravely. "I didn't see him that well, but I want to do this while it's still clear."

Detectives Anderson and Morgan conducted the interview with Sylvia. They were in there for about twenty minutes, asking what she'd seen, when did she notice the individual following her, that sort of thing. However, Detective Morgan's questions became more loaded, more concentrated towards the suspect he had in mind. His tone became deranged, obsessive. Mrs. Hardey asked if the meeting could go on without Morgan, to which he initially consented. I watched him go and get a glass of water from the cooler. I went over to say hi, to ask how Sylvia was doing, but for some reason he didn't respond. He seemed to be staring at something in the distance behind me.

Then suddenly he charged back into Sylvia's hospital room like a man possessed. He put down photos that he had of the suspect and could be heard loudly yelling, *'Is this the person who attacked you? Look! Look! Is this her?'* When Sylvia tried to get up and leave the room, he seized her and manhandled her back into her chair.

At this point, he was forcibly removed from the room by Detective Anderson and Mr. Hardey. Detective Morgan could be heard saying, *'I know she did this!'*

After this, Detective Morgan was removed from the Red Killer case and put on immediate suspension for distressing the frightened young witness. It was the sad end to what had been a brave new career. And of course, it would be just a week later, that Detective Anderson was able to use Sylvia's and my own testimony to identify Randall Kayne as the Red Creek killer and capture him before he managed to flee from town that cold September night.

Morgan has argued many times that Sylvia Hardey's testimony is false as she was highly distressed and running for her life in the dark. He has also made false and disgusting allegations that I would say or do anything to sell my books. Which quite frankly is offensive to my integrity as a journalist. He has to this day, spoken out in defence of Randall Kayne and has a restraining order placed against him by the young suspect he so believed to be our Red Creek killer.

Chapter Nine

Interview with Randall Kayne' The Red Creek Killer'

Brankowski: But of course, you admitted to the murders, didn't you? You pleaded guilty in court and confessed to all of the killings.

Kayne: I know.

Brankowski: So, I mean you have to understand, to suddenly change your story after so many years, it doesn't look very...

Kayne: I was in the woods that night. I was...It was where I'd keep. It was where I kept some...some things of mine.

Brankowski: Yes, the box of images was found just two years ago.

Kayne: I knew it wasn't right to keep them. So I kept them in a box buried in the woods, nice quiet spot. Knew it was wrong to even want to look. Knew it was sick and depraved...

Brankowski: And this spot in the woods, was?

Kayne: I'd go out there to...pleasure myself while looking at those pictures. I wasn't hurting anyone. It was just pictures, not like I would have done that to an actual kid, an actual child. I wouldn't have. Don't look at me like that. Please. You said you'd come here to help me, please...

Brankowski: Please compose yourself, Mr. Kayne.

Kayne: (sobs)

Brankowski: You were afraid that they'd find the pictures.

Kayne: I was. And my lawyer said they had some much evidence... so much stuff that said I'd done those awful things. I'd been at the diner when that girl, Lacey something, was hiding out. I'd been seen...I'd been almost everywhere, seen by lots of people. They said it would be better for me if I pleaded guilty.

Brankowski: But you confessed.

Kayne: I felt like I deserved to be punished. For what I was...what I am. Save anyone knowing.

Brankowski: Then when the pictures were discovered, it was all for nothing.

Kayne: They linked them to me. Now I'm not just the murderer, but I'm a paedophile too. My poor sister doesn't visit no more. She doesn't come, even after all this time. Just another thing that makes life a little worse. And in here...Do you know what they do to guys like that in here? Do you know—! (breaks down)

(Brief intermission)

Brankowski: So, Mr. Kayne, you're saying that you didn't do any of this?

Kayne: I didn't. I know what that book said, that the killer had to be a loner, I know that I fit the profile. I had no friends, nobody to vouch for me when the police came. Nobody to say I'd been with them on those lonely nights. But I wouldn't have hurt someone. I was a big guy back then, but I couldn't have cut anyone up like that. The sight of blood makes me sick. I grew up on a farm and my daddy called me weak, I couldn't watch any of the slaughter-ing. I couldn't even sheer the sheep. It's not who I am.

Brankowski: But you were there the night Sylvia Hardey was at-tacked?

Kayne: I was...finishing up what I was doing in the woods when I heard someone scream. I hid the box and went running out to see what was going on. I saw this young girl with big curly hair—that Sylvia, she comes staggering out of the tunnel. And there was this flashy red car. The girl is screaming and she gets inside. I try to go over there to see what was happening—and the lady driving sort of lurches towards me. I fall on my ass and they shoot down the tunnel and out of sight.

Brankowski: And this is what you told Detective Anderson initial-ly, right? About someone else being there.

Kayne: There was someone there! I saw him. Figure stood by the undergrowth at the end of the tunnel. They had their hood up and a red scarf over the lower part of their face. I could see a knife.

Brankowski: This was the new part of your story, how you now say that your prints ended up on the knife that cut Sylvia Hardey. You say you gave chase. Why did you do that? There was a killer on the loose, you believed you were face to face with them?

Kayne: Well, they'd cut that young girl and I was right there, like right there in front of 'em. It was like…a fight-or-flight instinct or something like that, I suppose. I had to try to stop him. Like I said, back then, I was a big guy. And right there, in the dark, even with the knife, this guy looked…kind of short and scrawny. So, I got up and went after him, think I yelled, 'Hey you' or something like that. And they ran. They went and ran into the woods. But because of my—erm, secret box, I knew that part of the woods pretty well, so I could keep up with them, even in the dark.

Brankowski: And you said to your lawyer just last month, that you caught up with them?

Kayne: Yeah, I grabbed his scrawny little arm and pulled him back towards me. We scuffled, he nearly cut me in the chest. I dropped him on the ground and tried to scramble on top of him. He kicked me between the legs, but I managed to get hold of the knife. I took a swipe at him, I was panicking. I was scared, my heart was thumping in my ears. I was shit scared. But then I heard him say…

Brankowski: He spoke to you?

Kayne: He sounded like a kid. He said to me, he said, 'What about your special little box?' He knew those woods too, you see, and he'd seen me, seen what I was doing there (voice wobbles). He knew about me. Said I should toss his knife and go home.

Brankowski: And you did?

Kayne: I convinced myself at the time, that this person was a kid. He couldn't actually be the Red Creek killer, just some stupid kid trying to scare a classmate. So, so, yeah I…I let him walk off and I tossed the knife into a bin. That was how they found my prints on it.

Brankowski: And you didn't report it at the time.

Kayne: How could I?

Brankowski: You think it was a boy you spoke to that night? A boy, you're sure?

Kayne: I mean, I think so. It sounded like someone in their early teens. I guess it might have been a girl.

Brankowski: I know it was dark, but you were in close quarters, I'm going to show you a photo of a person of interest in the investigation at the time. This is Sarah White, she was around fifteen then. Could this have been the person you spoke to?

Kayne: I'm sorry, it was too dark. I couldn't see a thing behind the hood and a red scarf. But I mean, I would have said it was a boy rather than a girl I mean, girls don't do stuff like that, right? It's not in their nature.

CHAPTER TEN

I wake up to a pain in my head and my skin aches like I've been lying out in the sun. I raise one leg and admire the track marks of the groves of my nails along my thigh, deep and red and etched on. I roll onto my side and ignore the buzzing of my phone.

My mother isn't home. I just know. The house is quiet and outside the room is that red door just waiting for me at the bottom of the stairs. I cover my ears and drag the covers back over me for a second of relief.

Stop ditching, Sukhy has sent in a text. I'm going to let Lisa become my new BFF.

I smirk and lie there considering going back. I scroll through my texts and see nice messages from everyone. Except Beth. The last time she texted me was the day of the party, something stupid about Lisa getting on her nerves.

Hey, what's new with you? I type and then delete.

Miss me?

Delete.

Beth, can we go back to normal?

Sent.

And now, feelings of immense regret.

I don't want her to look at me like that. It's a look I know too well. It's the same look I give my mother every day she comes home with that cello case weighing slightly more than it usually does.

I don't want anyone to look at me like that again.

. . . .

Downstairs is quiet. I stick something stupid and repetitive on TV. I eat my mother's cereal because I know she hates when I do that. Her cereal is bland and has too many raisins in it, but the knowledge that she'd been inconvenienced slightly makes it worth it for me.

I look out the front and don't spot Pete the Hot Detective running past which makes me feel kind of lonely. Can't I be the one you come to see? I'm turning out to be a right chip off the old block after all.

Come on.

I sit in front of the TV for a bit, with a coffee and ignore the note she's left on the table about being back late tonight. Like I give a shit. It's not like I don't know how to cook for myself. When I was a little kid, she never left me alone. I think I had a babysitter like once. Probably didn't want people nosing around the house, maybe checking out the basement. No, until I was like ten, she would either leave me at a friend's, if I was lucky, or drag me along with her.

So many memories sat drinking shitty lemonade, watching her mess around in someone else's garden, being bored out of my mind, so she can have her little let's pretend job as a gardener green fingered wonder witch. Having to nod politely when the sucker who hired her, inevitably comes out and says, 'Ooh, is someone helping Mommy at work?' Even though you want to say, 'No, I'm sat on my ass. I didn't want to come here, stupid.'

I absolutely hate adults. It's like you get to a certain age and then you just talk in general clichés or speak about the weather like your life depends on it. Growing up has so many pit-falls.

. . . .

Beth doesn't text back and the TV doesn't get more interesting. I lie out on the couch and try and distract myself with literally anything. I'm bored and I resent my friends for staying in school. I wonder what everyone is talking about. I scratch my leg bloody imagining Beth saying awful things about me and eventually, even Sukhy starts to think, hey, maybe Beth has a point. Maybe we should report this to someone.

Maybe we should be worried.

Maybe we should talk to someone.

The doorbell rings and I dig my nails into the sides of my face, terrified that it's the police. I hug my knees to my chest and try and calm down my heart.

Shut up! They are going to hear you!

The doorbell rings again and I find myself getting up and walking over to answer it whether I want to or not. I put on my mother's ugly red shawl because it'll cause problems if anyone sees what I do to my wrists and knees.

"Just a second," I call.

I peek through the tiny glass window in the door and spot two people. A broad shouldered and well-dressed woman and a sheepish looking man. They aren't police. Maybe collecting for something?

I open the door.

"Hello," I say, doing my best 'Oh you just woke me voice'.

"Sorry to disturb you, miss," the sheepish looking guy says. "Could we trouble you for a few minutes of your time?"

"Sure."

"My name's Adam Morrison," he says. "And this is Alice Sanders."

Sanders.

You know, Riley had her exact bone structure, I remember how tough that firm jaw was to remove.

"My son Riley is missing," she says. Her tone is stiff but her eyes look tired, red, exhausted. "He's been missing for two weeks. The police are...looking." There is the slightest sneer in her voice, disbelief. "But so far, they haven't found any leads. We are asking for volunteers to help us search the woods for him. Perhaps you've heard about this?"

"Erm, well, like, yeah, it's been mentioned on the news, right? And I go to school with Riley," I say. "I'm just a freshman, but we all know the football team."

"Oh right, you know Riley a little?" the sheepish man says. "Are your parents' home at all, Miss...?"

"Taylor," I say. "And no, my mom is out right now at work. I'm only here because I've got the flu."

I can see those big strong hands of hers shaking.

"My son," she says, then seems to trail off, her words stay still in her throat before she manages, "He can be a spoilt and reckless boy at times," she says. "He's run away before. Just once, he had a fight with his big brother...But never for as long as this."

She is so worried about him and so angry with him for making her worry like this.

"I know a lot of the kids at school are planning on going along. Like I said, my mom is out at work at the moment, but I'm sure she'd be interested in joining the search party too. Don't worry, Mrs. Sanders, I'm sure that Riley can't have gone far."

The sheepish looking man smiles. "Could we possibly take a contact number for yourself, Miss Taylor? So, we can contact your mother with arrangements?"

"Sure, do you have a pen?"

As I write down our house telephone number and my mother's name, I keep shooting glances up at Riley's mom. After her stiff, sad little monologue, Mrs. Sanders seems to have retreated back into herself. She holds her hands stiff and still by her sides. Her bottom lip is still and frozen as if someone has drawn it on. She focuses on things that are far away and doesn't dare look me in the eye. I can see you, I think, trying not to cry.

And I want to feel guilty when I look at her. I want to fall to my knees and beg for her forgiveness when I see her suffering. Arranging a search party for him that will never provide any kind of closure, just more worry, more pain and more hopelessness. I want to tell her that I'm so sorry that I had to kill her precious son.

But when I look at her, all stiff and frozen in her pain, I find myself really holding in a smirk, a chuckle, a full-blown hysterical laughing fit. I can feel my sides shaking. I wait for them to go, I watch them walk down my street. I close the door, lock it up and double over on the sofa, laughing and laughing until there are tears running down my cheeks and soaking up the cushions.

. . . .

After I re-open a nasty gash on my knee and fiddle with it, I head back onto the roof and check out the photo album Sukhy discovered when she was last here. I can see that photo again of Mother and her old family. Looking in more detail, I can see that she is the youngest. And there's the sister she's never mentioned, the parents she never talks about. The brother, the dead brother, I know about a little, Robert 'Bobbie' White. He looks sweet, grinning cheekily at the camera, his hands in his pockets. A wild head of curly hair and bright brown eyes. He holds his mother's hand. At this height, he is neck and neck with Mother, who is his complete opposite. She frowns, she's blank. She doesn't belong in this happy picture.

I want to ask her about them, about him in particular, who Detective Fatso seemed to have some pretty fucking big opinions about.

There's a chapter about little Uncle Robert in that stupid book Mother keeps at her bedside. Chapter Seven – Little Bobbie White: Red Creek Draws First Blood. It's short and Mother tells me it makes a lot of assumptions, but I think she gets a casual mention. Then three years ago, it turned out that guy, Randall Kayne was a massive paedo, so Winnie Gails wrote another book about Red Creek— Mother had it pre-ordered on Amazon—and that had a massive section about Little Bobbie White and the implications of his death etc etc.

I've never read the books, I think she wants me too.

I hide the photo album to upset her, just in case she comes and looks at it.

. . . .

I don't like the basement. Not even when I was little. Most kids hate rules. 'Don't ever go in the basement' might as well mean putting a 'Welcome' sign on the door in neon letters 10 ft high. But not me though. Don't go in the basement meant that I don't go anywhere near it. Not even when my mother was down there—I just yell from outside the door.

The basement was…is the sound of a drill, or a kind of scraping and darkness. Darkness where my mother pours so much of her time.

I know that lovely Detective Pete is looking for when he looks this way. I know it's what he's after when he stares at this house.

But anyway, I suppose rules are meant to be broken, whether you take them seriously or not. And despite everything, I did go down there once.

Or, at least I think I did. I might have dreamt it. Some childish anxiety that mixed with a memory, or my mother's rules or…It doesn't matter, I remember it.

Sat at the bottom of the steps in the dark, the scratching sound of chains dragging along the floor, a screech of metal. A dull groan of someone else, some other person sat with me in the dark. And there is this ache in my chest, like my heart is about to burst free of my body. I cover my mouth to keep my voice trapped deep inside. But the noise seems to vibrate from me. And there's this pounding my ears that I'm sure the person in the dark can hear too. Then, there's this shuffling sound again. I tuck my legs close to my body. The shuffling gets closer and closer. I try and climb backwards up the stairs, not turning away from the darkness in front of me.

There is a grunt. In the dark someone staggers up right, swaying.

I can see the shape of them moving around.

Then I start screaming, 'Mommy! Mommy! Mommy!'

That is how I know it was a dream. I am absolutely certain that I've never once called out for her.

So, it has to be.

Mind you, it always ends the same way, this dream, with light and red and her arms around me too tight.

. . . .

I find myself standing outside the basement as the sun begins to set. I watch the red door, watch the way the wood holds together. I press against it and listen to see if something, anything is listening too.

She was right. I have run out of skin. So, I scratch at my wrist and start to nudge the door open with my foot. The arrogance of that woman, of course she'd never lock this door. It's dark, the fading light of the living room only illuminates half of the steps. My fingers fumble around uselessly, trying to find a switch or a hanging light or something. I stumble nervously onto the first step and squinting, manage to spot a hanging light at the end of the stairs before everything dissolves into pitch black.

So, I close the red door behind me and submerged in darkness, I cling to the banister as I make my way down the creaking steps. The ground aches under me and the deeper I go, the more stagnant the smell gets, like rusty metal and something wet that I know too well. I can hear breathing, the breathing the red door always seems to have when I go to sleep at night, waiting for me in the morning in my otherwise silent house.

I find myself at the bottom of the stairs, standing on cold concrete instead of weak-willed wood. I reach for the dangling light and tentatively tug it down towards me. There is a crackle and a dim light flickers on in the centre of the room.

And I mean, it's pretty much what I imagined.

It's dark and well organised. There's a crude operating table. A small furnace. Two simple grey urns. A six pack of bottled water. Some pink rubber gloves hung up from a hook on the far wall. The drill of that awful drilling noise, drill. There's a shelf filled with the rest of her tools and even more cleaning products. There's an overpowering smell of incense, which she tries to use to cover up the rusty smell of blood. Some old books and trashy magazines piled up against the wall. A CD player, she has it play white noise while she works. I hate the sound of it. Beth used to use it to sleep during midterm exams. Me and Sukhy went over for snacks and a sleepover with our science text books and all of our notes. It was fun, kind of. Or it was. Until we went to sleep. The white noise machine went on and Beth slept and Sukhy slept. But the sound of it made me vomit up the pizza we ate. It made my blood burn and my hands shake and then came the tears, the tears that came and stayed until Sukhy woke up and asked, 'What's wrong, Fiona? Was it a bad dream?'

There is a man she brought home in the cello case too. He's here for a short visit. She's already removed his arms. He sits in an arm chair covered with a plastic sheet, almost like he's resting. He's wearing dirty looking grey briefs and is pudgy around the middle but emaciated in other areas. His hair is starting to go grey and from the look of that beard, I'd say that he's probably a homeless man she picked up off a street corner somewhere. Perhaps he thought she would take him somewhere safe and warm.

Like that little cat lost in the rain.

Blue eyes open, delirious with pain. They waver around before finding me and staying with me. He recoils at first, thinking that it's her, come back downstairs to take perhaps a leg this time. He makes a hideous gagging sound and I can see that she's put some obscene looking device in his mouth that clamps his tongue down against the bottom of his mouth, rendering him speechless and drooling.

"Sssh, sssh, it's alright," I say. "She's not here. She's gone."

He shuffles around, tears brimming in his eyes as it dawns on him that his arms won't help him rise from his seat. He squelches against the plastic sheet. His legs flail uselessly under him. I crouch down in front of him.

"You poor thing, what has she done to you?"

He wheezes behind the gag and I sit up and manage to unlatch it where it's locked on under his chin. His lips had been cut from struggling against it. I wipe the blood where it reaches my hand. I toss the device away and he gasps for air.

"My name's Fiona," I say. "How did you get in my house?"

"The woman brought me here," he says. "She said she could take me back to the shelter. I wanted to go back. Never should have left. I just needed some air—" he gasps again and the tears come freely. "She cut me—! She cut me—"

"Ssh, please, she could be back any minute," I say. "Please, keep your voice down. I'll help you."

"What are you doing here?"

"She's my mom. She doesn't let me come down here. I thought it was her...workshop or something. I didn't know—! I came down here to find some cello tape or something. Shit." I'm doing my best freaked out voice, the one Beth uses before a big exam.

"Your mom? She's crazy! She fucking cut my arms off and diced them up like a cheese—! She's going to kill me—! She's going to kill me—" He started struggling. "Untie my legs."

Hands shaking as I bend down to undo the straps around his bony ankles. He is cursing, heart pounding in his chest. One leg and then the other. He scrambles to his feet with difficulty. I get up and glance around me, peering anxiously up at the stairs.

"Listen, she will be back any minute. We have to make a break for it. Keep behind me, ok?" I say. He nods, frantic and wild eyed. "I'm going to get you out of here." I can hear his heartbeat, he keeps close. He is unsteady, possibly from blood loss, possibly from lack of blood to his feet. He stumbles, his balance at a loss from his missing arms. He struggles to keep up as we walk the creaky stairs. I can see the red door waiting for us at the top. Our steps get heavier and heavier. I remember how Riley's body bounced on these steps and skidded across the concrete like a dead pig.

We reach the top of the stairs and I turn to him and say, 'It's going to be alright—" Before he slams his leg up into my stomach. I cry out in pain and fall back against the door. He kicks me again, struggling to keep his balance as his foot collides with my chest. I gasp out in shock, winded. He tries to wedge past me.

"Liar—!" he snarls at me. "I heard you two talking—! You knew! You knew—!" He slams his armless torso against the door, trying to wedge it open. His is frantic, bleeding over the floor as his old wounds open. "Come on—! Come on—!"

I lie there in pain on the ground, watching him struggle, watching him fight. I suppose that'd be how I'd want to go as well. Struggling and fighting. Not placid and gentle like the kitten. Not clueless and baffled like Riley.

Riley didn't expect me to bring a big knife to the party.

And this guy is the same. He figured out that I knew what she was doing down here. But he didn't know think that I would come down here with a knife in the pocket of my shorts.

The red door begins to wedge open behind me. He sees a glimmer of the fading sunlight outside. Maybe he thinks this is all going to be ok. Maybe he thinks he's going to be safe now, like that girl who managed to run faster than my Mother down that tunnel back in her little backwater of a hometown. Maybe he thinks he's won.

I can see that on his face as he steps over me to head out into the sun.

I cut the back of his leg, where his heel meets the calf. The tendon is severed in one slice and makes a sharp snapping sound like a tightly wound rope being recoiled all at once. He screams and staggered backwards, unable to support his weight. He sobs in agony and near-ly fall on top of me before his aching leg sends him backwards, crashing into the creaking wooden steps as he rolls hard onto the concrete.

I get to my feet and wince at the pain in my chest. I skip down the steps and shake off my bloody knife. It makes a very satisfying splat-tering sound against the wall. I see the fear on his face, the confu-sion, the agony. He groans because his ankle is broken in the fall and he will never be able to fight me off.

I smile.

He doesn't though, he just screams.

I think I see why she decided to use that gross looking gag.

The first blow stops that noise right away. The next is just for fun, puncturing a big hole in his face, just so I can see how deep I can go. Then I attack the body, deep in his shoulder, at his chest. I stab and I stab. Maybe Beth was right, maybe I am laughing. Maybe I'm laugh-ing so hard when I dismantle him. Like this, I can see how his whole body fitted together. He is so skinny in places, soft flesh for the tini-est centimetre, then bone so hard that it tries to resist my knife. He shits his pants before he truly and properly dies.

That was gross.

But it doesn't stop me working. That shocked me. I sit there, chopping him up into cubes, it's bloody and messy and nothing like chopping up that cow's heart. You can see how it all makes sense, how one thing works in relation to the other and how easy it is to destroy it so it can never ever make sense again.

I think about how crazy that is, how kind of majestic that is. How much he taught me about science, this weird old homeless man who thought he'd got the jump on me, before he died. I want to thank him, but I can't work out where his head is anymore. I'm sat there, covered in him, surrounded by his body and all of its pieces in the bad lighting of the basement.

The red door is open just a smidge but no light comes down.

Not for me.

Not anymore.

I lie down and feel that awful thumping in my heart has stopped and I can rest again. I can relax. The smell of the blood doesn't even bother me. I close my eyes and listen to how calm can be. How the world all comes together and makes sense when it's just like this.

Then I wake up.

She is stood at the top of the stairs, looking down at me.

And I realise that she's calling my name. She's frightened, I don't think I've ever seen that expression on her face before. Her mouth is drawn into a long thin line, like someone's drawn it on. And I recognise that expression from Riley's mother.

She is frightened that I'm dead.

She skids on the blood as she rushes down to me. She jerks me upright and I'm shocked at how strong she is as the blood rushes to my head. I don't remember the last time she touched me. Her hand strikes my cheek hard and the sound of blood splattering free from my hair is once again, satisfying.

"Stop it, I'm fine—" I say over her cries of 'Fiona, Fiona, wake up' over and over again. She really was frightened. Her eyes look like they are going to come out of her head. I can hear her heartbeat we are this close. "I'm fine—! Don't touch me—!"

"Did he hurt you?" She is inspecting me, pulling at my jaw, lifting one of my arms.

"He kicked me," I said. "None of this is my blood."

This seems to calm her down.

Her eyes go back to normal and she pinches the bridge of her nose. She goes back to being herself in a second. She sighs then looks down at me again. "You do realise that you're going to need to burn those shorts."

"Obvi," I say, getting up and instantly falling down, slipping on the blood.

"I don't know what that means," she says and gets to her feet. "I know I said you could join me in the basement, but this is ridiculous. Are you a toddler? Look at this mess."

"You chose to breed," I said.

She passes me a pair of black slippers. "Enough of that. Put these on and go have a shower. I'll take care of this."

The slippers feel soft.

I want everything to be soft now.

The sharp little trails I left on my legs and wrists are finally starting to sting.

I don't want to hurt myself again, I think, for the first time. I've had enough of that.

I rub my wrist gently. I want to protect myself. I want to be better than this, all this darkness and red down here.

My legs are shaking as I walk up the creaking steps and I see her taking out a mop and starting to clean up the mess I made of that man on the floor. I watch her as I reach the red door, scrubbing away, head down, calm and flat once again.

I don't want to be like you.

The shower is cold and eventually the blood comes off. I find bits of his hair and skin under my nails, even after I scrub and scrub and scrub. I sit in the bathroom and hold my hands over my face. I think I cried at one point. Yeah, I was crying. I don't remember why. Maybe it was a nervous reaction. Maybe frustration, it was so hard to get clean again.

Lying down in all that mess was a bad idea. But eventually I walk out of the bathroom clean. I see the beautiful Detective Pete doing his nightly jog past the house. I wander into my room and crash out on the bed.

I check my phone.

I want things to be normal too, Beth has said. I'm sorry. Please come back to school. I miss you.

I can be better from now on. Even Beth knows it. I forget about the mess I made downstairs. I manage to sleep without scratching. I manage to sleep without thinking of Riley and how good it felt to tear him into pieces.

I just sleep.

CHAPTER ELEVEN

I know that she doesn't want me to go back to school. And unfortunately, that made it the most appealing place in the world for me. I even dressed nicer for the occasion, sent Beth a snapchat of my school bag all ready to go.

Mother glares at me over the table but doesn't actually say anything. At one point while I noisily make myself a coffee, I see her open her mouth, then close it again, then start aggressively reading her crossword again.

Whatever, if you have something to say, say it to my face, I think but don't actually vocalise. I don't want her to try to talk me out of this. I mean, seriously, it's none of her goddamn business. Would she rather I was here where I make a mess that keeps her down in the basement all night long, or away, at school, out of sight and out of mind.

Detective Pete is quite bizarrely walking a dog, when I go outside for a morning smoke while I wait for Beth and her mother to stop yelling at each other over her algebra homework or whatever it is this time. He smiles and manages to draw the strong yappy dog to a halt.

"Ah, young Fiona, good to see you."

"And it's nice to see your lovely partner again, hello," I say, bending down to pet the dog's scruffy looking head. He licks my arm, and I wipe it back onto his fur carefully so Pete doesn't notice.

He chuckles to himself. "Albright made a good impression on you, I see."

"I mean, yeah, he was so sweet compared to you, you guys are a real good cop, bad cop cliché." I look up at him and see him smile at me before he bends down to pull back his eager, constantly licking dog.

"He can be intimidating. My first day on the job with him, I was so nervous I think I said three words."

We both laugh.

"So, is this your dog? Or a new member of the running club?"

"This is my sister's dog, Max, I'm taking care of him while she's away."

"Sweet, where did she go?"

"Disneyland, my little nephew's never been."

"Lucky kid, he's got one over on me."

"You've never been to Disneyland?"

"Erm, hello, could you picture my mother at Disneyland?" I say, and he frowns a little as if contemplating it, before nodding his head in agreement.

"Yes, I do see what you mean."

"So how long do you have Max for?"

"Two weeks. We've been a pretty good team before. I grew up with dogs."

"Woah, lucky, I was never allowed one."

"That's a shame. Allergies, is it?"

You know, if a random cat you meet outside goes missing, then maybe its owner puts up a poster for a bit, but then nobody looks for it. If you hit a cat with your car, you don't need to stop the same way you do if you hit a dog. I once killed a cat and found it had a little tag between its neck and its shoulder blades. I threw it in the river just to be safe. I think Mother's logic is that cats and dogs can go missing, but if you have pets, and people know you have pets and those pets keep disappearing or dying, then people notice that stuff.

And people who make movies just love insisting that negative, knife-happy behaviour starts with hurting animals for no good god-damn reason.

"I think she just doesn't like them. I guess they can be messy or whatever."

The dog has drooled over my shoes. Beautiful Detective Pete offers me a tissue.

"Yeah, this one sure can be, anyway. So, you're back in school?"

"Even staying at home gets boring, eventually. There's only so much trashy TV I can watch." I am wiping my wrist with his tissue when I notice his eyes narrowing on something and I realise he's just seen the deep crescent moon scratch marks on my wrists. I can feel my body breaking into a cold sweat.

"That looks nasty, are you alright?" he asks.

His tone is practiced, this is how they talk to kids they suspect are victims of abuse. His expression is kind, all 'you can talk to me', his tone runs true with this, but there's a kind of hunger in his eyes. That's disappointing. The concern is trained and practiced, but that's all it is. He wants to come into my house, and what better way to do that than a regular house call based on suspicions of child abuse?

"It's been hot lately," I say. "It's super gross, but I always scratch myself in my sleep when I get hot." I offer up my wrist to give him a better look. "It makes me look like some basket case, huh?"

He doesn't believe me. But he smiles anyway and says, "Owch, that's a nasty habit to get into."

"That's what my mother tells me," I say with a shrug. "So annoying, it's not like I can help it."

"No, I suppose not." He pets the dog again to make it sit. "When I was a kid, I used to switch my lights off twice. It was a really weird habit I picked up in school and carried on until I was in college."

"Less self-destructive," I said.

"Drove my folks crazy though," he says. "I guess kids always find a way to drive their parents crazy."

I want to ask him what he means by that when Beth comes out of her house and says, 'Awww, a dog!' loudly before bending down to pet Max on his shaggy head. She's gushing and excited, honestly, just like a four-year-old. Detective Pete laughs with her and asks if she's a friend of mine.

To my relief, Beth smiles and says, 'Oh yeah, we go way back.'

We're good.

"You girls have a good day. Glad to see you're back in school, young Fiona." He says, and I internally sigh as I watch him walk away.

"That was that policeman from school, what was he doing around here?" Beth asks.

"I think he lives close by, I've seen him jogging," I said, glancing back at her. I see that she looks nervous. "It's really good to see you, Beth."

She reaches out and hugs me around the middle. "The person who was probably the most upset by all of this was you, Fiona," she said. "I can't imagine how confused you must have been. I'm sorry that I was weird about it."

I smile and let her think that.

"So, we good?"

"We're fine. Come on, let's go to school."

The journey to school is better with the two of us. It's crazy how you can miss a week or two from a place you go every day, and somehow that improves the general experience. I listen to Beth chat about how boring it's been, I nod when she says that I can borrow her notes for English, but she doubts Jason would have anything productive for me to borrow in the other subjects. She said that since Riley disappeared, the girls were all confusingly given rape alarms, which had mostly been used to try and deafen nearby classmates in the lunchroom. She doesn't falter at the mention of Riley, which I was worried she would. It's almost like she just forgot.

I want her to forget.

I want to forget.

Things are going to be like before.

. . . .

"Fiona—!"

Only she says it like 'Fee-Ooooooh-Naaaaah' before she throws her arms around me and nearly knocks me on the ground.

"Oh, dear, I was so worried about you! How are you doing? I overheard Jason saying that you got hysterically upset and of course, none of us have really seen you since! I had suggested we go around to show our support, but the others didn't seem too enthused," Lisa gushes, moving her hand onto a lock of my hair.

I wonder how she'd look with that hand missing, but no, I'm not like that anymore. I glance at the others all looking over at me sympathetically as I play dead in Lisa's surprisingly strong grip. I mouth 'Thank you' for the avoided home visit.

"Well, you know, I'm fine now."

"If you ever want to talk, I'm a wonderful listener," she interrupts me slightly to belt out. Good listener, my ass.

She is babbling away about all the school gossip or whatever while the other share apathetic glances. Matt smiles shyly at me. I feel lucky. I lean back against the school wall and watch the playground while Lisa talks and talks. It hasn't changed. The other kids are here, some of them in their groups, others just talking shit or chasing each other around.

Riley is gone, and the school is still here, life goes on.

"How's it been recently?" I ask Matt. "Are any of those assholes causing you problems still?"

"No," he says. "They've really closed ranks, keep to themselves. It actually improves the whole shitty high school experience."

"And Fred, has he been in touch with you?"

"He tries to text me a bit, a lot," Matt says. "I never respond."

I hug him around the middle, and he rests his head on my shoulder.

"I'm really glad you're back."

Me too.

We go to homeroom without incident, just move through the corridors the same way we always do. Kids bump into us, kids yell over the sound of the intercom. So much has changed, and most of these people don't even realise that I was gone. And now I can be one of them.

I nudge past Daisy Jones so to get into the classroom first. I hear her say, 'Ergh! Rude! Watch it!' and a bizarre sense of peace comes over me. Everything is back the way it should be. And what I did to Riley and that man in the basement is long gone.

• • • •

There is a poster with Riley's face on the bulletin board when I go past at lunch. It's a particularly good photo, taken after one of his games. He looks ridiculously happy and excited, his hair brushed out of his eyes. There's that difficult strong jaw again.

"I have one of these in my room," Jason says, leaning down to whisper. "Got it hung up by my bed."

119

"Really?" I say, not interested.

He chuckles, "Oh yeah, it gives me something to look forward to in the morning."

"Hey, did Riley know you felt that way?" I say.

He smirks and nudges me. "Hey, come on, I'm serious here. Look how much nicer it is coming to school with that total axe wound gone."

He gestures to the lunch room; the football team is sat quietly around their table with their sympathetic looking girlfriends and well-wishers. It's quiet. You can hear yourself think. I spot Matt walking across the cafeteria to reach us, he passes their table without comment or attack.

"You did that," Jason said, whistling. "I can't believe it, honestly."

"Well, you were there."

"Fiona, you have to see how cool this is," he whispers a little too loudly. "I actually like coming to school. Matt is happier. Kids are less mean. Nobody's made an out of line comment to Sukhy. It's like all that negativity came from him."

"You're reading into it," I said, "Why not just enjoy it?"

Jason sighs and tucks his hands into his pockets.

"You're right, I guess."

"Yeah, I often am," I say.

"Still," I notice him glance back over his shoulder at Jesse Macinera, sat in Riley's old seat, at the head of the football team's table, he snorts loudly through his nose and his laugh rings out through the room, "It'd be a real shame if someone tried to fill the void Riley left."

I don't like the look on his face.

For some reason, his smile is...so much like hers.

· · · ·

When I was six years old, Beth had a birthday party at the ice skating rink. Me, Sukhy, Matt and Jason were all invited. She gave her invitations out in class, and we all got really excited about it. It was all we spoke about all day. Jason got nervous about being bad at it, he'd never been to the rink before—he'd never really done anything like that. His dad said that was girly stuff. Mr Danvers said that about virtually everything that wasn't fishing or cars.

Beth told him not to worry and invited him over to her house after school to try on her skates. I tagged along because I didn't want to go back to my house. We walked back, and Beth's mom was home, sorting out snacks and things for some dinner party she was having.

I remember thinking that Beth's mom was like the nicest person in the world when I was little. I wasn't as good at picking up on things when I was a kid. I didn't notice the pinch-faced ways or her weird obsession with grades and rules and all that other shit when I was little. All I saw it as was Beth's mom being super attentive and mom like, and my mother, who was scary and cold.

Unlike my mother, Mrs Green always smiled a lot and bought Beth pretty things to wear. She'd pat me on the head and say I was a good girl. I liked being liked, I liked being good. I really liked going over there after school.

The three of us got to Beth's house, and Mrs Green told us to make ourselves comfy in the living room. Beth rushed upstairs to get her skates, and Jason threw himself face-first onto the big plush cream sofa they had. He was rolling around on the cushions being silly. I was sat on the armchair—I knew Mrs Green didn't let Beth have her feet up on the sofa but didn't feel the need to explain this to Jason.

I liked being liked, and sometimes being liked was easier if someone else was being naughty.

Beth came rushing back with her skates, and Jason took off his dirty sneakers to try and put them on. This was when Mrs Green came in with cookies and snacks for us. She was always doing stuff like that before we turned ten and she became paranoid about Beth being overweight. I remember how she nearly dropped the plate of cookies when she saw what Jason was doing.

"Oh no, dear! Please, get those boots off the sofa!"

Jason looked baffled, he put his feet on the floor, and Mrs Green's hand rose to her mouth in panic. He started trying to pull one of the boots off, the colour rising in his face.

"Beth, dear, we don't wear ice skating boots in the house, do we?" Mrs Green said.

"Sorry, Mommy," Beth said in a tiny voice. "Jason is just trying them on before the party. He doesn't have boots of his own."

"For the party...Of course, I'm sorry. Here, Jason, dear, let me help." Mrs Green bent down and helped Jason get the shoes off his feet. His socks were dirty, and there was a hole around the big toe, I saw her mouth turn into a cross lipless line when she saw it. She was smiling a pinch-faced smile then as she asked, "So, Jason, I don't think I know your mommy. What's your last name, hon?"

"Danvers," he said. "You wouldn't know my mom. She lives in California with a guy who owns a tanning salon."

"Oh, I'm sorry to hear that," Mrs Green said, whilst not sounding very sorry at all. "So, you live with your daddy?"

"Yeah, he sells cars on Oak Street."

Mrs Green nodded and smiled, but I could tell that she was thinking about something. She was telling Jason about how careful he had to be not to put his feet on the sofa while me and Beth tucked into our cookies. I remember thinking it then—Jason won't be coming back here. Jason's dad picked him up a little bit later and had oil on his hands when he shook hands with Mr Green, who washed them the second the front door was closed.

Mrs Green patted me on the head and said, "I wish all of Beth's little friends could be as sweet and polite as you are, Fiona."

At the time, I felt happy. I felt relieved that Jason's mom lived in California with a guy who owns a tanning salon because Jason had no manners. And the Green's thought I was good. When I was little, all that stuff was really, really important to me.

Then I remember meeting Beth to walk to school the next day, she was red-eyed from crying and told me in a tiny muffled voice that her mom had told her that Jason wasn't allowed to come to her birthday party.

I remember her taking him aside on the playground and telling him that he wasn't allowed to come anymore. I remember seeing him go bright red in the face, I remember him shoving Beth out of his way and going and hiding in the shrubs until Sukhy convinced him to come out. He was red-eyed and sullen and wouldn't speak to any of us.

Then, I remember Hutch, Beth's dog going missing.

• • • •

After school Sukhy has debate and Beth has yearbook committee, so I head home without them. Matt has been getting picked up outside the school gates every day since the party. His mom had her shifts changed so she could always be there to get him. He rolls his eyes when he tells me that, like 'Oh man, can you believe her?' but I can see the relief in his expression.

I wish I could feel that safe with my mother.

"Jase, are you coming?" I ask.

He is sat by the bleachers watching the football team practice. His eyes follow Jesse Macinera as he runs along the field. And he has her expression, that horrible reptilian expression on his face. And this is just crazy because Jesse Macinera isn't even one of the bad ones. He never bothered Matt, he sure as hell didn't do anything to stop the others, but he isn't aggressive the same way. He smiles with all his teeth like a complete idiot. And he has always been...friendly. The kind of guy you could bring home to your parents, and they'd probably prefer him instantly. Whatever Jason thinks he's hunting, it doesn't exist in Jesse.

"Jase?"

He doesn't hear me when I call his name, so I say it again louder. He blinks like a rabbit in headlights.

"Sorry, Fiona, what?"

"Are you coming?" I say slowly.

"No," he says. "I'm going to hang out here for a little while."

I find myself scratching at my wrist as I leave the school grounds. My nail is red and bloody, and it's hard to wipe off on my sweater.

• • • •

On my walk home, I see Detective Pete is writing something in a little red notebook. He's sat in his car furiously writing, like he's cramming for a big test. I tap on his window and offer him my best go at a flirty smile.

"Ah, hey there," he says. "How was the first day back?"

"Good," I say. "Well, as good as high school can be, I guess."

"Your friend isn't with you?"

"Good observation, I get why they made you a detective," I tease. "No, she's at yearbook committee."

"Yearbook committee, already?"

"She's obsessed, anything to look good on her transcript, I guess."

He laughs and wishes me a good evening, tells me that they have a special offer on pizzas at MacLaren's today. I smile and nod and say something dumb about a plain cheese, mostly I pretend like I haven't been reading his notes from over the top of his hand. Something there about Mother's work in the Gregory's front garden, something about self-inflicted injuries.

I watch him drive off when I get to the front porch. Always these short little chats, Detective, I find myself thinking. I wish we could do them more often. Usually, all adults want to do is patronise or judge you. I like that he doesn't ask me about college plans or my grades like he's testing my worth as a person. I like that his questions are only prying to a point. And given the circumstances, he's prying for the right reasons.

I go and sit in front of the TV and mess around on my phone for a while. Sukhy is out at her aunt's birthday thing tonight. This will be a quiet night in. I lie on my side and think about sneaking a beer from the fridge when I hear her key in the front door. There's a scuffling noise, like something heavy dragging along the wood. The front door opens, and she huffs, exhausted. Then the front door closes, and she walks through to the living room, dragging the cello case with some difficulty.

When she sees me just watching her, she says, "Thanks for the help, Fiona."

"You seem to have it under control," I say.

She reaches the basement door and looks back at me, "Did you want to join me?"

"Yeah, in your dreams," I say.

"Well, that's what you said last time, and then I was up half the night cleaning up your little mess," she said. "So please make sure you're really sure before you say no."

"Goddamnit, I just told you no, I don't want to. I don't like this sort of thing. So can you just be quiet and leave me alone?"

I don't like how she's smiling at me. I throw the remote control at her and hear it smash into the wall before I start running up the stairs. I slam the bedroom door shut behind me and listen to the thump of that cello case on the basement stairs.

I ball my hands into fists to stop them from scratching at my wrists and legs. I squeeze them so tight that I feel my nails puncture the hard skin of my palms and I lie there, shaking and wishing that I could wake up and be someone else.

Someone good and polite and all those things that used to be important to me a long time ago.

CHAPTER TWELVE

Beth is back to her usual self. She looks nervous because of her mom finding out she's snuck out. Normal nervous. I can deal with her usual bought of anxiety. She is all smiles and jokes just like she used to; she rags on Lisa and groans in frustration at her constant jokes about her. She doesn't recoil when our hands touch as I pass her another ill-advised beer. We really are back to normal.

We are back to walking through the woods together, to quietly talking, all alone together about her embarrassing pinch-faced mother and how much it sucks when Jason doesn't read the book in English class. She is back to being able to make eye contact with me. I catch her gaze over them, and she smiles at me.

We drink whisky, and I find myself just listening to her talk, listening to her laugh. It was her silence before that made even this that I love so much, completely unbearable. It was some ghost at the feast bullshit before.

"So yeah, Lisa kept threatening to go round to yours," Matt said.

"No way!"

"Yeah way, with a gift basket and everything."

"She is so horny to visit people's houses," I said.

"Remember when she came to mine?" Jason said, rolling his eyes. "She acted like we'd give her rabies. She had this constipated look when she spoke to my dad."

"Or mine when she sucked up to my dad so much I felt like she wanted to swing with my parents," Sukhy said, rolling her eyes. "Beth, how do you cope?"

"I think about when she lived in England," she said, "And I only had to see her once a year at most."

"A happier time," Sukhy said.

"The golden age," Jason adds, scooping an arm around her shoulders.

Sukhy and Jason are back to doing that thing where they don't flirt, and it gets real awkward, real fast for the rest of us. It's been a thing that wasn't a thing since we were about eleven.

I don't think anything will happen, really. Just recently, it's become more obvious. Sometimes I'll text her, and she'll clearly be out with someone, but not say who. Then in class, Jason will let slip that he was out the night before and describe almost exactly the same thing Sukhy was up to.

This extra layer of closeness between them then never shows, until they drink together. They'd be doing fake waltzing together or singing some corny love song and all of a sudden, I'd be like, 'Oh shit, I'm gate-crashing their date'.

Usually, we notice it and Beth and Matt smirk at me. Sometimes I raise an eyebrow at them, and their weird flirtation of our friends is this big joke between the three of us. Only sometimes when I drink I forget to react and Beth assumes that I'm secretly upset about the whole thing.

'She'd still be our friend,' Beth says, 'Even if they start going out. Nothing would change really.'

But I'm not sad or upset about it, not at all. It doesn't make a difference to me. And it wouldn't be long term. Sukhy is going places and Jason...makes me worry.

Tonight, however, I can tell Matt is feeling sad about the lovey-dovey atmosphere. He sits there not making eye contact and drawing pictures in the dirt with a finger. His expression is vacant, and his eyes far away. His phone doesn't buzz anymore. He doesn't rush to check it.

I lay on the ground by the fire, one hand close to the flames. It always made me feel excited to do it as a kid, you know? Where you lick your fingers to knock out the flame? I used to love doing that. It always made my heart beat so fast I wanted to shriek. Beth is lying next to me, her eyes half open, looking up the stars through the trees. She is humming to herself.

I'm starting to think about calling it a night and heading home I hear footsteps, the trees rustling, and an old guy suddenly steps into the clearing, red-eyed and one hand on the front of his pants. He was in his fifties probably, and gross. I think he must have been pissing somewhere us and then swayed through to the clearing when he heard us talking. The waves of alcohol in my head start to clear, and we all kind of just stare at each other.

"Ew," Beth whispers to me, and I find myself smirking.

He is struggling to stay upright, pale, except his bright red cheeks. His hair is brown but starting to go grey, and he is balding on top. His clothes are dirty; I think I might have fallen over somewhere before he found us here.

"Is this where the cool kids are at?" He slurs and leans against a tree to prop himself upright.

None of us respond. Jason glances back at me like 'Ergh, read the room, old fart'. Why is it that entitled old men don't get atmospheres? It's fucking typical. He's a big man of the world who knows a few things. But we are dumb kids and could learn a thing or two from him and his whole Bachelors Degree from the School of Life.

He is entitled to our space.

"Lucky boys," he said as he leers at us. "Got some good-looking girls here, s-soooo, what are you kids up to?"

"Leaving," Sukhy said bluntly.

He laughs, it's a terrible kind of barking sound, "Oh, come on, let me join the party."

"Erm, yeah, like I said, we're kind of out past our bedtime," Sukhy adds sarcastically.

"Woah, hey, ain't your English good, hon," he said. He takes a step towards her and touches her hair. "Hey, this might surprise you, but I actually went out with an oriental girl before," he says, "Very traditional, very respectful, hey, does your daddy know you're out late?"

The closer he gets, the more I can smell sweat. Beth puts her fingers over her nose and Sukhy bats his hand away from her, her expression twisted in disgust.

"You're right, that does surprise me," Sukhy said, "You went out with someone?

"What was that?" he snaps.

"Think about it," Jason says as he taps the side of his head as he gets up. "Come on, guys, let's leave it for the night."

"Hey, hey, don't stop on my account," the guy says. "You're staying, ain't ya?" He goes to grab hold of Beth's shoulder, but she makes a frightened sort of squeak and leaps away, nearly knocking him flat on his ass.

"Come on, guys," he calls after us, "Daddy don't bite."

The five of us walk through the woods hurriedly, Sukhy leading the way. Our footsteps sound like an army we're walking that fast. We know the woods well enough not to need our phones. Matt and Sukhy head off in one direction, Jason follows them, just to make sure they get home safe.

"Don't need to worry about you, Beth," he says to her, grinning boyishly. "You've got a killer on the loose as your escort."

I start scratching at my wrist.

"Oh shut up, Jason," Beth snaps at him.

I watch them through the woods and hear the old man stumbling around in the dark, calling after us, promising a 'real good time'. Beth squeezes my hand as she leads me out through the woods and back to our houses. I hear him tripping over something a few feet away. We walk to the edge of the woods.

"I'm heading to bed," she says. "Ew, can you believe that guy?"

"I know, so gross," I said.

"Anyway, sleep well," she says. She hugs me around the shoulders before dashing off across the street. I watch her climb into her room like an incredibly nervous ninja. I wait for her light to go back off.

Then I turn back around and walk into the wood.

It doesn't take me long to find him. I spot him swaying around in the dark. I wait for him to see me and then I start walking again. I keep it slow and wait until he is definitely following me again. I hear his footsteps. He gets faster when I get faster. He slows down when I slow down. If he ran, he could reach out and grab hold of me.

"Where are you going?" He calls after me.

I ignore him and put my hands in my pockets.

"Hey! Hey, I'm talking to you, little girl."

My knife is in my hoodie, I run a thumb along the edge and enjoy the feeling of sharp steel against my skin.

"Hey! Don't you fucking disrespect me! I said I'm talking to you!"

He grabs my arm and spins me around to face him.

He is uglier up close, even in the dark, I can see that his stubble in uneven, he has an especially large black head at the end of his squashed looking nose. His breath smells, and he smells, but I just smile back at him.

"Where'd your friends go?" He asks, his hand gently moves down from my shoulder to my wrist.

"Not sure, I'm lost," I said.

"Is that right? We can fix that, hon, we can fix that," he slurs. He has three teeth missing, I notice. "Lucky you came back." Now he grips my wrist hard as he moves my resisting palm down to his crotch. "I've got somewhere you can be."

"Ew, gross," I said as I pull my hand free.

He keeps shushing me, spit on his lip. "You came back here to see me," he hisses at me. "Wanted a roll around the woods, didn't you?" He presses up against my struggling hand now, hard. "You're a fucking little slut."

I stab him in the face. I stab through his eye; I rip and tear until the eye comes away with my blade. He screams, but not for long. I cut his throat next. He staggers back and I kick him the crotch. Not the kind of treatment he expected in that particular area.

I lay down on top of his sweat-sodden body, and it's like fucking euphoria.

I take the skin off his face. I slice off his ears. I dice up the remaining eye in his skull. I punch him in the mouth and feel a tooth give way under my fist. I stamp repeatedly on his crotch and rejoice at how he writhes and wriggles under me.

And this time I hear myself clearly, crying and laughing and slashing off his fingerprints until suddenly I realise that I am not alone.

Beth is stood there with her mouth wide open in frightened shock. She must have looked out of her window and seen me walking back into the woods. She must have panicked and rushed out of the house to come and get me. She must have been scared and worried about me.

I'm so touched that she loves me this much.

But she didn't see him grab me or try and touch me. She has to come in at the worst possible time. Typical fucking Beth. Instead of finding me defending myself from a drunk old man, a potential rapist. She has to go and find me laughing and covered in his blood.

I get up and walk towards her.

She doesn't run away.

Running would mean that I'd have to chase her and I don't want to have to do that. So I hold out my hand to her and say, "Will you help me get rid of this?"

Her hands are shaking, and she covers her mouth with her hands.

And of course, she just cries and cries the whole time. I make her carry his feet. It's the only part not covered in blood. She cries all the way, but not once does she refuse, not once does she complain or call me a monster or pretend she's going to call the police.

"He attacked me," I tell her, though she doesn't ask. "It was self-defence."

We carry him to my garden, and I make Beth leave. She walks away like a zombie, covered in tears. I tell her that everything is going to be alright, and she nods her head too many times. I watch her climb back into her room, and the light goes out. I imagine that she's crying.

Then I drag him down to through the living room and toss his body down the basement stairs and just leave him there. I faintly hear the person she brought home whimpering and crying somewhere at the bottom of the stairs, but they don't interest me right now.

If Mother wants to criticise me and say I'm messy, then she might as well do it all herself.

After, I go to clean the blood in the woods. I burn my clothes; another nice outfit lost and go to bed. I leave my wrists and my knees alone. I sleep easily and try not to think too much about it.

. . . .

Beth doesn't come to school the next day. I try not to think too much about that either. I go about my day. I watch Jason watching Jesse again. I watch the way his hands go into fists when he sees Jesse and Sukhy joking around after they get out of Math at the end of the day.

I hope that his new crocodile smile is about that and goes no deeper than that.

Sukhy asks me on our walk home if I've heard from Beth and I say no. I persuade her not to drop by. I'm worried that Beth will say something to her, and I want to be able to control this narrative. I want Sukhy to see it from my point of view and not get confused by

Beth, who is probably not exactly in the right frame of mind right now.

Sukhy goes home, and I reach my street. I see Beth's blinds are closed. And beautiful Detective Pete is doing his afternoon jog again. Just what shifts does he work exactly? I sometimes worry about what Mother thinks about him being here. She knows, she's always known what he's doing. I dread to think of how much she knows.

Does she let him watch her as much as he does because she's...? I don't know, flattered maybe? I don't mean like a sex thing, ew. Her brain doesn't seem to work that way. She's never had anyone, never shown any interest in dating. I don't even know how she managed to conceive me, really. No, I mean, like she enjoys knowing that there's someone watching her, someone trying to catch her out. Does that make it more exciting? I think it'd make me feel like I was constantly about to have a heart attack.

What does she think when she sees handsome young Detective Pete, sitting in his car, driving around the block, walk up to the fence, pretending to casually jog or walk. What does she think about that?

We wave at each other but don't talk today. So I wait until he's back for his second lap before going outside. It's hot today, way too hot. Seeing myself reflected in his stupid shiny sunglasses really bugs me. I really really look like such a dork coming out to give him juice like he's my boyfriend or something.

"Ah, it's young Fiona, back in school for a whole week now, well done."

That smile always came so easily. He drinks the juice readily. He doesn't think I'd poison him. And for the record, I wouldn't.

"Thanks, it's hot today."

"Yeah, imagine how I feel, back in school, classes of thirty plus kids with no A/C? They could be subtler about torturing us."

He laughs at that one and leans forward against the fence.

"So you're homesick then?"

"Pretty much."

"What did you get up to on those days off?"

"To be honest, I just kind of moped around the house. I turn sixteen soon, Detective. Then I'll have to get a job and lose all the benefits of being a lazy moping teenage girl."

"Oh, of course, that makes sense."

"And you? I see you're still stalking my house."

"I am patrolling an area under my protection, so I suppose in a manner of speaking, yes, I am."

"Good thing I know you're a cop, otherwise I'd have to make a call about a really sketchy guy with a thing for houses."

His smile is like a Disney prince, and I always felt like a chubby cartoon side-kick in his presence.

"In that case, I'd feel obliged to let the police know about the girl at Number 28 who nearly never goes to school."

"Erm, yeah, but you'd still look like a stalker."

We both laugh, and I wish I was someone older, kinder, cleaner, and wiser. I wish I was someone else's daughter. Though to be honest, this is not an infrequent thought for me.

After he finishes his juice, he goes off to pretend that he isn't investigating my mother and I go back into the house to pretend that I'm a good person.

. . . .

"Are you there or not?"

The humming noise stops. Then there are footsteps. She stands at the bottom of the stairs, wearing those ugly brown overalls.

"What is it?"

"I'm going out tonight. Do you want dinner?"

She brushes her hands on her overalls and takes the keys from her belt.

"Sure, sounds good to me."

I suppose it's the one typical mother/daughter thing we do other than snap at each other. Sometimes we cook. I do the chopping, she does everything else. We have a system. We tend not to talk, but we sometimes listen to jazz. It's just about the only music that she can stand.

Not tonight, though. She unplugs the CD player as soon as she makes her way into the kitchen to wash her hands. So, we stand there in near silence, just chopping and pouring and simmering. And it's almost alright. Apart from...

"Your overalls stink, I can smell them over the onions."

"Do they? I hadn't noticed."

Of course not, things like smell or hygiene are always beneath my mother. Things like that have always pissed me off about her.

"Fiona," she said after a moment. I can see her glancing at me. "Where did you go last night?"

"The woods. Why? Are we doing that thing where you pretend that you sincerely give a shit about where I go?"

I notice her roll her eyes.

"I went to the woods with my friends. It isn't a big deal."

"The person you came home with didn't seem like a teenager."

"Yeah? So, what?"

"I am just voicing my concerns."

"Well, keep them to yourself."

"You were clumsy."

I drop the knife on the counter-top. She reaches across my body and hands it back to me.

"Be more careful in the future."

Now I can feel my hands start to shake.

"I don't know what you're implying."

"Don't be stupid." Her tone is like ice. She reaches across from me and takes the plate of onions and peppers.

"Stupid people get caught out in the end."

I slam the knife down on the counter.

"Look, you don't know anything. You don't know what I'm going through!"

"You forget that I was a young girl myself once."

How can she stand there and say a line like that with those big, dead eyes of hers? I can feel waves of nausea coming over me, and I want to tear my skin to shreds.

"You and I have nothing in common!"

Our one thing that we do together and she has to go and ruin it by running that big mouth. I slam the kitchen door behind me and faintly hear her say, 'Only blood, Fiona.'

· · · ·

I sit on my bed and sit there looking at the contact number for the good Detective for two hours. His card is in my jacket still. God, I'm such a stalker. Could he actually help me? I mean, I'd like to think that he would understand.

That man in the woods wanted to hurt me. I'd have been another statistic, another raped, dead teenage girl, another cautionary tale to be relayed to little girls to keep them indoors. As if my being outside is what would have gotten me killed. Not that pervert's inability to see me as a human being.

So, I had to cut him. I cut and I cut and I cut. In fact, I cut so much that I couldn't call you after all, Detective. A man in twelve pieces hardly looks like I did it in self-defence. And if anyone ever finds Riley, if they ever find any part of him, then he'd know that I was lying. He'd know that I'm bad.

So, his much mulled over phone number stays on his much mulled over card and out of my phone. Probably for the best. I'd rather be called clumsy by her than have beautiful Detective Pete look at me how I look at her.

But we are nothing alike. She is more like that man I cut into pieces. Old and selfish and incapable of empathising with anyone. That's the sort of woman she is, and yet she had the nerve to act like we are anything alike? I wouldn't hurt anyone if she wasn't my mother. If someone, anyone, had been clued in when I was a kid and got me taken off her. Mr and Mrs Green for all their long patronising looks, they didn't stop and think something was amiss? They didn't look at her and get goosebumps? Didn't watch her face and see that there was just nothing, nothing there?

God! Why didn't anyone want to help me?

When the food is ready, I take a plate to my room and eat in front of my laptop. She eats alone, just staring out of the window. She is so weird. That'll teach her to flash her opinions where they weren't wanted, I figured.

I get a text from Sukhy asking if I'm coming. A text from Matt asking if we are meeting tonight. And a message from Lisa that I don't bother to read. And renewed radio silence from Beth. She is frightened. I didn't see her at school, but I can imagine how she is, walled up in her room, pale and drawn and frightened.

But I have too much of a headache to deal with any of that. It feels too big for me. Sometimes I can't even see me, can't manage to think about me anymore. How the fuck can I also sort out all of the others?

I mean, I'm not stupid, deep down I know Beth is weak. I know so well that if questions are asked, she would slow down. She would crumble and take the rest of us down with her.

I think about how easy it would be for her to take a tumble in the deep dark wood, how fast the river on the outskirts of town runs. How she barely looks when she crosses the road. I lie awake at night thinking about all of those things. I think about it so much I don't realise when I've pulled a scab fresh from the battered crease between my wrist and my forearm.

And eventually, I realise that if I remove Beth, it would be hard to keep the others close. There would be no controlling the narrative with Sukhy then. They would never trust me again. Not even one of them.

There's also the fact that if I remove Beth, it would be hard to keep me, me. And I think that terrifies me the most. I need to keep hold of myself, cling on tight.

CHAPTER THIRTEEN

I don't realise it's a conscious thing to not tell the others about the man in the woods until I notice the way Jason barges into the guys at school. I watch him nearly knock Jesse Macinera on his ass for no good reason on the way to fourth period.

"The fuck, man?" Jesse snarls at him. "I've got no problem with you!"

"Yeah? Well, I've got a problem with you," Jason says, stepping towards him. "I think it's that scrunched up little face of yours."

"Whatever," Jesse says, rubbing his shoulder. "I don't need to jeopardise my place on the team cos you're bored. I've got places to be, things to do. Unlike you, clearly." He rolls his eyes and goes to turn his back when Jason barrels into him and sends him headfirst onto the floor.

I stand there and watch for a little while as Jason swings wildly, smacking Jesse in the sides while Jesse tries to wriggle away. The girls scream, and the guys cheer, or maybe it's more mixed than that. Jesse yells out in alarm, protecting his head as he tries to turn onto his back and kick Jason away. Two of his friends are already wrestling Jason off. He kicks wildly, nearly catching Jesse in the face with his scuffed up shoes. I notice scratch marks on the back of Jason's neck as Mickey Jameson yanks him back by his collar. I notice crescent moon shaped groves on his wrists as he swings back his fist for another punch.

Mr Davis comes running, and Jason laughs in his face when he roars down at him. The fight disperses, and Jason and Mr Davis walk off to the principal's office. I get nudged in the arm by Kelly, and I realise that it's time for me to walk away now.

Jason is bloodthirsty.

I think he's just going to get worse.

And that's when I realise why I didn't tell the others about that man in the woods, it was because of Jason.

I saw it on that night as he helped me dismantle Riley completely. I saw it in the glee on his face when he looks at the missing person posters. I can see it in the corner of his eye every time he smiles that crocodile smile. He wants to hurt someone, the way I hurt Riley. Like how I've been literally itching to do it again, it's made Jason desperate to try it out for himself.

When I think about that summer Mrs Green made Beth uninvite him from her birthday party, I think about how Hutch, Beth's dog went missing the day after the party. I remember calling for Beth at her house that weekend, I'd brought crayons over, and Mrs Green asked me to go back home, Beth wasn't allowed to play today. I remember tearing up, my poor little child's brain panicking that Mr and Mrs Green didn't like me anymore, but Mrs Green bent down and patted my hair.

"Of course you haven't done anything wrong, Fiona sweetie," she said. "This is to punish Beth. She can't do nice things with her friends if she's in trouble."

Of course, they'd blamed Beth for Hutch going missing. They said she must have left the back door open. She was always forgetting things, like in the spelling competition, or her gym clothes. This was another failure on her part. They didn't care how worried and upset she was about Hutch being missing. They wouldn't even let her use a photo for her missing posters, her desperate attempt to get him home. I'd seen her tearful face around school. I'd seen her weeping loudly as she put up hand-drawn missing posters on her walk home.

I felt bad and helped her put them up.

Mostly I felt bad because I knew exactly where Hutch was. Jason had taken him away.

He gave Hutch treats and opened the gate for him to come out. He walked him into the woods behind my house and bashed its head with a rock. He skinned it slowly to see how it all went together. The dog was pink and soft without its fur. The skin on its belly so fine you could see the organs inside.

I found him doing it.

It was...a nuisance to me.

I could tell that Jason would have walked home like that, covered in blood. He would have just told Beth, if for some reason she'd have asked, that he had been the one who hurt her doggy. He would have just sat there and watched her cry and not understand why he'd done it.

I held out my hand to help him up, and he just stared at me like a blank, useless idiot.

Honestly, he could be so stupid. So I cleaned him up and helped him bury the dog in the woods. It would shock Beth how many times she's walked past Hutch's final resting place since.

I let Beth get into trouble for the dog going missing.

"She was mean to me," he said after when the two of us sat on the sofa watching cartoons and waiting for his dad to come and get him. "You all went skating without me."

"You can't do stuff like that," I said to him. "Besides, Beth wanted to invite you, idiot. It was your fault for putting your feet on her mom's sofa, stupid. Grown-ups hate stuff like that."

Upon noticing my mother returning from the basement, Jason quickly removed his dirty trainers from the sofa and put them carefully on the floor.

I should have been more careful. I could see how he'd see this whole ugly situation. I knew exactly how he'd take it. Getting to kill Riley and then instantly killing someone else, forgetting the man in the basement, would have been unfair to Jason.

So I won't tell him. Ideally, I would have preferred for nobody to know, it would be like the time in the basement, or that's how it was supposed to be, but Beth had to go and see me.

The group of us meet in the woods, I see Beth leave without me, walking off with her head down and her hands in her pockets. I let her go. I don't want her to get scared and chicken out. I take the long way through the woods. I don't really want to talk to any of them yet. I watch Beth disappear up the hill into the clearing. I watch Matt creeping around in the dark and nearly trip and fall on a branch before finding his way. I'm about to head back myself when I hear Sukhy and Jason coming.

"You can't keep getting into fights," Sukhy said to Jason quietly.

I was watching them in the dark just a few feet ahead of me, keeping my footsteps steady on the rough earth.

"Whatever, it's not a big deal."

"It is a big deal," she said. "You could get really badly hurt if you keep picking fights with people bigger than you."

"I can handle myself, Sukhy," he says bluntly.

"I don't care if you can or you can't. Look, whatever, you be like that if you want, but I think it's gross and awful and stupid." She brushes past him and walks quicker, nearly disappearing into the undergrowth.

"Sukhy wait, I'm sorry, hey," he says and rushes after her. I hear them stop and stand together, very close in the dark. I can't hear what they are saying. But he wraps both of his arms around her, and I hear a soft, almost wet sound. I find myself looking away, embarrassed.

"Don't get into fights," she says, her voice firmer and bolder now. "Or you can't do that again." She pushes him away and dashes towards the clearing, laughing now.

"Sukhy!" he calls, laughing and rushing after her.

I follow them, slowly and quietly and watch them in the clearing through the branches for a while. Matt and Sukhy are laughing about something; Jason is nudging them, helping to light the fire. He says something to Beth and she ignores him.

"You know, Beth, you've gotten kind of rude since that cousin of yours moved here," he says louder. "Hello, don't ignore me."

She looks nervous and says in a tiny voice that I can't help but overhear, "Guys, I have something I need to say."

I walk out of the bushes and loudly introduce the beer I brought with me. Her nervous rambling is forgotten, and the rest of us are drinking and chatting and laughing while she sits there and panics.

I see you, Beth. I see you. What would you have said if I hadn't been waiting all alone in the dark?

I watch her from the other side of the campfire. She doesn't touch the beer. I can see how terrified she is. If she hadn't seen me that night, then all of this ugliness would have been nearly forgotten. Sukhy isn't even fazed. Matt is getting softer and happier again, his bruises are gone, and nobody will hurt him again. And Jason, eventually this rage will go away, just like it did after Hutch.

I might have been able to laugh about how easy it was. How stupid everyone was. I'd smashed Riley to pieces, and even now, we all smiled, except Beth, she just sat there wanting to destroy all of our happiness just because someone like Riley, and someone like that old man, was dead.

She's the fucking worst.

So, I let her sit there hating herself while we all laugh and talk. And when it's time to go, I watch them all. I watch Beth to make sure she stays silent, I watch Jason to make sure he doesn't do anything stupid. I watch Matt to make sure he stays safe. And Sukhy, I don't need to. Have never ever needed to. I trust her completely. In fact, as the two of us walk arm in arm through the dark, dark night, I give her that man's wallet to dispose of.

"Can you use that incinerator at the hospital again?"

In the dark, I think I see the faintest trace of a frown. But she slides it into her jacket anyway, and I know I'll never need to look at it again.

. . . .

You know one of those dreams where someone or something is chasing you? And you, right, you're running and running trying to escape. It might be in a dark city, dashing through the back alleys. Or maybe in a creaky old mansion? Or perhaps, in the woods?

You keep turning corners, ducking and dodging but that person or that thing on your tail, it keeps finding you. You get so scared, but you can't wake up. And just when you're about the give up hope, you hear that reassuring voice. Maybe it's your lover, your best friend, your big brother. A kindly police detective.

Anyway, you hear them call your name. They say, 'I'm here! Don't worry! Follow my voice, I'm right here, come on! You'll be safe with me!'

And by this point, you are nearly in tears, and you run to that voice, thinking, 'I'm saved, thank God! I'm saved!'

You turn the corner and expect to find them there.

You expect to find light, a way out, a hand to take yours and take you away.

Only, instead, there is this portable CD player on the floor. Like the one we have at Sukhy's and knock out when we decorate. It's on the floor in front of a wall.

It's a dead end.

And you get real cold, real fast when you hear that loop of reassuring words spiralling back at you.

"Hey, it's alright, I'm right here. Follow my voice."

You turn around to run, but that thing that's chased you your whole life is waiting, blocking the only way out. And then your only hope is to wake up before the dream ends.

I wake up scratching at my skin again, nails bloody, gasping for air. I hear her shuffling around outside my bedroom door.

"*Go away!*" I scream.

The shuffling moves back to her own room. I cover my face with my hands and try and calm down, just one breath at a time. Everything can be fine.

I guess everyone has nightmares, right?

I wonder if now the others have them about me.

. . . .

The dream is an omen, I guess, because the next day in the afternoon, they found Riley's arm.

It was partially decomposed. But eventually identified as his from that dumb woven bracelet he wore on his wrist. I got so mad when I heard that detail. I remember myself, clearly, very clearly, telling Beth to remove it before she got rid of it. Also, I told her to get rid of it. Not put it in a fucking public trash can like she was throwing away a packet of fucking chips! No wonder she cried so much, she buried Riley in a public bin, a small one that hadn't been cleared out for a few weeks due to some public service issue.

Beth panicked and put her piece of Riley in the first thing she passed on her way out that morning as the sun rose. There was no security camera near that area. She tossed it in and ran home. It was covered in shopper's litter for a while, and then as the trash-can wasn't cleared, the smell became more prominent. A shop keeper complained, and when the town council finally came to clear the bin, Riley was discovered.

It was all over the news by lunchtime.

I had already read about it when I got a call from Beth, who was hiding in her parents' bathroom based on the acoustics. Whispering to try not to draw their attention, I'm sure. I could hardly hear her over her tears and half-formed erratic sentences.

"They found—! They saw—!"

"Beth, you need to calm down. What are you saying?"

Say it, I think. You say it, you complete fucking idiot.

She manages to calm down. Then she mumbles something about Riley, something about an arm. Then she weeps as loudly as she can, muffled behind her shirt, I can see her vividly. It's a pose I know well for her. Snivelling and panicking like I'm her cruel pinch-faced mother.

"You didn't put it somewhere sensible, did you?"

"No," she wails.

"And you didn't take off his bracelet?"

"N-No, no, I-I forgot."

"Beth…"

"They know he was killed. His parents…I saw his mom on the news."

"That doesn't matter, Beth, I thought you understood now, he was a thug, and he wanted to hurt Matt."

"Why did you have to cut him up?" she snarls.

Her rage is surprising. I guess I hadn't realised it before, but just behind her cowardice was rage, pure and unhesitating rage. I guess it's easier to say that stuff over the phone.

"Why did you have to do that? You say you were protecting Matt, but you didn't have to keep cutting him and cutting him. He was scared and drunk. He was just eighteen."

"Beth, what exactly are you saying?"

She stops crying.

"Are you saying that I was looking for an excuse? That I perhaps, just like hurting people?"

"No." She says defiantly though her tone says the opposite.

"Then, enlighten me, please. Why do you think I cut him so many times?"

"I think…you're not well," she said, her voice trembles. "I know you wanted to protect Matt, but I just think…if we told the police, they could help you. They'd get you to t-talk to someone."

"Oh, someone like a judge? Or a warden? Or convicts? Do you want me to go to prison?"

145

"That man you killed probably had a family too," she said.

"He might not."

"I don't care if he might not! It's not normal. First Riley, then that man! I mean, who's next, Fiona? You need help! This is not normal, this is scary! Normal people find this scary!"

"I had help," I say quietly. "You helped me, Beth. You did a shitty job the first time. But the other night you were a huge help shifting the body of that disgusting man."

"That's not what I!"

"And I had help from our friends too. Good friends, not like you. The others all helped me hide the rest of Riley. So, do you think the police could help them as well?"

She is crying quietly.

"I feel sick every second of every day."

"Then grow up," I said. "If the rest of us get caught, it's your fault. What were you thinking putting it there?"

"I want to kill myself."

"Don't be so stupid."

I hang up the phone and wait for her to text to apologise. And just when I start to worry that she won't, it buzzes through after ten minutes. She never changes. Beth has always been a–two-steps-forward-four-steps-back kind of girl.

Once Beth's panic has worn off, my own kicks in. I mean, I'm not a monster. The police finding Riley's arm is scary. I sit there and panic and vomit, worrying that I hadn't done a good enough job cleaning Matt's hair and blood from Riley's fingers. I mean, can you ever be sure that you've done a thorough enough job for that kind of thing? Or what if the others fucked up, what if they find the ashes of my burnt clothes, what if they identify me from the outfit because of a picture of me on Instagram, smoking cigars with Sukhy and Jason sat on the garden wall? What if they bring all of us in for questioning? What if Detective Pete starts to get a hunch? What if he's been talking to me more because of the hunch?

What if…?

I mean, eventually, it's all pointless. I go for a walk and buy gum. I wave at Detective Pete as he drives past with his partner, Detective Fatso. I leave Mother a vague note about running away to become a tree forest person before putting on a jacket, stealing the liquor that

Mother never even drinks and heading out into the woods. I jump out and scare Beth as she walks miserably through the undergrowth. She cries miserable tears, and I wait for her to clear them up before we go in and face the others.

Matt arrives, nervous and pale from the news. Sukhy looks rattled, and even Jason is void of that awful crocodile expression. They look nervous, so I act calm and casual, I crack a stupid joke about Beth being confused about the definition of a trash person, and we all laugh, except Beth, of course. We tease Beth about her shitty hiding place. Making light of it made it less real. We drink too much, and star gaze and Matt rolls his eyes and nudges me when Jason leans down and kisses Sukhy on the side of the head.

Beth walks home first, quiet and pale.

"Do you think she'll be alright?" Sukhy asks for the third time.

"Oh, she's just being nervous as usual," Jason says. "It's like when she has an exam coming up. She flunked out, and now she's scared of getting in trouble."

"It is disturbing," Matt slurred. "How quickly you normalised the whole body parts thing."

We all laugh and struggle to drag ourselves out of the woods and back home. It's all normal and fine, and Beth is just...weak, like I always said. I try not to think about how I flinch at every siren.

· · · ·

On Monday morning, I can't bring myself to get out of bed, so I skip for the day. Beth is still doing the same, even though I hear her pinch-faced mother ranting about it when she takes out the trash. I bet a lot of people did. Now everyone can actually grieve for Riley. Fuck, I wouldn't be surprised if they light candles around his picture like he's Mother fucking Theresa instead of a gross dead high school has-been.

I sit there, enjoying the breeze and thinking about that, pretty much, when I notice beautiful Detective Pete pull up outside my house. I am enjoying the view when my phone buzzes and I get a text from Sukhy that a patrol car was outside the school. My nails bite into the soft skin of my neck, and I think, 'Oh God, I'm caught. This is it. This is...'

But then beautiful Detective Pete drives away and the moment passes.

I wipe away the blood, clean up my hands, I find out high necked tops. I put one on and ignore my mother's cold gaze when she passes me in the corridor. I let it wash over me. So what if they found Riley? So what?

. . . .

Then the next day, Mother's favourite, Winnie Gails is on the radio. Our local radio. We are eating dinner at the table and not talking to each other. The radio is on because I put it on and hid it in a cupboard underneath the butter dish.

"And tonight we have with us, the lovely Winne Gails, Ms Gails, please say hi to our listeners tonight."

"Hello, Mike and thanks for having me."

"Ms Gails is here tonight to talk about the recent tragedy that's struck our small town, folks, this, of course, being the grisly murder of young Riley Sanders, which took place just a few weeks ago."

"Those of you who have followed my career must know, of course, that I kick-started my stardom in journalism with my ground-breaking book about the Red Creek Killer. Red Creek and I go waaay back, not too far back mind." She laughs nervously, and I cringe at how like the back cover of her book she is. "When I first heard about this case, this small town in a crisis, a poor boy's family waiting for him to come home, I felt this creeping sense of nostalgia. This feels like the work of an old friend. This feels like Red Creek."

Mother drops her fork.

"The way in which young Mr Sanders' arm was found is typical of how Red Creek disposed of his victims. Police are yet to find the remaining pieces, but I have a hunch they'll have luck in the woods surrounding this town."

"Ms Gails, Winnie, may I call you Winnie? This surprises me immensely, it was, of course, your eye witness testimony that helped put Randall Kayne behind bars."

"And I stand by that, Mike, I truly do. Anyone who's had the pleasure of devouring my published work knows what kind of monster Randall Kayne is. However, due to the disruptive nature of the police investigation at the time, the thought of a partner didn't even crop up. What if Red Creek wasn't one person, but say, several people, all working together? What if Randall Kayne was just the weak link that put that monster into its cage for a while? What if now, the beast is out, and it's hungry for old habits?"

Mother gets up from the table, opens the cupboard, lifts the butter dish, and switches off the radio.

"Fiona, I'm going out for a drive."

"Like I care."

I don't expect to see her rattled. But, then the next morning the school issues a warning that all of us kids are meant to be indoors by ten and are, under no circumstances, to wander anywhere near the woods alone.

And when I go home and find Mother's cello case empty, when I open the door and yell 'Hellooooo' down into the basement and hear no reply, no breathless sobs, no smell of rust and incense, I think 'Holy shit, they really do think that Red Creek did this!'

The rest of us all take a deep sigh of relief. Well, all except Beth. She stops coming out to the woods late at night. She stops answering my texts. She ignores the others too. She closes up into herself.

But she stays quiet.

I can handle quiet.

CHAPTER FOURTEEN

About a week after that, Beth hasn't come back to school. We try going over but get no results. She won't even talk to Matt, who she has always secretly confided in when she feels Sukhy, Jason and I are leaving her out. I keep my messages short and sweet, I snapchat the same stuff as usual.

No change at all to how we interact, minus her replies. It's my way of saying, 'Just checking up on you'. Please, I am all about passive aggressive observation, who do you think raised me?

I volunteer to go along to the Green house after school to check on Beth.

She knocks and I wait.

Mrs Green comes to the door, pinch-faced and smiling.

"Oh, girls, hello, it's so nice to see you."

"Nice to see you too, Mrs Green," I say. "We just wanted to check on Beth."

"Oh, Beth," she says, the irritation is creeping into her expression. "Beth still isn't quite herself. She's barely left her bedroom. Her father and I are both a little worried."

A little, not a lot.

"We brought her some notes," Sukhy said, "And my copy of To Kill a Mockingbird. It's going to be on the exam."

"Well, isn't that just so kind," Mrs Green says. "I'll be sure to tell Beth you dropped by."

I notice Beth staring at us from her bedroom window. Sukhy waves and Beth closes the blinds.

"Well, this isn't great," Sukhy says with a sigh.

"Yeah, this sucks ass."

We go back to mine, and we climb up onto the roof to smoke. We sit there in silence for a while, just staring out at the quiet woods. I wonder if Detective Pete is down there, looking for an excess of Riley. I try to banish that thought from my mind and wonder about what coping strategies Beth is using right now. Unconsciously I go to itch my arm and only realise I'm doing it when I feel Sukhy's hand on my forearm. I look up and see concerned brown eyes staring over at me before she turns back to the woods.

"Sorry, I didn't realise I was…"

"The teachers have been asking about you," she says.

"Bully for them."

"Ha, yeah, but seriously, Fiona, you need to stop doing that."

"I guess."

She blows a cloud of smoke into the air and leans back against the tiles.

"Do you think things will be different when we're in college?"

"I hope so."

And I do. I really really do.

The two of us are going to go to the same college, I'll manage to get in somehow. Maybe I'll study and get good grades and all that proper shit. Somehow, I'll make it work. I'll move out and take my stuff and leave my mother alone with her dirty overalls and the basement and whoever she has trapped inside. It'll be different when it's just me and Sukhy. We'll room together, re-invent ourselves and never have to come back to this shitty place. I'll become a vegetarian, get a cat, cut my hair really short and sexy and will never carry a knife with me when I go out.

If Mother has been arrested by then, I'll change my name from 'Taylor' to 'Henderson' or 'Miles' or something vague and non-threatening like that.

We won't even think about Beth, she'll move on with her life, get a boyfriend, get some shitty job in an office. Every now and then she'll panic and get upset about what happened this year, but it'll wash over her.

We won't see Jason anymore, he'll stay in this town, maybe knock someone up, maybe work for his father, maybe get arrested for joy riding or something. Whatever is happening now with him and with

Sukhy, it won't last. She's destined for bigger and better things, and it's me that she's taking with her. Not him.

I'd like to keep Matt with us for as long as we can. But otherwise, me and Sukhy will make new friends, we'll throw parties, get good jobs, live it up, and when people ask where we're from, we'll just roll our eyes and say, 'Some shit-hole' or something along those lines.

This will be the past and none of it will matter.

I'll never speak to that woman again, and we'll both be happier for it. If she doesn't get arrested, she'll probably make do, hurting people and landscaping ugly gardens for the rest of her life. Maybe one day someone will ask if she had a daughter and she'll just say, 'No'.

"I'll be happy when I'm away from here," I said.

"Me too. But sometimes I worry, I get scared that we're wrong, that we'll feel just as shitty in a new place. Like the problem is just us."

"That's an uplifting look at things."

Sukhy lies flat on her back, raising one leg high. I suddenly become aware of just how much bigger and taller than me she's grown. I remember when we were the same size, like we could fit inside each other.

"Did you get rid of that wallet?"

I pretend that I don't notice the uncomfortable look on her face.

"Of course I did. I couldn't get through to the one at the hospital, so I dropped it in the incinerator in the art room. Bye-bye Mr Wallet."

"That's good. I really appreciate it."

"Lisa nearly saw me."

"Did she say anything to you?"

"Nothing of note. Does she ever say anything worth hearing?"

"Right. Ok, that makes sense. Sooo, you think it's 100% certain that Beth won't be coming out later?"

"Well, that should come as absolutely no surprise."

"Yeah, it's too bad, though. I wish she'd just...talk to us. Hey, you should bring your mom's guitar and we can do a campfire singalong. Nothing more wholesome than that. Reckon that would change Town Councilman Butt-Face's mind?"

Well, it's a cello, but I'm tired of correcting her on that. I swear now she just does it to annoy me. Though I find myself panicking whenever Sukhy goes to help my mother carry it inside or to her car. I don't want her to feel the weight and notice that it's never the same.

"What? Start singing Old Mac Donald? No thanks."

She laughs again and sits up, brushing back her long dark hair. "Ok, perhaps not."

She is chatting excitedly about something stupid that happened in the debate team meet-up the other day. I listen and nod, but mostly, I look carefully at her. I wish I could read people better. I am pretty good with strangers, pretty good with people like Beth. But Sukhy, who I should know best in the whole world...there are times I can't read her at all.

I mean, I know that her and Jason sneak off to eat face. And that's cool, kind of weird and gross, but whatever, that's their business. I know that she sometimes frowns when I ask her to get rid of wallets and boy's body parts. But she also smiles when she sees me, she nudges me, rolls her eyes, takes my hand in hers and physically stops me from scratching marks onto my skin.

So why can't I tell if Sukhy is frightened of me now? With the others, I can see it, I can see how they feel. They wear their feelings on their faces. Like I know how Matt loves me for saving him, how it almost stops him from hating me for bringing him into my ugliness. He jokes around, he laughs, but there's a fear there that just didn't exist before. Beth smiles like I'm holding a gun to her head and now she has withdrawn from all of us just to get away. Jason is just as fucked up as me. He isn't scared the way the others are. And I need to keep him in line because he got reckless.

But Sukhy, Sukhy is my best friend. She has always been at my side. She is going to get out of this shitty town with me. I know, I know so much that it would hurt when I start to notice the fear in her face whenever she looks at me. I don't want her to leave me alone. A future with her, away somewhere else, is the only future I can imagine for myself.

The hand on my arm again, restraining my itching fingers.

"You look tired," she says as gently as she can.

"I am."

"Well, you have no excuse for that. I saw you napping in home-room earlier." She climbs through the small attic window and back into the house. "Wake up, we're going to the woods."

I can hear my mother drilling when I close the back door behind me.

Bye-bye, Basement.

• • • •

"Have you guys really not heard from Beth?" Matt asks as we sit in the low light of the campfire. "I kind of hoped…"

"No, her mom wouldn't let us see her," Sukhy says. "She saw us from her window but she wouldn't come out."

"This is so weird. She seemed so much better," he says. "I don't know what's changed so suddenly."

I do.

"She just needs time," Sukhy says, lying back and resting her head down near my knee. "I mean, this isn't exactly something you can talk to someone else about."

"She used to talk to me," Matt says. "The last time we talked about it…she stared at me like I was a monster for being able to see past this." He looks disappointed and confused. He doesn't respond when I touch his arm. I wish I knew some more useful words to say to him. Matt coughs and sighs before lying back down. "Speaking of absent friends, where's Jason, Sukhy?"

Heat flashes in her face, and she swats at him. "Hey! How should I know?"

"Well, I don't," he says, "But I'm sure you have a few ideas." He wriggles and swats back at her. The two of them dissolving into help-less laughter. I pretend I understand the joke and rest my head on Matt's shoulder. The three of us laugh and eventually fall quiet, star-ing up at the sky.

It's dark outside, cold and crisp and clear. I can see so many stars. Matt and Sukhy are whispering about that, about the views here, about their favourite places to go stargazing. Matt is talking about how positive this makes him feel like all the small stuff is small. And I really wish I felt something when I look up at the sky like that. But the stars are just stars. This is just a view, no different from another. I wish I was wired differently.

The expression on their faces is hard to copy.

Sort of misty in the eyes, wide, stupid mouth, or sometimes a half smile. I'm glad that they are looking up there so they can't see me copying them. I close my eyes and curl into Matt's shoulder, rolling onto my side. My arms and legs don't itch. My feet sting a little from the cold. Sukhy drags a blanket over the three of us, and I find my eyes getting heavier and heavier.

I never feel this safe.

. . . .

"Fiona, wake up," Matt is saying, shaking me gently. "Fiona, come on, it's time to go home. Hey, come on."

I blink and see that the sun is starting to come up. I can see Matt fumbling around with his jacket, hissing as he glances at his phone. Glancing over his shoulder in the dim light, I spot Sukhy and Jason fast asleep on the ground, covered by his leather jacket.

"When did Jason get here?" I mumble.

"Oh, ages ago. He came by real late with extra beer. You slept right through." Matt leans over and shakes Sukhy gently. "Sukhy, we've been out here all night. Come on. Wake up."

She blinks and bodily shifts away from Jason before rubbing her eyes. "What? No, it's only…" She glances at her watch. "Oh fucking hell, my dad is gonna go crazy."

Jason slurs something and rolls back onto his front. She elbows him hard in the ribs and staggers up to her feet. He groans and rubs his eyes, dissatisfied. He looks over at me and smiles. "Oh, hey, Sleeping Beauty."

"Hey yourself," I say and scramble to me feet. "Damn, I can't believe we stayed out."

"I am going to be so screwed. I'm surprised the police didn't wake us for how much this will have scared my mom," Matt says, running a hand through his hair. "Right, I got to dash. See you guys at school, I guess?"

"I'm not going," Jason mumbles. "Too sleepy."

"Yes, you are going," Sukhy snaps at him. "Oh, God…"

Matt waves cheerfully before disappearing into the undergrowth. I hear him saying, "Mom, I'm fine! Honestly! Hey!" before his voice trails off into the distance.

Jason snorts loudly, shaking his head.

"What? Your dad didn't call you?" Sukhy says, smirking at him.

"Oh, yeah, to ask me where the twins are, he has no freaking clue." Jason rubs his head. "Maybe I was meant to be watching them. It was kinda unclear. Oh, man, I am so tired."

Sukhy smirks and shakes her head dismissively.

"Sukhy, tell your dad that you stayed at mine and forgot to call," I say. "We're close enough to mine, anyway."

This seems to calm her down, and she smiles, nudging me. "Always thinking on your feet." She shakes some of the leaves from her hair awkwardly before stretching. "I might grab a shower at yours though. I look gr-immm!"

We walk ahead, leaving Jason frowning and browsing through his phone by the leftover campfire and bits of broken twigs.

· · · ·

Right now, I find the school to be…an unsettling place. Riley's picture covers just about every surface, his eyes haunting every corridor. It should be some ghost at the feast bullshit. I should be struck with guilt whenever I see that face. But…instead, I am filled with a different train of thought.

Mostly, that this is overkill. There actually is a large photo of him right by the school entrance, surrounded by flowers and nice notes. It looks like a celebrity's gravestone. I've seen like four girls crying in front of the picture. This is ridiculous. His locker is made up like a shrine. I hate walking past it. It's like when there's a tragedy, like a school shooting, and all the adults in charge say 'thoughts and prayers' but don't actually do anything. It's lip service.

Like, I wonder if they would deck the halls of the school the same way if, say, Tommy Bannister had died instead? Would we be seeing his gloomy, spotty face everywhere?

Somehow, I doubt it.

Lisa hugs me when I approach the others on the playground that morning before flinging me aside and clinging to Sukhy. This was not something that I feel either of us particularly enjoy. Matt offers me a sympathetic wince, I expect the others had the same treatment.

"It's so good to have us all back together," she says, reaching over to touch a strand of my hair. "It's been such a tough time recently, hasn't it?"

"Wait, all back…Is Beth here?" Sukhy asks.

"Oh yes, she's in the bathroom," Lisa said. "Auntie Rebecca called me last night and insisted that I get Beth back in school where she belongs. Anything to take her mind off things." She lowers her voice to what a sympathetic person might call a stage whisper, "She seems to have taken the whole Riley Sanders thing very hard."

As if on cue, Beth appears from the back doors. Matt waves in greeting, beaming at her. The corners of her mouth lift into a smile, but she won't meet my eyes. She is limp in Sukhy's hug. She is… flat.

"Part of the reason I managed to drag Beth back here is because of the memorial assembly for Riley today," Lisa explains. "I'm so glad that you could make it, Beth. Everyone deserves a chance to say goodbye."

If I hadn't been the one to end his short and quite frankly overrated life, I would have told her to get a hold of herself.

But it made sense to smile sympathetically and nod in agreement.

Yes, poor, dead, garbage-fire person Riley.

"I wouldn't have missed this for the world," I say and catch myself wondering if I look at all like her when I do it.

· · · ·

In first period, Jason, who is bleary-eyed and tired and smells strongly of grass and dirt, tells me that Beth has tried to talk to the others about going to the police. He seems reassured that I didn't seem surprised.

"She's a coward," I said. "Of course, she wants to run away."

"And just so you know, none of us are going to the police. The world is a better place without Riley in it. The others know that. Beth needs to get her head together. Seeing all this corny shit at school doesn't help either."

It often reassures me that they all helped me get rid of the body. Beth knows that turning me in will implicate them all. And if she turns herself in alone, she's a murderer. I don't need to get rid of her. Her cowardice will keep her quiet until she moves on and forgets. And she will forget.

Just like that old man in the night, or whatever Mother brought back to the basement. It isn't worth remembering. It's just not. I laugh and say Beth is an idiot because it makes it easier to think about that.

We go from maths to Riley's assembly, which, by the way, is the most contrived thing I have ever seen. We walk in and sit down around the auditorium, and there is this huge photo of Riley, posing in his football gear. A bunch of the girls are crying, and his teammates are gathered up at the front with the teachers like we're at some general's funeral.

Jason snorts a little too loudly and manages to turn it into a kind of whimper when he senses pairs of eyes shooting up towards him. I notice Detective Pete, beautiful Detective Pete, looking even better because of his immediate proximity to Detective Fatso, stood at the back, watching.

I fix my face into something sombre like I'm thinking hard about how lucky I am not to be dead like apparent school hero, Riley Sanders.

"Now, welcome, everyone," Principal Anderson says, tapping the microphone. "Welcome to this special assembly, where we will honour the memory of your classmate, Riley Sanders, whom we all miss very much."

Somewhere someone lets out a hysterical, loud sob.

For fuck's sake. They talk about him like he was going to grow up and be Bill Gates or something, instead of, you know, an abusive father working the sales in some shitty supermarket or maybe a supervisor somewhere if he played his cards right. I try not to let this show on my face and sit there, composed and thoughtful. Sometimes when I worry that I'm smirking, I raise a hand over my mouth, and anyone watching might just assume I'm crying.

I spot Matt sat a few rows down. Matt wouldn't be in this room right now if I hadn't done what I did. And I bet they wouldn't have held an assembly for Matt. I find myself covering a hand over my mouth again to hide a bemused smile.

After half an hour of listening to Principal Anderson rambling on, after listening to the football team mutter incoherently about what a great guy he was. After nudging Jason in the ribs when he snorted when Jesse Macinera said that he was sad that Riley was gone...After what felt like hours of keeping my face still and careful, Principal Anderson asked for people to come up on the stage with him to say the thing they would miss the most about Riley.

A lot of his football guys got up again. Jesse Macinera with a kind of calmness that makes me think he should go into politics or at least reporting on tragedies on the news. The others are not as polished, most of them struggling to get a clear sentence out through their tears. A few hysterical girls came on. I notice that no girls who found their names attached to him, not even one, comes up on the stage to say a few words.

Lisa, who didn't even know him very well at all, gave an Oscar-worthy speech about him.

Now that's fucked up, in my opinion.

She had literally only spoken to him once at the party he died at, and her speech would have you thinking they were practically child-hood friends.

Principal Anderson seemed to be winding it down, when a trembling, pale hand bolts into the air and to my shock, I see Beth staggering up from her seat and walking, shaking like a baby deer, up onto the stage. I see Sukhy freeze. Matt glances back at me with this nervous, 'What is she doing??' look on his face. Jason's hand finds my arm, and he starts squeezing very, very hard.

"I'm sorry," Beth said. Her voice is quivering in the microphone, her breath comes out almost like a high-pitched wheeze. "I'm sorry," she repeats, one hand coming to her throat. "I'm sorry, I'm sorry...I know that Riley wasn't a close friend of mine, that he wasn't always a nice person..." She lets out a slight sob. "B-But I'm so sorry that he's gone. I can't even—" Her expression crumples, her face reddened from crying. She heaves now as she speaks. "I'm sorry! I'm sorry! I don't know what to do!"

Chapter Fourteen

My hands are shaking in my lap, and I realise that I'm aware of my fists rapping against my knees because the whole hall is silent as Beth just cries and cries into the mic.

And I'm so angry with her for going there and making a scene.

How could she get this stupid over a guy who wanted to kill Matt?

Principal Anderson eventually acts and puts a doughy arm around her and gently leads her off the stage and out of the hall, Beth still sobbing and apologising. Jason is staring after her with his mouth wide open, and I realise that he isn't the only one. People are looking. Detective Fatso is muttering something, beautiful Detective Pete is jotting something down.

Mr Davis jumps up onto the stage and wraps up the assembly quickly before sending us back to class.

We walk back to class, we get on with our day, but my brain is fried.

What was he writing down?

Had they spoken to her?

What had she gone and said…?

Every time someone walks by my classroom, I find myself panicking that someone is coming to get me, someone is coming to take me away with the police. She has opened her mouth and all sorts of things have come tumbling out.

I need to talk to Beth. I'm bursting with it before lunch, Jason laughs at me for rushing on ahead, but I don't let it bother me. Matt and Sukhy are already in the courtyard and much to my dismay, I find Beth missing from our table and Lisa in her place.

"So this is where you guys always come," Lisa says. "It's nice on a day like this, but I usually prefer the canteen."

"And what drags you from the canteen today?" Jason asks, taking a seat next to Matt.

"Oh God, Jason, what are you trying to get rid of me?" she says, laughing and swatting him.

He looks very much like he wants to wipe that particular section of jacket clean. Which is funny as he was literally sleeping on the floor on top of it just a few hours ago. "Oh, who would," he grunts.

"Whatever," she says, rolling her eyes. "The canteen is soooo gloomy today. Lots of people crying, very sombre. And of course, it's such a sad occasion, but I needed to get away from it, you know?

Have some air to breathe! And how often do we get to have lunch together?" She nudges Sukhy playfully and begins rattling on about some gossip she heard in Math earlier.

I hate the way she calls it maths, with a nice long 'ssssss'.

"Where's Beth?"

"Oh, didn't you hear? Poor Beth went home," she said. "She got so upset in assembly. Even I was shocked! She's usually not one to cause a fuss." Lisa sighs and fiddles with her salad. "I guess she must have been holding a torch for Riley. I mean, soooo many people did. He was such a dreamboat."

"Speak for yourself," Matt says.

"Not your type, Matty?" Lisa says, pouting. "Not even with those shoulders?"

"Can we not sexualise a dead guy?" Jason says. "It's a bit weird."

"Hey, I'm not! I'm just getting 120 questions now about my cousin and Riley. Where they dating? Did he ever take her to make out point, etc.?"

"Make out point isn't a thing," I say.

"Well, maybe you've just never been there," she says, smirking at me. Then she spins off into ranting about something she heard from Casey Andrews and Lara Finn, and I switch off completely.

So, Beth isn't here.

That's fine. I can get hold of her later somehow.

At least everyone assumed that her strange little outburst was due to her having some sad little crush on big football star, Riley Sanders.

· · · ·

I'm walking past the reception on the way to gym when I spot beautiful Detective Pete, talking to Beth in one of the side offices. He has his officer face on, professional, calm, reassuring. Beth is still crying, and he pats her hand gently.

I wonder if she's said anything about me.

No.

She's clearly been there for a while.

Someone would have come.

There would be more police here.

Beth suddenly turns her head and glances right at me. I freeze up. She looks away quickly, and I see Detective Pete looking now as well. He smiles at me, and I have to force my face to smile back.

It takes everything I have to move one leg, then the other. And my whole body feels stiff and pinched as I walk away.

. . . .

After school, Jason and Matt come back to my house as Sukhy has debate practice again. They are going to Washington later this year for nationals which means more practice, and to Jason's dismay, more time with Jesse Macinera.

"I can't stand that guy," he says as we walk. "Did you see him?"

"Where?" Matt says.

"In assembly, talking like he was the governor of some forest fire state. All lip service. He didn't even care."

"Well, at least he was coherent," I said. "Riley's friends could barely get their words out."

Matt rolls his eyes. "Well, they are usually so coherent."

Jason snorts and stretches before kicking a pile of leaves and stomping through like a child. Matt shrugs and follows him, and I walk alongside, wondering if we will see Beth by her window again. We turn the corner at my house, and I notice Detective Pete jogging past. He stops for a breather, Mother is home, so of course he does. He smiles when he sees me and waves.

"Hello, Fiona," he says. "Got some gentleman escorts with you today."

"Oh yeah," I say. "I'm pretty lucky like that."

"Any plans for tonight?"

"Probably just pizza and a movie. Basic teen stuff. My mom is pretty casual about me having people over. How about you? Hot date with a log cabin or something?"

He chuckles and shakes his head. "Oh, very funny as usual. Well, have a fun evening." He jogs away, and Jason swats me and Matt for watching him go.

"God, you two are such weirdos," he said, laughing and shaking his head. "Take a picture, it'll last longer."

"Who was that?" Matt asks, elbowing Jason hard in the ribs.

"He lives by here, goes running. We chat sometimes."

Matt nudges me and smirks, "Reckon he could jog near my house?"

"He's like forty," Jason says, scandalised.

"Oh, he is not," I say. "He's probably thirty at the oldest."

"Yeah, that means when you were born, he was our age. It's weird!"

Me and Matt share a look. He raises his eyebrow.

"So, you're saying we should go for people our own age?"

"Like...Sukhy, for example?" I say.

"Hey, you shut up," Jason says, kicking leaves at us.

We shriek with laughter and rush ahead up the steps to my house. I can hear the faint sound of drilling in the basement. I guess the initial fear must have worn off. Swallowing heavily, I open the door and mockingly bow. "After you, fine gentlemen."

"And to you, dear lady," Matt said, bowing back.

Jason flops down onto the sofa, kicking off his shoes and leaning against the pillows. Matt laughs and jumps on top of his legs. They squirm around, laughing and kicking at each other before Jason sits properly.

"Drink?"

"Coffee, please?" Matt said.

"Juice?" Jason says.

"You're such a kid," Matt says.

"Coffee tastes like ash," he grumbles. "And it rots your teeth."

"Woah, what are you, a dentist?" I say sarcastically before moving into the kitchen to get down the mugs from the cupboard. I can hear them arguing over the TV, Jason laughing loudly. I glance down at my wrist as I reach down to the fridge for the milk and see that my wrist is finally starting to heal. I rub it gently and fumble around the fridge for the juice.

Then comes the creak of the door I know too well to be the door down to the basement.

"Hey, Ms Taylor, do you want a drink?" Matt calls.

All the blood seems to drain out of me.

"Ms Taylor?"

I hear the creak of the stairs.

"Dude, it smells funny down here," Jason mutters but his voice echoes.

My feet pound so hard on the floor that I can imagine the ceiling creaking over her head. My heart is in my throat and my head burns. All of my injuries seem to be inflamed like I'm bleeding something poisonous.

"Hey!" I yell as I yank back the red door and stand there, panting at the top of the stairs. Matt and Jason turn back to look behind me, baffled expressions on their faces. And at the very bottom, I can see her, wiping her hands on her brown overalls and that crocodile smile comes back into place.

"Fiona, there's no need to shout," she says. "A coffee would be lovely, thank you. Fiona, if you wouldn't mind?"

I don't move.

"Erm, nice overalls, Ms Taylor," Jason says. "You drilling or something?"

"Yes," she says. "I'm just sorting through some little maintenance chores."

"Need a hand?" he offers brightly.

"Oh yeah, if you need help, we're ok with our hands," Matt says, waving his hand lazily. "I helped my dad fix our kitchen table last year."

"Well, that is impressive," she says.

Jason takes a step forward.

There's a knife in her pocket. I can see its outline through those ugly overall pockets. I can always tell when there's a knife in her pocket.

"Erm, what do you mean, Fiona, if you wouldn't mind?" I snap. "I would mind. Make your own goddamn coffee." I turn and stomp out, knowing that they will follow. Shaking as I pray inside that they will come after me.

"Fiona, oh my God," Matt says, half shocked, half laughing. He clambers up the stairs after me. "Fiona! Hey!"

"Sorry, Ms Taylor," Jason says. "We're doing our best with her, really."

I breathe a sigh of relief as Jason follows me.

I keep going until we are in the kitchen. Jason is laughing, Matt looks concerned, I feel his hand on my arm.

"Fiona, hey-"

"I've told you not to go down there!" I'm yelling at him before I can stop myself. "I've fucking told you both that!"

He blinks in genuine surprise. "Fiona! That was like...when we were kids."

Jason has stopped laughing.

"Fiona, don't cry," he says in a voice I would have thought too gentle, too kind for him. "Hey, come on."

I touch my cheek and realise there are tears, streaming down my face and dripping down onto my sweater. They are both staring at me with visible horror on their faces. Matt's hands have fallen down to his sides, and Jason leans forward and hugs me gently around the shoulders.

"Hey, we're sorry," he says. "We didn't know."

"She doesn't like people going down there," I mumble.

"She was fine," he says. "She didn't mind."

"I say these things for a reason," I snap, holding my hands over my face.

"We won't go there, Fiona. Please don't cry," Matt says.

"Man, what is happening to everyone?" Jason says, laughing and shaking me a little. "Beth's gone fucking nuts, and now you're crying for no sane reason."

"Hey, shut up," I said. "I've got stuff going on."

"Don't we know it, you lunatic," he says. "Come on, give us a smile."

"No way," I say and laugh as I shove him off.

"I'll sort the coffee," Matt says. "You go and sit down. Help Jason pick a movie. Please nothing gross or scary, I'm really not in the mood."

I feel embarrassed on the sofa, Jason picks something laid back about musicians to watch. He keeps asking me if I'm ok to the point I want to tell him to drop it. Mother comes up to collect the coffee from Matt after the kettle boils. She passes me on the sofa without looking and thanks Matt—calling him 'young man' as she has no idea what his name is. She takes her drink upstairs with her and vaguely says something about going out tonight.

"Do what you want," I call after her. "Nobody cares."

Jason laughs as soon as my mother is safely upstairs. Matt shakes his head at me, exasperated. "Fiona, can you please not be so horrible to your mom?"

"It's just how we talk to each other," I say. "And besides, she's getting on my nerves. Whatever, let's order pizza. We have a few hours before Sukhy gets out of debate. I think she's meeting us in the woods."

. . . .

"Hey, I remember where I saw that hot jogging guy," Matt says suddenly, looking up drunkenly from his beer. "He was giving out interviews about Riley. He looked different without the uniform!"

"Oh shit, yeah, that guy is a policeman," Jason says. "I recognised him from the Riley talks."

"Erm, you did not," Matt said.

"Whatever, man, you were too busy drooling over him," Jason says. "Like Fiona was any better."

"What's this?" Sukhy asks.

"Fiona's got a special grown-up friend."

"Ew, like a 'show us on the doll where he touched you' thing?" Sukhy says, wrinkling her nose.

"Gross, no," I say. "It's just this guy who goes jogging in the area. Sometimes we chat."

"Yeah, we saw him earlier," Jason says. "He's the cop investigating Riley's gruesome end."

"Oh him, yeah, I've seen him a few times around this area. You've talked to him, isn't that right, Fiona?" Sukhy said.

"That's right. He's investigating Red Creek. I've seen him patrolling near my street."

Of course, he's never specifically said he was after Red Creek. But, come on, he comes by my house every day. He writes notes on where we go and what we do. What else was I to assume?

"I can't believe the police really think that Riley was taken out by Red Creek," Matt says.

"Randall Kayne is haunting these woods, stalking for new victims," Jason says.

"Oooh, spooky," Matt says, waving his arms stupidly.

"Randall Kayne isn't even dead," I say.

"Winnie Gails thinks the real killer could still be at large," Sukhy says. "I heard her on the radio the other day."

"Oh man, I've read her book," Jason said. "She's hysterical."

"Erm, should a book about a serial murderer be funny?" Matt said.

"Well, it's not haha funny, but her writing style sucks," he said with a shrug.

"And since when are you a literary expert?" I ask.

"Since when do you not tell us the police are sniffing around you?" he asks and there it is, the crocodile smile is back.

"Hey, he goes jogging near my house," I say. "He's not sniffing around me."

"Sniffing around who?" Beth asks as she steps out of the bushes.

"Oh, hey!" Matt gets to his feet and hugs her. "I was so worried about you."

She leans into it and shrugs her shoulders.

"Didn't think we'd see you tonight," Sukhy says.

"Well, I'm here."

"What was that at school?" Jason asks. "I thought you were going to like…point around the room and out us all. No offence, Matt."

"It's fine, Lisa," Matt says, rolling his eyes.

Beth sits down on the log stump and shrugs her shoulders again. "I got upset."

"But you seemed really upset," Sukhy said. "Beth, I said you could talk to me if you needed to."

"I know," she mumbles. "I didn't know I was going to get like that. It was just hard, coming back to school, seeing all the pictures."

"Seeing the weird shrine," Jason said.

"Jase," Sukhy hisses.

"Yeah, it was a bit much."

"No need to act like the Exorcist though," Jason says. "You scared me."

"We should be scared," she says. "I mean, a guy is dead."

"Beth," I say.

She looks up and glares at me. "What were you saying about some detective again?"

"I think there's a guy investigating Red Creek sniffing around Fiona," Jason says. "I mean, seems plausible. Fiona, did you travel back to the eighties to hack up some bodies?"

"No," I say. "Thanks for asking though."

We laugh, and Jason bumps his fist against my knee.

"I mean, it is lucky they seem to snatch it up to Red Creek," Matt says with a sigh.

"Not if the real Red Creek gets mad at us for copying him," Jason said, laughing.

Beth shivers and the rest of us laugh at her.

The Red Creek murders have a beginning, middle, and an end, so normal kids like us don't feel scared. Thirty confirmed kills. Randall Kayne is a household name, but he's like, been in jail since before any of us were born. Our parents were teenagers. People don't shudder at the mention of the Red Creek Killer. I mean, it's not like mentioning it will make that household name urban legend appear. This isn't like Bloody Mary.

But I mean, even I can't pretend that her legacy doesn't create a stir. I heard once that Randall Kayne gets fan mail from really sick weirdos, or ladies wanting a death row wedding with him. I heard talk about a movie a while ago, God knows what that would do for her ego.

Most of the known victims were found in Read Creek, all chopped up into bits, lodged under rocks under the water. That place has been known as Red Creek ever since. People have morbidly defaced the sign for so long that I think the local authorities have just stopped trying. The media coined the whole Red Creek thing and as more victims followed the same pattern, the murderer became known as the Red Creek Killer.

There have been books written about the killer, better writers than that hack, Winnie Gails, Mother has read them all and pretends that she hasn't. I've seen a list of suspects as long as my arm before they settled on Randall Kayne. There was another suspect, the head detective lost his job over it.

And just so you know, thirty doesn't even scratch the surface of what Red Creek did.

Nobody even noticed when she got back to work.

"It'll be fine unless they start to suspect that it's a copycat killer," Sukhy said. "That always happens in films, right?"

"I mean the whole chopping him up is just practical, I guess," Matt said, "But it's actually really lucky that doing that is just Red Creek's style."

There was the other reason they think it was Red Creek who did away with Riley. It was the fact that his skin was covered in multiple stab wounds, like whoever chopped him up did so in a stab-happy frenzy. If it was one cut and then I'd put him in chunks, I bet those guys never would have bothered connecting his death with Red Creek.

"I should get home," Beth said suddenly.

"What, already?"

"Curfew," she said. "Sorry, guys."

She staggers off, back through the woods, her head down.

"Well, that was sporadic," Matt said.

"It can't have helped that you guys wanted to talk Red Creek," Sukhy said. "What an excellent topic for our glitchy traumatised friend."

I notice Jason staring after her, frowning.

I kick him to make him focus.

"To be fair, she brought him up," Jason said suddenly.

"Who?"

"Red Creek. Beth brought it up."

"She was just trying to join in," Sukhy said. "The next time she comes back here, we talk about…like literally anything else. God, when did we get so gloomy?"

The night goes on, and we drink and laugh, and the topic turns away from serial killers with knives, victims underneath the water. We joke around about the shrine, we laugh at the way Mr Davis ran up onto the stage. We talk about what we want to do over the summer.

Then, as Matt mutters drunkenly about not wanting to sleep out here on the floor again and Sukhy starts blinking too slowly, nearly passed out from whisky, Jason leans over to me and asks, "Do you think Beth was wearing a wire?"

I frown and ask him what kind of world he thought he was living in. We both laugh, and he shoves me playfully as we both stagger to our feet. My head spins, and I hope that this will be the end of it.

"She seemed kinda like she was wearing a wire," he slurs to himself as he makes his way through the woods.

CHAPTER FIFTEEN

My headaches and my knees feel stiff as I make my way out of bed and downstairs to get a cup of coffee. Way too much to drink. I'm going to be practically fucking comatose for all of school. I want to just not go.

But it will look bad if both me and Beth keep ditching together.

I spot her sipping a glass of water and eating her plain, horrible tasting cereal at the kitchen table when I come down. She doesn't look up, so I roll my eyes and walk past her to get to the kettle.

"Good morning," she says.

"I'm not speaking to you," I say and ignore her bemused expression.

The kettle boils, and my hands shake from the urge to throw its contents over her. I was glad she wasn't back when I got home last night because I don't know what I'd have said.

"Is this about your little outburst yesterday?"

"I mean it," I say. "Don't even start with me today."

"I never expected tears from you," she said. "You hardly ever did that when you were little. So I was surprised to see that side of you."

"You don't threaten my friends again," I snarled at her. "They're mine. You don't get to hurt them."

"I didn't do anything to your little friends," she says. "What a rude accusation."

"You had a knife on you."

"They came into my workshop."

"You invited them down there."

She looks up and there it is. Just like a crocodile.

"My friends are off limits to you," I say, wanting to be braver than I feel.

"What made you so sure I had a knife?"

"You were down there, weren't you?"

"No, Fiona, dear, you said that I had a knife on me. What made you so sure?"

"I can tell," I said. "I'm not dumb."

"I'm not implying anything of the sort."

"I can just tell," I snap. "You had a knife. And inviting them down there, I can't believe you'd do that. You know how important they are to me." I feel my heart pounding in my chest.

"I was alone down there, they wouldn't have seen anything incriminating," she said in that detached voice of hers.

"Bite me," I hiss and feel my hands shaking as I stir my coffee.

"Can you always tell…" she asks, "when I have a knife?"

"Yes," I say flatly. "Call it a skill for life."

"You might live longer for knowing it," she says.

"So why not give yourself a big pat on the back, Mother?" I sneer at her.

"How about now, Fiona?"

I glance at her briefly over my shoulder and see that she's now stood up from the table.

"How about now, what?"

"Am I holding a knife now?"

She takes a step forward, coming towards me. I grab hold of the little red knife that I use the cut carrots and spin around, lurching forwards at her. Strong dark hands reach up and grasp hold of my wrists and slam me sideways into the kitchen cabinet. One hand restraining my knife hand, the other forcing my free hand against the kitchen counter-top.

I hear a frightened whimper come out of my mouth and hate myself for it. Her expression is completely blank. Her eyes are empty, without even that crocodile smile on her face. She's…empty. Is that what those people saw before she ripped them into pieces?

"Fiona," she says. "You were wrong. I don't have a knife."

Then she lets me go.

Panting, I look at her properly and see that her hands are empty, her pockets are flat against her skin. She is unarmed. Only that blank, thin smile on her face.

"I fucking hate you!"

"You're too paranoid," she says. "But, in the future, please ensure your little friends don't come down into the basement. It can be pretty unsafe down there." She dusts off her clothes, dumps her bowl in the sink and walks up the stairs. My hands are still shaking as I double over and vomit on the kitchen floor.

· · · ·

My head is still spinning as I walk the route to school. Turning the corner, I spot Beth is a few feet ahead of me. I see her with her head down and her hands in her pockets. Her mother must have forced her to go back in. I bet her eyes are all red and puffy from crying. I think catching up with her would send the wrong impression.

I watch her wander over to Lisa, who is holding court on the far corner of the playground with some other perky looking girls who have strangely all worn the same coat.

Maybe they'll be her friends now.

I wish it didn't need to be like that.

Whatever. I go through the school gates and notice that the others aren't here yet. Feeling kind of dejected and lonely, I wander around the school corridors aimlessly until one of the teachers angrily tells me to go outside. Ergh, get a life. I am about to head outside towards our usual spot by the big bins when I hear Matt's voice in a hushed, angry whisper.

"I've said I don't want to talk to you!"

"Matt, come on. Please."

It's Matt and Freddie Hankerson in one of the classrooms. I stand outside the door, frowning.

"I don't want to see you."

"You have to tell me what happened that night," he says.

"No, I don't. What, did you just start to care?"

Freddie's voice softens. "You know that I do. You're the one who won't answer my messages."

"I told the police what happened. Your buddy Riley beat the shit out of me then he walked off drunk. I crawled home, got found by my friends and spent the early hours trying to make sure they didn't call the police. Happy?"

"And you didn't see anyone?" he asks. "There was nobody else there?"

"I was kind of busy getting beaten up. Sorry, didn't spot the monster that killed your best friend the fucking maniac."

"He is dead, you know," Hank said. "Don't talk about him like that."

"I'll talk about that fucking asshole however I want!" Matt snarls. "If he wasn't drunk off his face, he would have killed me. It sucks for his parents or whatever that he's dead, but I won't act like I'm sad that he's gone! I'm actually pleased! I manage to get from A to B without him and all your other asshole friends physically attacking me."

"I'm sorry, alright?" he says. "I'm sorry."

"No, you only came here to bombard me with this shit! Did I see something? Are you fucking serious?" Matt sounds like he's crying. "You left me! You left me there with him."

He sobs.

"I didn't want to," Freddie says. "I was...scared and stupid."

"I was scared! You know, you say you want us to date, but I'd never let my friends hurt you, right? But you let your friends call me names, push me around and actually try to fucking kill me every day! You just walked off and left me there with him." He shoves him hard into one of the desks because I hear it scrape across the floor. "Leave me alone, ok? You were real good at that before."

The door opens, and Matt comes rushing out. I leap back but he sees me. His eyes are small and red, and he rubs a hand frantically across his face.

"Were you listening to that?" he asks, voice raw and angry.

"No," I say.

Hank comes rushing to the door as well, he reaches for Matt and I knock his hand away. His eyes widen in surprise, and for a second, he looks just like Riley, thrown off guard. He thought he was untouchable.

"He's asked you to leave him alone," I say slowly. "So, can you manage that or do you need some help?"

"What the-" Freddie snaps, rounding on me. "This is a private conversation." He grabs hold of my collar and pushes me back.

It's strange. I have the exact same knife that I used to dismantle Riley in my coat pocket today. I feel my fingertips against it when Matt forces his way in between us, his arms splayed wide.

"Stop!"

Freddie looks startled and steps back, he lets go of me instantly.

"I'm sorry," he says. "Matt, please. I really need to talk to you. I need-"

"No," Matt says. His hand finds my sleeve, and he tugs me along after him, pulling me outside. He is walking faster than I've ever seen him move. Freddie Hankerson probably thinks that he's crossed a line, that Matt was protecting me from his big horrible ex.

But it's the opposite.

Matt is shaking. He won't meet my eyes, just like Beth.

No, Freddie. He is protecting you from me.

His hands are shaking violently as we stop and stand outside. He won't let go of me. Like he's trying to hold me back.

"Matt," I say.

"It's fine," he says.

"Was he bothering you?"

"No."

"What did he ask?"

"Fiona, it's fine. He is just being stupid."

"Was he asking about Riley?"

"He did. But it was a dumb, round about thing."

"Do you miss him?" I ask.

He covers his face and nods.

"I'm sorry, Matt."

He won't look at me, he just crouches down onto his knees and keeps his face covered, breathing very fast. I know that look. I'm glad he's too distressed to recognise it. This was how I felt when he and Jason wandered down into the basement with her. I'm glad he's covered his face.

I don't want to see my expression on his face.

"Are you guys ok?" Sukhy asks, appearing from behind us.

Matt rubs his eyes. "Yeah, I'm fine. Honestly. Just hungover." He makes a vomiting noise and Sukhy laughs and helps him to his feet. "Noo, don't move me," he groans, resting his head on her. "I'm so done."

"Better pull yourself together," she says. "People might talk." She glances over at me and frowns at my expression. "Fiona, what's the matter?"

"Nothing."

I know she doesn't believe me, but she does drop it.

. . . .

Jason calls me late at night to tell me that he'd seen Beth on her phone. She looked upset and was talking quickly and quietly. She was talking like she has a secret, he said.

"When did you see her?" I ask.

"Through her window," he said.

"Through..." I rub my head. "Jason, that's weird."

"There's something up with her, she's talking to someone," he snaps at me. "You have to see that, right?"

"Beth helped us hide it," I say flatly. "She helped us do that. You know she'd be in trouble as well."

"What if they've made a deal with her?"

"Jason, come on."

"I'm serious," he snaps. "Fiona, I'm not being funny, but you deserve to get caught if you aren't going to think about this stuff."

"There's nothing to think about."

"You were on your phone tonight too. What was that about?" The suspicion in his voice is ridiculous. I want to roll my eyes. I want to close my fists around his windpipe.

"Are you watching my house too?"

"Well, I mean, it was right there," he says. "Why won't you answer?"

"I was chatting to my mother about dinner," I say.

It's none of his goddamn business. I remind myself to close my blinds earlier.

"Have you chatted to her about anything else recently?"

"Fucks sake, Jason, what have you been smoking?"

"I'm just trying to keep this group safe," he snaps at me. "Whatever. Enjoy your evening with your mom."

When he hangs up the phone with a huff, I glance out of the window and through the blinds; I spot him walking around Beth's street, peering up at her bedroom window. I wonder if this isn't the first time he's done this. I wonder where this will end. As my hands bruise my healing wrist, I wonder if this actually has nothing to do with Beth being some kind of police nark, working tirelessly to put us all in prison. I think the itch had just gotten too strong. I think, like me, he's up at night, digging blunt nails into flesh to try to get rid of the thought of tearing something into pieces.

I should have helped him better.

CHAPTER SIXTEEN

I've drunk more than I realised, I think and hold my head upright with some difficulty. Sukhy and Matt are playing cards, and I realise that I was meant to be refereeing. Don't ask me how you referee a game of cards, but it's always been something we do.

In the background, I hear Beth quietly mumble something about curfew. She nearly stands on my hand as she staggers through the group of us. Her phone light flashes on, and she begins to stumble uselessly through the woods.

Of this, I am half aware.

But then I suddenly realise that Jason isn't with us anymore. I lean back and see Jason wandering off into the woods after her.

"I'mma go pee," I say to nobody in particular as Sukhy is explaining a possible illegal move to Matt. They are laughing and don't seem to notice as I leave the group as well. Away from the safe light of our fire and after the crunching of footsteps over leaves in the dark.

I follow them because I knew he hadn't stopped thinking that someone on the police had given her a wire. He was adamant that the police were watching, desperate to wheedle a confession out of one of us. I noticed him tailoring the conversation carefully when Beth was near, whenever that night came up. I notice the way he stares at her, sneers at her.

Like he doesn't know her.

Like we haven't always been together.

I find them quickly, rushing through the clearing when I hear something scrambling around like animals in the dark. Using my phone to light the way, I spot them clearly. He is leaning over her, snarling like an animal, his voice a frantic whisper. He tugs at her jacket, trying to find the wire he has imagined. She is struggling, trying to wriggle out of his grip. Her hand swings back, and she slaps his face as hard as she can. He releases her and staggers. Beth looks shocked at her own strength. She hesitates before she goes to run.

I watch them for a moment, watch her turn to run, Jason collect himself, and with the very same knife he used to once kill her dog, Jason reaches out and slashes Beth across the forearm. He muffles her petrified scream with his hand and sends her to her knees easily with the force of his hand. The blade comes up, and she wails, twisting her face out of his grip.

When he doesn't strike with the knife again, she thrashes and kicks. Jason sits on top of her, trying to restrain her with one hand and keep hold of the knife with the other.

"Where is the wire?" He snarls. "I know you have one! I know you're with the police, Beth!"

"I don't know what you're talking about!"

He thrusts the knife down close to her face, and Beth lets out a terrified shriek like an animal before he muffles it with his hand. He holds the knife above her left eye and starts to laugh while she dissolves into tears.

"Ergh, is that pee?" He shifts up, gasping in disgust, before sitting down on her chest. "Beth, what the actual fuck?"

She doesn't reply. She just sobs, her body heaving.

"Don't scream," he said, removing his hand. "Now, what did you tell the police?"

"N-N-Nothing," she wails. "Jason, why...?"

"Don't fucking lie to me," he hisses. "What did you tell the police?"

"I told them that...I didn't think it was Red Creek who killed Riley."

He is panting. "And why did you do that?"

"Fiona is mentally ill," she whimpered. "I t-think she needs help, I think she's not well. She k-killed Riley and she killed t-that drunk man from the other night, and I think..."

"Hey," I said, stepping out of the dark shrubbery. "What's going on here?"

Jason freezes, looking up at me. He puts the knife down, but he doesn't move from sitting on top of Beth. Beth just lies there, crying and stinking of piss and sweat. Her arm is bleeding badly.

She is going to have a lot to explain to her pinch-faced mother.

"This fucking rat's been talking to the police about us," Jason said. "No wire, like you said. But she's got a pretty big mouth."

"Jason, what would Sukhy say if she saw you pawing all over some other girl?" I said, offering him a hand. "Let's get you up."

"Fiona, Beth is going to get us all fucking arrested. We need to get rid of—"

I see Beth's hand jerk out faster than I can react, she snatches the knife up and surprising everyone, even herself, stabs Jason in the thigh. He howls like an animal and leaps up off her, uneven on his bleeding leg. Beth rolls onto her front with all that softball practice and is on her feet, clasping hold of the knife, she brandishes it in front of her like a woman possessed.

"Keep away! Both of you! Keep away from me!"

"Beth, don't be stupid."

"I won't be a part of this! I won't! I won't! I won't!"

"You little bitch!" Jason snarls. He lunges at her and dodges as she tries to slash at him. His fist catches her in the right cheek, and she falls to the ground. I step forward to stop him as his foot slams back and forth, kicking her over and over and over again until she stops fighting. He is panting, exhausted and reaches down to snatch the knife from her unconscious body.

"Don't," I said. "Don't bother."

I know the others won't help us get rid of her body. I know Matt would never forgive us for this. I know Sukhy would run. She's always been the smartest one.

Jason, on the other hand, stands over her, bewildered.

"What are we going to do?"

"We take her to the emergency room."

"Are you joking?"

"You have zero follow-through, you know that? Help me get her upright, you absolute fucking idiot."

. . . .

It bothers me how much I imagined this situation. I'd thought about getting rid of her whenever things got hard. But there was always a reason not to. Even though she was weak, even though I knew that if she was ever suspected, she'd break and give the game away. Even though I knew all that, I couldn't bring myself to accuse her of that, to actually try to hurt her.

Beth is a coward.

Though perhaps not as much of a coward as I'd first thought.

I sit there in shocked disbelief where three days pass since Jason and I dropped her off at the hospital, saying that she'd been found on her walk home, and the police don't come, nobody calls around our house with accusations and fear. Nothing happens at all. We have a statement at the hospital after dropping her off and then nothing.

Mrs Green comes over to our house, and my mother provides her with coffee and avoids the fact that she has no idea which of my friend's mothers this is. She nods sympathetically and for some strange reason, puts her hand on Mrs Green's arm as if to reassure her.

"We need to keep a tighter watch on our kids, Sylvia," she says, wiping her eyes. "I had no idea Beth was sneaking out again. I would have expected she had more brains than that..." She seems to restrain herself, seeming to remember that this is the same brainless Beth in a hospital bed with knife injuries.

"I'm sorry, Mrs Green," I say before Mother calls her 'dear' or 'you' again. "We never usually have problems. We just go there to kid around."

Strangely I think the fear of Beth being attacked and potentially left for dead, is overriding her rage that we snuck out, that we were drinking. That we had been doing all of the things she disapproves of so badly.

"If you and the others hadn't heard her scream," She says in a wobbling voice, "I could be like that Sanders woman right now."

"That's a dreadful thought, Mrs Green," Mother says, once again, tapping her gently on the arm. "It is lucky that Fiona was there."

I stand there and learn, much to my shock that Beth has gone out of her way to surprise us all when I hear from Mrs Green that she told the police that she left us to go home, saw someone waiting in the clearing, this person rushed at her and attacked her. She said that she didn't see their face, it was too dark. She didn't even get flustered when who I guess must have been Detective Fatso (Mrs. Green referred to him as a deplorable overweight man with side-burns), gave her the third degree that he gave me back in school. No, Beth kept insisting that she bumped her head really hard and besides, it was so dark, she was confused. Before Mrs Green did her classic scary mom 'I want to speak to the manager' deal and had the interview terminated.

I guess even pinch-faced mothers like Mrs Green have their uses.

· · · ·

"So, Fiona, was it you who beat up your little friend, or was it somebody else?"

She is washing bloody hands in the sink.

"Watch it, I'm cooking here," I said.

"From the way you're chopping up those onions, I'm assuming it wasn't you," she said. "Not got any mindless acts of violence on the roster at the moment?"

"Shut up."

"Now, whoever it is, they are just ripe for getting caught if they aren't careful." She wipes her hands dry on her overalls. "But you'll be careful, won't you?"

I could have told her to be careful all those times she was slicing up bodies in the basement. All it would have taken was a tearful chat with a teacher and I'd be in a home and she'd be in jail.

She should try remembering that sometime before she lectures me.

I don't say that to her, though.

"It won't matter. She hasn't said anything."

"The next one might," she said. "If whoever it was is incapable of finishing them off, then I'm sure you could help them out."

"I'm not like that," I said.

She chuckles, and the basement door closes behind her.

185

. . . .

The hardest part of the whole Beth fiasco is Sukhy and Matt. The two of them genuinely believe that she was attacked by someone. The second I'd gotten rid of Jason's knife, we both started yelling at the others for help. They were worried about her. I can see Sukhy and Jason sat together on the playground, he has an arm around her while she talks in a quiet, miserable voice.

He really is a total fucking idiot with zero follow-throughs.

Mostly what scares me is that I know another surge would emerge in Jason. No longer would he stare impassively at the playground. His temper had always been bad, but now it had more bite. Now I could feel the hairs on my neck standing up when someone said something stupid to him in class, I'd panic when someone nudged into him. Now he comes to school and stares like a hunter. I'd find him looking at Lisa with a kind of hunger she probably mistakes for attraction. She would try to flirt with/insult him, and he would smirk at her like he was imagining all the ways he could hurt her.

We are walking from the science labs back to the canteen to get lunch when Jason draws away from me and ploughs straight into Jesse Macinera, who is coming out of a classroom with Sukhy and a group of other debate kids. Football instincts coming in, Jesse straightens his shoulders and steadies himself against the blow.

"Watch it," he snaps at Jason.

"Sorry, you're in the way," he says, straightening up.

"How are you friends with this guy, Sukhy?" Jesse says sarcastically, glancing down at Sukhy. He is doing that politician sneer smile, before Jason's fist jerks up and bobs him right in the mouth.

Sukhy shrieks as Jesse staggers back into the guy behind him.

"Jason, stop it!"

Jesse is holding his bleeding mouth, eyes burning with rage. I see his arms tighten and everything in him must be roaring to hit Jason back. But he doesn't. He stands there, rigid, glaring at him. Jason raises his arms, daring him to go for him again. He looks right past Sukhy, who is trying her best to get physically between them.

"Come on then, tough guy," Jason says. "Come on, hard man."

"Seriously?" Jesse says.

"Not going to without your asshole friends here to protect you?"

186

"You're white trash," Jesse says through the blood. "Why don't you just drop out of school? It'd save the administration the paper-work."

Jason removes Sukhy's hand from his chest and pushes her aside, sending her hard into the classroom door, he lurches forwards, fist raised, going for Jesse again. I step forward and grab the short, deli-cate hairs at the base of the back of his neck and pull as hard as I can. His fist swerves and he howls, eyes watering and frantic, peering back at me in shocked betrayal.

"Come on, stupid," I snap at him. "We're going outside."

"Fiona, let go."

I tug again, and he pulls back to avoid the hairs being pulled.

"Ah! Ah! I get it! Let go of me!"

I release him and wipe my hands on my jacket when we get to the bike sheds outside the canteen. He is glaring at me, aggressively rub-bing the back of his neck.

"You're such a bitch."

"What the fuck is that?" I snarl.

"I can't stand that guy."

"Your temper is out of control." I step forward and snatch the knife out of his jacket pocket. "And why the fuck do you have this with you?"

He doesn't respond.

"What, were you going to use this—because you don't like the football captain being on debate with Sukhy? Boo-fucking-hoo, Ja-son," I snap at him, tossing the knife on the ground and stamping on it. "What was the plan? Stab him in the chest right here in school or just wave it around and get expelled, anyway?"

"Shut up!" he yells at me. "Give me that!" He yanks the knife up and rubs it with his t-shirt before stuffing it back into the pocket of his jacket. "It's none of your goddamn business, ok?"

"Do you remember how difficult it is to get rid of someone?" I ask, jabbing my finger into his chest. His mouth opens. "No, don't interrupt me. Do you know how hard it is to get rid of someone com-pletely?"

Jason glares back at me.

"Didn't matter when you cut Riley to pieces. It seemed pretty easy with all of us working together."

"And how well did that go? Beth got caught out."

"Yeah, and the police think it was fucking Red Creek," he yells, eyes wild. "It worked out great!"

"You need to stop this," I said. "You try that shit again and I won't stand for it. You start something at school then you're on your own! This is broad fucking daylight, you brainless sack of shit! And by the way, if you aren't strong enough to finish the job, I won't hold your hand through it. And you are so fucking lucky that Beth was smart enough to keep her mouth shut! You should thank her because you'd have exposed us all!"

He shoves me hard then. It shocks me and sends me crashing against the wall.

"Speaking of Beth, yeah, Beth said you killed an old man. Gee, it sure must be nice to act so high and mighty when you're getting rid of whoever you want."

"Beth was lying."

We hold each other's gaze for a little while and then the hand on my arm slowly moves up to my shoulder and stops at my neck. He doesn't squeeze, just holds it there, staring at me.

"Maybe Beth was a warm-up, maybe I feel like I could finish the job now."

He leaps back as my knife flashes across his vision. He brandishes his own at me, hands shaking.

"Did you seriously just try and cut me, Fiona?"

"Did you seriously just threaten me?"

He smiles.

"Damnit, Fiona, why do you always have to be so freaking scary? And what did you literally just say to me about bringing a knife to school? Such a hypocrite," he says and laughs at me. "Can I borrow your chemistry book by the way? Totally bailed on the homework."

I hand it over, trying to stop my hands from trembling.

This is my fault.

I should have done more.

That day when I found him with Beth's dog, I should have pretended to be shocked. I should have screamed and called for a grown-up.

Only the only grown-up around was my mother.

And nobody could convince me she wouldn't have done anything better.

I'm going to have to get rid of him.

He'd lived his whole life wanting to hurt somebody, and I know from experience how lonely that life can be.

I'm so sorry, Jason.

But I choose me.

CHAPTER SEVENTEEN

Before we get to Chemistry, with Jason's haphazard homework that slightly resembles mine, Mr Davis comes and takes him away. Jason stuffs his knife into my jacket pocket before he follows him to the principal's office.

He smirks at me and laughs as he starts getting lectured before he's turned the corridor. I feel a shiver go down my spine. Back there, he scared me. The others didn't come out to the courtyard at lunch, so the two of us sat there together. It was like the conversation minutes before hadn't happened. Just sitting with him after while he sat, copying out my homework assignment, I was trying to keep my hands from shaking. He was smiling, chatty, rolling his eyes and joking around. I dug my nails into the palms of my hands until I could feel the old scars starting to break.

He had actually managed to scare me.

There's only one person I can manage being afraid of.

I can't handle living in more fear than that.

I pass the art room on the way, sneak past Miss McLaughlin, who is wrestling with one of her flashy displays and put his knife in the incinerator.

Let him find something else to hurt people with.

· · · ·

They call for me before Chemistry has finished. I ignore the other kids sneering and laughing and follow Mrs Kein back to the principal's office. I spot Jason sat on one of the red sofas, stretched out and smirking like he thinks he's fucking David Bowie.

"Yo," he calls to me.

"Jason, you be quiet," Mrs Kein snaps at him.

"I don't have to listen to you," he says. "You're not even a real teacher."

She rolls her eyes and knocks on Principal Anderson's office door abruptly, her lips in a thin, angry line. Principal Anderson opens his office door and beaming, offers me a hand.

"Hello, Miss Taylor. Do come inside."

His smile isn't really befitting the situation, but whatever.

I have actually never been to Principal Anderson's office before, which would sound like a good achievement if I wasn't a freshman. It's very red. Red walls, redwood looking desk, even the cushions on the seats are red. Principal Anderson settles himself back behind his desk and offers me the chair in front of it.

Pfft, as if I can sit anywhere else.

There is a poster behind his desk that reads 'There is No 'I' in Team' on the background of a river, which makes me want to barf.

"So, Miss Taylor, I'm sure you can imagine why I've asked you here today for this little chat," he says.

"I guess this is to do with Jason Danvers. I mean, he's sat right outside," I say.

Fortunately, he laughs.

"I don't think I've had to call you to my office before," he says. "You and Mr Danvers are friends, aren't you? I seem to be seeing him every other day."

"I can't keep tabs on him everywhere," I say. "Not for lack of try-ing."

"So you witnessed this event today, isn't that right?"

"Yes," I say. "We were walking to the canteen to get some lunch—" The knife feels very heavy in my pocket. "And he went over and started trying to cause trouble with Jesse Macinera."

"Had Jesse said anything to Jason to provoke the attack?"

"Not initially," I said. "Jason sort of walked into him. Sukhy tried to get him to back off."

"This would be Sukhy Khan?"

"Yes."

How many other Sukhy's go to this school?

"Right, so Miss Khan tried to resolve the incident? I understand she runs around with your little group too?"

"Yeah, we've all known each other a while. Sukhy tried to calm Jason down and get him to back off. And Jesse made some comment like 'nice friend you have there' to Sukhy and Jason punched him in the face."

"You definitely saw him do it?"

"Well, yeah. He punched him and Jesse started bleeding everywhere."

"What happened next?" He is making a note of it quickly on a piece of paper in front of him. "Did Jesse hit him back?"

"No. He called him white-trash and then Jason tried to hit him again. He shoved Sukhy out of the way to get to him. She was stood in between them."

"What else happened?"

"Nothing really."

"A few of our sources said that you managed to wrestle Mr Danvers away from Mr Macinera and Miss Khan?"

"I guess I did then."

"Miss Taylor, I just want to know what happened exactly before we punish anyone," he said.

"What did Jason tell you?"

"He said that you scratched him. He has some troubling marks on his wrists. Scratch marks, that kind of thing. Did you do this?"

He is staring at me now, and I don't like the look I'm getting.

"I pulled his hair," I said. "Right...there, at the base of the neck?" I turn my own head and kind of point. "It hurts a lot more if it gets pulled there."

"You didn't scratch him?"

"I don't go around scratching people," I say bluntly.

"Right, after you pulled him away, where did the two of you go?"

"We went to the bike sheds, then the courtyard after he'd calmed down a bit."

"And did Mr Danvers retaliate—did he lash out at you?"

"He pushed me," I said with a shrug. "But he didn't mean anything by it."

"Another one of your friends, Miss Green, she's been hospitalised recently," he says. "I have to ask, does Mr Danvers make a habit of shoving his friends around like he did with yourself and Miss Khan?"

"No," I said. "I think he just has a chip on his shoulder at the moment. He was with me when Beth got attacked. It's all been kind of scary for us at the moment."

He smiles sympathetically and touches my hand, which I really, really hate.

"Of course, I understand. That should be all, Miss Taylor. Thank you for coming in today."

Again, like I had a choice in the matter.

. . . .

"He's been expelled," Sukhy says as the three of us walk home.

"Shit, really?" Matt gasps.

"I didn't think they actually expelled people anymore," I said.

"Well, it's a last-last resort," she said. "Jesse went ballistic. He reported him, he was covered in blood. They called me in to make a statement." She sounds miserable. "I couldn't do anything. Everyone saw him push me."

"He pushed you?" Matt says. "Are you ok?"

"Yeah, I'm fine."

I grab hold of her arm and pull her sweater collar to the side. A bruise is already starting to blossom upon her shoulder.

"Sukhy!"

She gently pulls away and rubs her eyes. "What the hell is he going to do now?"

"Another school will have to take him," Matt says. "I'm sorry, but I can't believe he shoved you. That looks painful." He squeezes her hand gently. "I'm shocked he'd do this." He glances back at me. "Where did you grab him again?"

"His hair, the bits that are right at the back of the neck, try it, it hurts like a bitch," I say.

"I'm good, thanks, got to take your word on this one." Matt smiles and hugs Sukhy around the shoulders. "Why don't we go to the diner in town? It'll take our mind off things. We can have pancakes?"

Sukhy's phone starts to ring. She takes it out, and I see Jason's name on the screen. She hesitates, so I take it from her and decline the call.

"Just the three of us today," I say. "Let him stew. He hurt your arm."

"Pancakes, Sukhy, come on," Matt says brightly. "No distractions."

· · · ·

After the fiasco with Beth, the woods are closed off to us. We go to Matt's house sometimes, at others, Sukhy's. I say that Mother is decorating because I don't feel safe having people over right now. It's a shame, we can't stay out as late and we have to watch our mouths as there are nearly always parents present.

Matt's mother winks a lot and asks us about boys. She leaves lipstick stains on Matt's cheeks when she comes by with snacks and drinks. She wants to know the hot gossip, what everyone is talking about in school.

Sukhy's mother is always marking and asks us about college a lot with her frowning eagle's eyes. Her father sternly asks if either of us have seen that thug Jason Danvers around lately, whenever Sukhy is out of the room.

"You tell me if he comes sniffing around, Fiona," Mr Khan says, "I want to give that boy a piece of my mind."

"Violence is never the answer, dear," Mrs Khan calls from her office.

"A piece of my mind," he calls back. "I mean with words."

It's nice, and it's a change of pace. But it doesn't exactly take my mind off things. I still worry about Jason. We aren't talking to him, and I can't keep tabs on him at school. It's very annoying how depressing school has gotten without him.

So yeah, now, when it gets dark at night, I start leaving the house at night to track Jason. What is he doing now that he can't sit outside Beth's house and panic about her being on her phone like every other teenager in America? Or out all night with us, sleeping amongst the fire and the leaves in the woods. How does Jason Danvers spend his time?

I've made a few observations.

Beautiful Detective Pete made a house-call. I saw that much. I wonder what they had to say to each other. I worry for a second that he's spotted me, stood out by one of the trees. But then the moment passes, and he returns to his car and drives away.

Mr Danvers came to school to get Jason's stuff. I saw him by Jason's locker, grunting and furious when he opened up his locker to find a bunch of scrap paper and sandwiches he hadn't eaten.

"Boy's a fucking animal," he grunted before slamming the locker shut and stuffing its contents in the nearest bin.

He spotted me and Sukhy stood watching him and awkwardly putting his hat back on, he muttered something about being sorry and embarrassed for the spectacle his son caused. I nod and say its fine and Sukhy quietly asks if Jason is doing ok.

"Who cares," Mr Danvers grunts. "I sure as hell didn't raise him to behave like that. God knows, got to find somewhere else to hoist him off now." He grumbles to himself and storms off outside. We rush to the nearest window I spot Jason in the front seat of the car and hear him yelling, 'Dad, where the hell is my stuff?' through the open window as they drive away.

He has a black eye now—I suspect that to be part of Mr Danvers' own grown tough love to teach his son how wrong it is to use violence. I'm sure it didn't go over Jason's head...

Jason doesn't respond to messages on our Whatsapp group or texts or anything. His phone is on radio silence. It makes me wonder if he even has it anymore.

From listening in at the Danvers home, his dad only communicates with him via yelling.

He seems to sleep all day and only comes out to play at night.

Tonight, I watch him at his house. I watch his dad sleep on the couch. I watch the twins sneak off through the upstairs window using the outdoor shed to cushion their fall. I have no idea where they go. They seem to elude both Jason and their father.

I watch Jason leave the house and walk to Sukhy's place on the other side of town. He opens the back garden gate and crouches in the bushes, frantically texting until she comes outside and asks him to leave. It's been the same these three nights I've kept tabs on him.

And again, I can't hear what they say to each other very well. Sukhy keeps shaking her head. At one point she angrily brandishes her shoulder at him, pulling aside her cardigan. He holds up his hands in defence, talks in a frantic and miserable whisper. She keeps pointing at the open garden gate.

He has tears in his eyes when he leaves.

After being rejected by Sukhy, I watch him walk into the town centre. He avoids the woods, probably because of all the increased police. I keep a comfortable distance from him. It's not difficult; Jason is kind of clueless, especially when he's in a mood. He stomps in the leaves, frowns and occasionally mutters 'God I'm so stupid' under his breath.

It's strange to see how his life would be without any of us.

He wanders, friendless and alone through the streets with his head down. Sometimes he goes and sits in one of the downtown diners and orders juice and coffee that he doesn't drink. He frowns outside at the weather and gets snappy with the sixty-year-old waitress who keeps asking if he actually intends to order food this time.

Other than her, people don't pay him attention.

He walks through alley-ways, past the back of houses. Sometimes he enters people's back gardens just to see if he can. Once I saw him trying to back door of some family's home. It scared me the first time, but fortunately, the house was locked.

What would I have done if it hadn't been? What would he have done?

Sometimes he sits in alleyways in the dark, watching a waiting. He doesn't carry a new knife with him now. He has something new on him, but I still can't seem to work out what it is.

To be honest, I'd rather not have to find out.

This is just people watching.

Usually, he walks around and around and eventually just goes home. He can't get into any of the bars, so what he can do is pretty limited. He usually goes home, gets in just before the twins, who use the garden shed to propel them back into the house.

But tonight is different.

Tonight, I followed him to the diner and the dark alleys and all of his favourite little weirdo spots, and at around two in the morning, he is walking through town when some middle-aged guys come out of one of the bars and being stupid with him. One of them hooks an arm around his skinny neck and hoists him down to rub the top of his head.

"What are you doing up late, kiddo?"

"Let me go," he snaps. "Same as you drunk bastards."

They laugh that one off and release him.

"Nah," one of them says. "You should be home with mommy and daddy."

"Got school in the morning, kid," another one says. "Best run home."

He glares at them. "Why don't y'all mind your own damn business?"

They laugh at him again. One of them, the drunkest from what I can see, jabs Jason on the chest with his thumb. "You should show your elders some damn respect, boy."

"Why, you someone important?" Jason asks.

The guy shoves him hard now. He loses his footing and lands on his ass on the ground. His new friends howl with laughter.

"More important than you, kid."

"Kids these days," another says. "Leave him, Carl. He's wet behind the ears."

They turn to go when Jason is suddenly on his feet and dives at one of them. I can see he's got some kind of metal rod in his pocket. He smacks the old guy on the back of the shoulders with it. The man yells in pain and turns around and hits Jason as hard as he can in the gut. Jason groans out in pain and curls into the foetal position on the floor.

"Little bitch hit me with a stick," the guy gasps.

"What the fuck?"

"You hurt, man?"

"He hit my back."

One of them picks up the fallen rod from the ground.

"It's some kind of little gay baton," he says before bringing it down on Jason four times, quickly, panting from the exertion. "How'd you like it?" He nudges Jason with his foot. Jason has his hands over his head, shaking.

"Leave him, little fucking bitch."

The rod gets thrown down on his head.

Jason flinches and stays there until they walk away, laughing and sneering and spitting.

My hands are shaking. My nails dig into the skin of my hands. Sitting here in the dark was hard. But...this is possibly a best-case scenario. He's tried picking on someone his own size and it hasn't worked.

I close my eyes and pray, pray that he'll realise that this isn't for him.

· · · ·

"Our little group has really shrunk," Lisa says dramatically, as if she were ever part of the group.

"Hm," Matt says.

"Yeah," she continues, "Things are really quiet without Jason."

"Why don't we talk about something else?" I say when I notice Sukhy's face fall. "Lisa, how are your grades?"

"What are you, my mom?" she says, laughing. "It's all Auntie Rebecca cares about too. Who's going where, how good is the school. We're freshmen, what's wrong with just enjoying school?"

"We can enjoy school?" Matt says, looking up at me and raising an eyebrow. "Nobody told me."

"Matty," Lisa says, shaking her head. "I love how sassy you are, oh my God."

"It's something you're either born with or not," he said bluntly. "So, have you heard from Beth lately?"

"She's still in hospital," Lisa says. "She's quiet. It's sad, really. You guys should come and see her, I know it would cheer her up."

"I've been," Matt said. "Her parents were kind of funny about it."

"Well that's because they think it was Jason who stabbed Beth," she said. I hope my face doesn't show anything in response, particularly as Lisa is staring right at me as she sometimes does. "I mean, what a crazy theory, right?"

"That's fucked up," Sukhy says, speaking for the first time since lunch started, "That's a really horrible rumour, Lisa."

"It's just what Auntie Rebecca and Uncle Howard think. And I've heard a few people saying it around school."

"Jason would never do something like that," she says.

199

It's sad because she really believes that.

"I'm just saying what I heard," Lisa said. "And to be fair, Sukhy, he does have a temper."

. . . .

"I can't believe that horrible little bitch," Sukhy says and in a very Jason like way, aggressively kicks the leaves in her path. "Nobody is saying that, I guarantee, it's her spreading those rumours."

"She's always been awful like that," I say.

"I know, but imagine if he hears people saying that."

It's just the two of us tonight. We are walking to my house because I know Mother has a prior engagement at some pretentious garden party. The perfect excuse to have her over and not think about any of that other dumb stuff.

"He is lucky enough not to come to school anymore," I say. "So no dumb rumours for him, especially as his phone seems to be incognito."

"I guess that's the one perk," she says, though she knows that this isn't the case.

"Speaking of, guess who managed to bump up her English test to an A-," I said, shrugging my shoulders. "I'm not doing too shabby now I don't have Jason to distract me."

"Wow, two perks," she said, before hugging my shoulders. "Nice one, Fiona!"

"Well, I need to bump up my grades if we're going to the same college," I say. "We're in this ok, you know?"

She grins at me. "Thanks for cheering me up."

"What are best friends for?"

We cross my street when I spot Detective Pete out for a run. He waves when he sees me and slows down.

"Hi there, Fiona."

"Hey, Detective Pete," I say. "You're eyeing up my house again."

He laughs and glances at Sukhy. "She is convinced that I'm out looking for a date with her house. How do you put up with her?"

"Oh, it's a best friend thing," she says, offering her hand. "I'm Sukhy Khan, by the way. I take it you're Fiona's special grown-up friend?"

He shakes it and laughs nervously. "I don't even want to know what that is."

"Oh no, you definitely don't," I say, elbowing Sukhy in the ribs. "So, when can we go back into the woods, Detective?"

"Soon, we hope," he says. "It's a dangerous time at the moment, girls. You two take care of each other."

"Oh, we will," Sukhy says, linking her arm through mine.

"Well, I won't interrupt your evening. Take care," he says, before sprinting off down the street.

Sukhy glances back over her shoulder and shrugs. "I guess I see why you like him." She shoots me a grin before bursting out laughing. "Why on earth are you talking to him about that weird documentary about house humpers?"

"It's kind of an in-joke," I said, "He kept staring at my house."

"I guess there's not a normal way to flirt."

"Yeah, you know, stand there, laugh at anything he says and flap your eyelashes around...Or keep suggesting that he wants to take your front porch to bed. I mean, they are so similar."

"Shut up!"

We sit around on the sofa and watch some shitty TV. Sukhy finishes her biology homework. I can leave her comfortably in the living room while I get drinks without worrying about her suddenly deciding to explore the fucking basement.

She doesn't mention Jason and his late night visits, and that's fine.

I notice that he tries to text her a few times, though.

I debate going and watching the whole thing unfold again. I like to think that tonight that will be his only visit out of the house. Maybe he'll go back to his dumb drunk dad, and the two of them will actually properly notice that the twins are missing for once. Maybe they'll actually look at sending him back to school. I lean against Sukhy's shoulder and close my eyes.

Then as the night starts to fall, I become almost certain that my Jason worries are over.

Not that I won't follow him tonight.

I have to be sure.

I didn't get this far without being paranoid as fuck.

"My folks will worry if I'm not back soon," Sukhy says. "Doesn't it feel weird that like, literally last week, we could just sneak off without all this drama?"

"I know what you mean. Here." I reach across and pass her my spare umbrella. "In case it rains, you know?"

"Oh cool, thanks, Fiona," she says, fiddling with a switch. Then suddenly she looks back at me and says, "Fiona, where do you go at night?"

"What do you mean?"

"Can you please just answer the question?" she says.

"I just...wanted to go for a walk," I say. "To clear my head."

"There's not...some reason you want to be out of the house, is there?" she asks, carefully. "You're always welcome to stay at mine."

"No, I'm fine," I say again. "Honestly, I've just been getting a little bit restless at night. It's no biggy. I'm always careful, you know?"

"Ok."

I choose to ignore that she doesn't look convinced.

My mother is home before I leave. She drags her cello case from the car with much difficulty. Detective Pete is on another run and stops as she gets out of her car. I watch him smile and offer to give her a hand, and I see her eyes narrow.

"No, I'm fine, thanks."

"It'd be no bother, I can see you struggling there," he says.

"Why do men always choose to ignore clear instructions?" she says. "I am fine. Thank you." She offers him a disarming, charming smile and continues to struggle to carry whoever it is, up the stairs and into the house.

I wonder how many people have died in our house, while Detective Pete obsesses over his notebooks.

He must know what's going on.

I smile at him and wave before he jogs around the corner again.

"I'm going out," I say to her as she reaches the basement door.

I am pretty sure she says something in response, but I don't entirely hear what it is.

. . . .

I follow Jason out of the house. He goes to Sukhy's house, this time she doesn't come outside but her father does and chases him away.

He sits with his head in his hands by her street sign. I watch him get up and walk with his head down into town. I watch him stick to the alley-ways out of sight. I watch him go to the diner. This time he is approached by a middle-aged guy who gives him an envelope. Money is exchanged, and the man leaves.

Jason then leaves and walks into one of the shadier looking bars in town, he flashes what appears to be a fake ID and goes inside. I watch him from the window outside. He sits by the bar and orders a beer and sits there, minding his own business for a while.

It's boring, and my legs are starting to hurt. The cold is biting, and I have to keep ducking down into the dark when men notice me stood there alone and try to speak to me. It's harder to blend in around here. I'm so cold. So I start thinking about going home, as Jason might after he finishes his third beer.

Then just when I was starting to believe that my worries were ungrounded, and it was time to find a new nightly hobby, a very drunk girl, of about college age, starts talking to him. I can see them laughing, he has a strange expression on his face. He almost doesn't look like Jason anymore.

They buy each other drinks, and as it gets later and later, I notice her hand slide across his thigh. They move to a booth where I can scarcely see them, and I notice them kissing, pressing up against the wall at the back of the bar.

Maybe this is what he was after. He's given up on Sukhy and killing, and he's just going to be one of those guys—like he's started the breeding and joy-riding storyline early.

I watch them leave and head out into an alleyway, her tugging on her warm looking coat. His eyes are wild like an animal's. I duck behind the bins as they come crashing into the alley that I'm lurking in.

"It's cold out here," she says.

"Come here then." He kisses her, pushing her up against the wall. She's laughing, kissing him hungrily, she has one hand down the front of his pants.

I look away as I see her get down on her knees for him. He runs a hand through her hair with one hand and pulled out his new knife with the other. I see the glint of it in the dark. Her eyes meet mine for a second and she goes to say something like 'Hey, what are you looking at' when he cuts her throat.

He's used the same tactic that I had for Riley. He clamps a hand over her mouth to stifle the last sound she'd ever make.

I see all the blood.

He is shaking, trying to ease her onto the floor, onto her back. But she struggles against him. Her hands reach up, trying to claw at him, grasping and struggling. Long-nailed fingers flail and try to clutch at the wound on her neck. She pisses herself and croaks like a baby bird as she tries to call for help. Her other hand reaches for me in the darkness.

Jason kicks her body, dropping the knife on the ground.

He is panting and keeps stamping on her over and over, long after she has stopped moving.

He gasps for air. He smooths his hands through his short hair, then he bends down and picks up his knife. He stamps on her hand as he walks off into the alley-way, leaving her there for anyone else to find.

I hear him whistling as he walks away, off into the night.

Probably to have the best night's sleep that he's ever had.

And at this point, I am practically vibrating with rage. The idiot just walked away and left her there. He left a body. He was pale and twitching and trying to wipe the blood off his hands, but his expression was flat and calm, so calm, calmer than I'd ever seen him in his whole life.

So I did what any good friend would do.

I cut her into little pieces with my knife and mother's little saw which I took from the basement. It was hard to do in the dark—I was scared that some drunk person would wander down here for a piss. It was like walking out of your house nude to cross the street and hoping that nobody would see you.

It was quick enough to do. I think I've gotten the hang of it by then. I dismantled her and wrapped her up in the plastic sheets I brought in my backpack just in case. She was heavy, but I didn't have far to go.

I walked home and left the bits of Jason's girl in the basement for Mother to get rid of. I found myself itching at my cuts and scratches as I tried to calm down this feeling of anxiety and dread in my heart.

At least he chose to do it with a stranger.

At least he didn't do this to someone we know.

• • • •

"Was that yours?" she asks in the morning.

"No," I say.

She purses her lips. "This isn't a funeral home, you know."

"Blow it out your ass," I snap. "I'm going to school."

"Let him get caught next time," she calls after me. "Someone like this is bound to get caught."

As if I don't know that already.

Why do adults always feel the need to state the obvious?

CHAPTER EIGHTEEN

"You're on your own today?" Detective Pete asks. He is coming out of Beth's house when I get back from school.

"Yeah," I say. "Sometimes even I end up alone. How is Beth?"

"She's doing much better, still rattled, but that is to be expected after going through what she did." He glances back at the house. "Still, I think it'll be awhile before she's up to rejoining you at school."

So she's finally home.

"You're making house calls now?"

"She said it would make her feel better, and I had the time," he says. "She's a tough young lady. Kids today are scary."

"Don't say kids like you're like…ninety," I say, nudging him. "I bet your partner calls you kid."

He smirks at that and folds his arms. "Maybe the Sheriff has called me the intern a few times. I can't help this baby face," he says, pinching his own chiselled cheeks like he doesn't know he looks like a Greek God, one of the hot ones.

"I bet you still get asked for ID."

"All the time," he says. "Everyone tells me to take it as a compliment, but mostly it just gets scrutinising stares. It's a bit unfair, I mean, I'm an officer of the law."

We both laugh, and I imagine reaching forward and brushing back his soft brown hair.

"So, I should get back to the station before they start wondering where the intern has gotten," he says cheerfully.

"Erm, Detective, can I ask you something really quickly?"

He smiles. "Of course, Fiona, what can I do to help?"

"Has Beth asked after me?"

He frowns a little. "Well, I can't really discuss anything to do with the case."

"Surely this isn't about the case," I say gently. "I haven't seen her since she was in the hospital. We're all worried."

"She has spoken to me about you. I think she's worried about all of you as well," he says gently. "You guys are a very...close-knit group."

And I can see it on his face.

She's told him something.

Not everything.

But enough.

She's told him that she thinks I'm fucking crazy.

I can feel heat and embarrassment in my face. He's humouring me. He thinks I'm some depressing teenage basket case. And look who he thinks my mother is—he is looking down on me.

"So, erm, you best get back to the station," I say, "Sorry for holding you up."

"It's no trouble," he says, and he smiles, and I feel that little bit more pathetic.

I watch him drive away and suppress the urge to go and scream in Beth's face. How dare she speak like that about me? I'm fine! I'm the one who's fine! Not her, who has huge public melt-downs and falters the second things get hard. I bite my lip until I taste blood and stomp back on over to my house until the pounding in my head subsides.

I'm...hurt that she'd told him I was mentally ill.

I mean, how would she like it if I said something like that about her?

Rude.

And what was that comment about our group?

Of course, the police would have to go and turn a spotlight onto our group.

Is it because of who my mother is?

Did Matt's bruises give us away?

Did they recognize that...murderous look in Jason?

Did he smirk when you mentioned Riley was missing or did his flat cold expression give him away?

Or, maybe, is it something I did?

Chapter Eighteen

. . . .

I think about confronting Jason. I imagine that conversation, I revise text messages over and over again, but delete without sending. I imagine how the call would go in my head.

But it doesn't make sense.

It always goes badly.

And from the look on my mother's face, I believe her, I really do when she says that she won't clean up after him again. I'm not ready to manage the clean-up on my own. I don't want to be ready.

I am sat on my bed, scribbling away at my art book half-heartedly when my phone screen flashes on and to my shock, I see Beth's name.

"Hello."

"Hi, Fiona," she says.

"Hi," I say again, because I don't really know what to say.

"How's school been?" she says awkwardly.

"Ok, you've missed a lot of To Kill a Mockingbird."

"Sukhy gave me her copy," she says.

"She's good like that."

"I know," she says. "She told me you've bumped up your C+ to an A-."

"Yeah, just the other day."

"Nice."

It's weird talking about school like this. I imagine Beth in my head, sat awkwardly on her bed, probably fiddling with her clothes. She coughs quietly. I can almost see her hand go to her hair.

"How's your head?" I ask.

"It's good," she says. "I'm feeling normal again. The arm is healing too."

"I'm glad. I was worried."

"So," she says before going quiet again. "So, erm, why did you stop him?"

I don't know what to say.

"You must have stopped him...I mean, I'm still here."

"Beth, why would you even ask that?"

"Well, I mean..."

"I wasn't going to let him," I said. "I tried to...talk to him about the whole wiretapping thing. He's crazy."

"Yeah, I heard he got kicked out of school for fighting."

"Oh yeah, you're really missing it all," I say.

She laughs, and suddenly I can hear her crying.

"I'm sorry, Beth," I say.

"I know."

I stay on the phone and dig my nails into my knee.

"Why did you have to cut him up?" she asks.

"I wanted to," I say. "I suppose I just really wanted to."

"But why, Fiona?"

"I think it's how I was made," I say.

"And Jason?"

"I think it's how he was made as well."

"I think he's going to hurt someone else," she says, not knowing how right she is about that. "I...I've been worrying about not telling the police. I mean, what if he kills someone?"

"He won't," I lie. "It's going to be ok now."

"And you...will you do it again?"

"I don't want to."

I hope I mean that. I really hope that I do.

. . . .

There is a knock at my bedroom door. I can hear her waiting on the landing. I roll my eyes and yell, 'Yessss, what?'

She pokes her head around the door and stares at me with that awful, flat expression. "That stupid boy is here," Mother says flatly.

"Yeah, he's stupid, not deaf," I snap, barging past her and tugging on my dressing gown. "I was in bed, Mother, God. Can't you just tell him to leave like a normal person?"

She doesn't reply. She loiters upstairs as I descend to find Jason lazily rummaging through the kitchen cupboards.

"Man, you've been out of school for like two weeks and you're already falling into bad habits."

He smiles at me brightly. "Thought I'd get you a drink."

"Nah, I'm good." I fold my arms and glance over at him. "How is non-school?"

"I mean, it'd be fun if I could actually do anything. Or if I didn't live with my dad. Right now, it's kind of like having the flu."

"Sounds troubling," I say.

"Well, you've seen my dad. Did you see that he just dumped all the stuff in my locker? He got rid of my swiss-army knife and my Ramones CDs."

"Woah, maybe you can get a job and buy an iPod and get over it."

He frowns a little, leaning against the counter-top. "So, you don't like me anymore, is that it?"

"I saw Sukhy's arm," I said. "Kind of put all of us off."

The colour rises in his face.

"I said I was sorry."

"I'm sure her bruises healed on the spot."

"She's been talking to me," he said, shyly now. "I mean, I don't expect her to forgive me, but we're talking."

"What do you want, Jason?" I ask. "I really don't get why you're here."

"I wanted to talk," he said. "I mean, you didn't even say hi to me last time I saw you."

"Yeah, I was being called into the principal's office about you beating up a kid unprovoked, so I didn't have time to stop and chat."

But then he smiles that crocodile smile again.

"No, I mean, the other night. By Fryman's bar."

I frown at him. "Like I'm old enough to go to a bar."

"Well, it must have been awfully cold outside," he said. "So, you see, I'm not all talk, no follow-through after all."

I snort. "No, I mean, you had it all figured out. You butcher up a girl who's had her hands all over you all night. DNA evidence isn't a thing, right?"

"Didn't think I needed to," he said. "I mean, you were there."

I glare at him. "Excuse me?"

"Yeah, you'd followed me, you saw it all go down. You even dealt with it for me." He smiled. "I would have had no clue if you weren't there."

"It's not happening again."

"Right," he says. "Sure, whatever you say."

"I'll let you get caught," I say. "Clean up your own mess."

"See, if I was to get caught," he said. "I mean, I'd be caught. I wouldn't have much left to lose. So, I might start mentioning Riley, what really happened that night."

"And have Sukhy sent to prison too?"

"We'd all go. You girls would be together, I'd look after Matt. I think it could be fun. We'll all get out early on good behaviour, I'm sure in prison we'd be motivated enough."

I roll my eyes.

"You know that you're the dumbest person in the world, right?"

"Yeah," he said. "Prison might be a bummer, so, you'll need to help me out."

"No."

"Fiona, I love this," he said, reaching forward and taking my hand. "I've found something I really, really like doing. I feel more confident, happier, more relaxed than I've ever felt." He squeezes my hand, holding onto it. "You must know what that's like, right? Like your whole body is going to burn."

I don't answer him.

I don't need to.

"I'm making the world a better place, just like you did with Riley."

"You didn't even know that girl," I say. "You got drunk and fooled around with her and then hacked her up. It is not the same."

"So, you've never hurt anyone for no reason?"

"Riley was attacking Matt."

"And that old man?"

"He was a creep. He groped me."

Jason's eyes narrowed. "When?"

"In the woods."

"I was there. He didn't get near you."

"After you all left."

"You went back in," he says, smirking. "Didn't you?" When I don't answer, he grabs hold of my head and forces me to meet his eyes. "You're just like me, aren't you? We're the same?"

"My mother is upstairs."

"She never listens to us," he says, shaking me and causing my eyes to water. "Fiona, come on, you have to help me. You have to! You know what it's like to feel like this." His eyes are crazy. He's not looking at me with fear like I used to worry. Somehow this look is worse.

"Jason, I can't—"

"Why?" he demands. "God, why? Why won't you help me?"

"Let go of me!"

I see her at the top of the stairs and manage to wrestle out of his grip by stamping on his foot before she can reach us with that big knife. Jason is panting, he's about to reach for me again when he notices her and steps back, smiling and polite again.

The knife is tucked behind her back.

"Sorry, Ms Taylor."

"I think you'll need to go," she says. "Yes, you'll need to go now."

"Right, yeah, I guess," he says.

"Use the back door," I snap at him.

Both of them turn to stare at me. He doesn't respond, so I take his hand and march us over to the back door that overlooks the woods. I can hear her following us, she's light on her feet. I see the glint of the knife. I fumble with the lock and shove him out onto the back porch.

"Get out of here!" I say.

Jason looks confused as he shrugs and walks away.

My hands are shaking as I look back at her. She has put the knife down on the counter-top and glances at me like she can't believe how stupid I'm being. She rolls her eyes before going to make herself a drink.

"I've told you—not my friends."

"He needs to go," she says. "Before someone else does."

"He's going to stop."

"Are you dating him?" she asks.

She genuinely has no idea. It really does baffle me, often, how someone so fucking oblivious could evade the police for as long as she has.

"No," I snap.

"Good," she said. "So, you don't have to fool yourself into thinking that he'll stop."

"He will stop," I say.

I know he won't. But if he has to go, he doesn't have to go with her.

"He was going to hurt you," she says.

I roll my eyes. "What, do you care about me now?"

"You're very tactless, Fiona," she said.

She looks up at me, and I find myself not recognising the expression on her face. She almost looks...human.

. . . .

Sukhy texts asking everyone to meet in the woods. She says it's safe again. Beth instantly turns the invitation down. She says that her parents are keeping a very close eye on her. That much is definitely true. I spotted her and Mrs Green leaving the house for a drive this morning. Mrs Green didn't look pinched, she wasn't yelling. She looked...like all of her edges had been smoothed down.

They came back later with McDonald's, Beth was chatting, bright-eyed and waving her arms around. Mrs Green was even laughing. I've never seen them like that, not even when Beth was really little.

I wonder why I sometimes want that; sometimes think I'd want that.

I get there early, I want to see if I can find lazy, leftover police tape, or anything to indicate what the cops might make of this situation. Beautiful Detective Pete hasn't been jogging past for a little while.

I am finding this to be a wasted trip when I hear a noise in the dark, whispering, giggling. I walk past the daisies that have sprung up and wild in the undergrowth and spot Sukhy and Jason sat together on an old fallen-down tree. They look surprised to see me but don't spring apart.

"I'm early," I say.

"Us too," Jason says.

"Wow, stating the obvious much?" Sukhy offers before smiling. "So, me and Jase have talked it out...And we're cool now."

"You're cool?"

"Cool as," Jason says. "I'm really embarrassed about how I acted." He touches her formerly injured shoulder very gently. "I'd never...do anything to hurt you guys." I remember Beth's terrified face. "I want things to be like they were before."

"They will be," Sukhy says.

"I had a lot of...anger," he says. "But I've had some time to think and I'm seeing everything differently."

She leans up and kisses him on the cheek.

"So, erm, yeah, that's the other thing."

. . . .

We sit there around the campfire, me and Matt and Sukhy and Jason. It should be like before, no parents to watch over us and ask questions, no school and Lisa and football players. It should be better, but it's not.

Jason has this relaxed, confidence that he completely lacked before. They kiss when they think we aren't looking. He laughs and jokes around and keeps his arm around her, Matt teases him about getting expelled. Sukhy looks...serene. And it's all wrong because he's a deranged murderer and I can't get him to leave. He makes eye contact with me and smirks.

He knows that he's got me.

This will be fine for a while. But soon he'll want to get out and hurt someone again. And I will just have to sit there and clean it up. All the while, he's holding my best friend's hand, calm, relaxed, like he deserves to be here.

Also, no, Beth, you were wrong before, it is weird now that they're a couple. We've known each other since we were five, since we had to sing songs about flushing the toilet correctly and making things out of pasta. It's weird that they're dating. And yet, I'm the only one that seems to think so, as Matt whispers to me, 'Well, it's about time', when the two of them leave as it starts to get late.

I nearly text Beth to update her about this.

But I can't deal with all her fear. I'm afraid enough.

I know whatever comes next is going to hurt.

If he won't stop, I'm going to have to stop him. And like I said, I've known him since he was five. I'd never let anything happen to him.

But I'll always choose me.

She is right. He has to go.

I know it's going to hurt Sukhy a lot.

．．．．

They are inseparable.

He walks her to school in the morning and waits outside the gates at the end of the day. He waves brightly and ignores the stares, ignores the remarks. Sukhy, of course, doesn't tell him that Jesse Macinera took her aside after debate and asked her, politely in that politician style of his, what on earth she is thinking?

I overhear the conversation on my way to lunch.

"I don't mean to be disrespectful," he says, "But...Jason Danvers is out of control. He has a temper. The way he manhandled you was just—"

"Jesse," Sukhy interrupts. "I appreciate your concern. You're a good friend." She stresses the word 'friend' carefully. "But this thing with Jason, I can't really explain it. And I don't feel like I should have to."

"No," he says, flustered. "I'd never mean to imply—"

"It was implied," she said. "Look, really, I know what I'm doing."

She comes out of the classroom and links arms with me, whispering in my ear that I'm such a creep listening at doors. I nudge her and grin.

"He wants to bang you."

"He...wants to bang himself," she said. "Come on, let's go and get lunch."

Matt is glued to his phone, Sukhy is texting Jason, so I am stuck with Lisa. Lisa, who has taken the news that Jason is dating someone very badly.

"Sukhy," she says, drawing out the 'eeeee' part of the name for way too long. "I can't believe you didn't tell me!!!" After this, whenever their relationship is mentioned, she sulks and glares at Sukhy when she's not looking. She asks strange, probing questions, and when Jason is there at the school gates—not allowed on school grounds, Lisa walks past him with her nose in the air.

"I think she's taken your breakup very hard," Sukhy teases him.

"She wishes," he says, kissing the side of her head.

We walk home as a group, without Matt, whose mother still comes and meets him at the gates. I see Freddie Hankerson following him.

He stops the second Matt's mom gets out of the car and fixes him with the frostiest look I've ever seen on her usually cheerful face.

We walk home without Beth now as well. Her shadow seems to stretch out over the town. Sukhy says that she misses her, Jason smiles and nods along and says he does too. I wonder how long he has been able to lie like that.

Fortunately for me, Jason leaves us at the top of the street at Sukhy's house. He waves goodbye, glancing cautiously around for a sign of Mr and Mrs Khan. I guess that explains that question. They don't know. That seems to hang between us as well. I like the Khans, they are strict but kind. They've always made me feel welcome. I am glad I can keep calm and keep my face relaxed when Mr Khan asks if that no-good Jason Danvers has been around lately.

I'm not used to feeling this much guilt.

Lying to my own mother is easy to do but difficult to pull off. With the Khans, it's all hard.

They don't know, and their daughter is in danger.

"Do you think it's weird we're together?" Sukhy asked me. "Me and Jason, I mean." We have snuck a beer from the secret box in her brother's room and sit drinking them on her bed.

"A little bit," I said. "I mean, he's Jason. He used to pick his nose. We've seen him go through puberty. There's so much to unsee."

"Yeah, but he's seen me with braces and you with really bad hair."

"He's nuts."

She had this distant look on her face. "Yeah, I suppose he is a little."

"But you've always liked him, haven't you?"

She smiles at me, pulling her knees to her chest. "Yeah."

I sip my beer and stared vacantly at her TV. "Will he have to come with us to college?"

"What?"

"You know, when we go to college, get out of this town and start fresh. Reckon Jason will come with us?"

"Oh yeah," Sukhy said, brushing back her hair. "I don't know. Early days really. Right now, we're good. I never thought he'd actually make a move."

I try not to notice, try not to let it show.

But I can see it there, in her slightest hesitation, that she's planning on leaving without either of us.

My fingers dig into my arm, and she reaches across and loops her hand through mine, resting her head against my shoulder.

"Please don't," she says. "Everything is ok, really." She pauses and asks very quietly as if she can't find the right words. "Fiona, that thing with Beth," she said. "That wasn't you, was it?"

"No, it was Jason."

Her expression doesn't falter.

"Why?"

"He thought she was wearing a wire for the cops."

"Yeah, I was worried about that." She put her beer down and carefully got to her feet, stretching herself out. "I'm glad it wasn't you. I figured that we'd stop all of this now, right?"

"It's all I want."

Please don't leave me alone.

I shouldn't have lied to her.

But, come on, I know as well as anyone that I'm lying to myself when I say I want to stop, when I say that this isn't who I am anymore.

I know that when I say, 'It's all I want', it means, I'll stop doing it in front of all of you, I'll stop involving you. This is my thing, and I'm careful. And I won't be caught out.

Like Jason, I know I can't stop.

I want to cut things to pieces.

I just do.

But I'll do it far away.

Not in this town.

I'll find people in a city, in the next state.

I'll restrict it to one a month.

I'll clean up my own messes.

I won't cause you any more problems, that is what I wanted to tell her.

Sukhy smiles at me and gets up to pull on her jacket.

"Shall we go then?"

"Sure."

I feel guilty as we leave her room and dash off outside into the night. I want to tell Mr and Mrs Khan that their daughter is in danger.

I want to warn Sukhy about Jason, but I'm scared she won't believe me.

I imagine myself speaking the words out loud about him and that woman in the alleyway, but then I'd have to tell her about the disgusting old man I butchered, about the man in the basement. About the basement and my mother and suddenly I'm digging my fingernails into my lips because there are just too many things to say.

So, I just say that stopping is all I ever wanted and leave it at that.

· · · ·

The night goes on. We meet in the woods and dance around the clearing. Matt takes off his shirt and does a crazy dance. His phone beeps a lot, and I half-heartedly notice that all the messages are from Freddie Hankerson. Sukhy laughs and leans onto Jason, and the two of them start to blur together like a snake.

Sukhy breaks apart from him and tugs me onto my feet to dance with her, and I fall down and kick over the beer. I groan and bend down to start clearing it up, but the twigs and leaves all get in the way. Sukhy is laughing, cheerful, and she tries to pull me away.

"Leave it, it's fine."

"Fiona, it's not a carpet," Matt says.

"I've gotta clean it," I say, maybe twice. Maybe just once.

"Fiona's good at cleaning up a mess," Jason says.

I look up and see him smirk.

"You're a fucking asshole," I say, but it's slurred and drowned out over the music.

The others all start to get up and go. Jason pulls me upright onto my feet. I struggle and swat at him. Sukhy takes my hands and I fall flat on my face. I feel her hands on my ankles and his under my armpits. I struggle and they laugh and my ass bumps against the undergrowth. My head hurts. I lean over to vomit and fall on the ground.

I'm lying still, looking over at the daisies that have sprung up high.

Somehow there is blood on them, dashed across the flowers. My body burns and I taste dirt in my mouth. I roll onto my back with immense difficulty.

"Sukhy," I groan. "Sukhy—"

But there's no answer.

"Did he hurt you? Oh God, oh God—"

I realise now that I am alone.

Sukhy and Jason were with me, but now they are gone.

I realise steadily that I've started to cry. It fills the woods, and I don't hear the footsteps until they are beside me.

"Fiona, is that you?"

Beautiful Detective Pete is stood in the clearing. He crouches down next to the bloodied daisies and offers me his hand. I'm unsteady on my feet and cling to him in a way I never thought I would have dared.

"You've been drinking?"

I start sobbing loudly.

"Hey, hey," he says so gently. "It's alright. Come on, there's no need for any of that."

"I don't know where my friends are," I say.

"How long have you been by yourself?" he asks.

"I don't know."

He is even more beautiful up close.

"Come on, let's get you home. It's ok now."

He helps me walk, shaking and unsteady, red-eyed and tearful through the woods and out into the clearing by my house. His hands are warm and keep me safe. I wish I could stay like this, one arm around his waist, head against his chest. His heartbeat is steady.

I think at some point I must have stopped crying.

"You should be more careful," he says when we reach my front door. "There's a lot of horrible things out there." He hesitates, he's not moving to go away.

I imagine myself saying, 'Come inside', feel the words get heavier and heavier on my tongue until I can scarcely make a sound. I just nod my head pathetically. He smiles at me and squeezes my hand gently.

"There's nothing wrong with a little youthful indiscretion every now and then, but you have to keep safe, ok?"

"I know."

"I'm sure your friends are fine," he says. "Maybe text them in the morning, once your head clears up."

Please help me, please help me, please.

"Uh-huh."

"Take care, young Fiona. You have some water to take to bed with you."

"Gotcha."

He walks off into the distance, and I curl up by my front door, scratching at the wool of our carpet, burying my face into my scratched-up knees. The tears come then. Because what happens next is going to hurt.

And there's nothing I can do.

This is how I was made.

CHAPTER NINETEEN

"Where are you going?"

Lisa looks back, affronted. She folds her arms across her chest. "What, Jason?"

He smiles at her. "You wanna hang out?"

She smiles then. "I mean, sure, what's going on?"

"Well," he says, while the rest of us stare in horror. "We usually go to the woods. We set up a campfire, drink beer, tell spooky stories, the works."

Matt is nudging me quickly. His elbows are surprisingly sharp.

"It's pretty lame," Sukhy says. "I mean, I've heard it's going to rain. It makes my hair so humid. Humid, so annoying." She tries, knowing that humidity affected hair is one of Lisa's least favourite things.

"That sounds fun," Lisa says.

My heart sinks.

"What the fuck?" Matt whispers to me as Jason and Lisa start chatting about camping and who was providing the beer—were any of the cheerleaders invited. etc.

"I knew you guys were always up to something," she says.

She berates Jason for getting kicked out of school on the walk over. She nudges him, asks Sukhy what on earth she sees in him. She calls Beth halfway there and asks if she will come out. Beth nervously says something about it raining later before hanging up.

"She has gotten so weird lately," she says dismissively.

"Why did he invite her?" Matt whispers to me.

"Maybe he missed her. I mean, it's not like she can irritate him at school anymore. Maybe he needs his 'I-Hate-Lisa' fix?" I offer. But I doubt that very much.

I know why he invited her.

I mean, look on his face. It's so obvious.

I remember how he watched Beth's house every night, how he scratched into his skin, wanting to hurt her, wanting to punish her. He had his chance and he couldn't do it. And now Beth blocks his number, she avoids him. She is guarded, watched by her parents. She won't join us out in the woods ever again.

But Lisa will.

With Lisa, it will be easy. He doesn't have any childhood memories of Lisa to hold him back. Lisa doesn't laugh at his jokes. He's never carried Lisa around on his shoulders. He doesn't send Lisa something on her birthday every year.

With Lisa, he won't chicken out.

With Lisa, he can follow through.

I'm so sure that I'm right.

This is powerlessness again.

This is stood in the kitchen, frozen to the spot while Matt and Jason wander down into the basement.

This is being seven years old and terrified of the five of us being too noisy at my birthday sleepover in case it provoked her.

This was being a little kid and knowing I could never have a dog or a cat because God knows what she'd do to it.

This is living in fear like I have every day of my life.

I love Jason with all my heart. But I wish he'd never existed. I wish we'd never met. I won't live in fear with someone other than her.

We sit here in the clearing, gathering wood for our campfire. I watch as he smirks at Lisa as she insists on his jacket to sit on. I watch his eyes glaze over everything she says. I watch him itch at his skin when she shoves him or teases Sukhy or says something dumb to Matt.

He wants to hurt her.

I could kill him. He thinks he can have his cake and eat it too. He will get to be with Sukhy, he'll get to hurt whoever he wants, and I will clean up the mess and keep him out of harm's way.

Dead fucking wrong.

Only my skin feels wrong around my body and my nails are too blunt to dig as deep as I need. My brain is burning.

"Fiona, are you ok?" Matt asks.

"I just have a headache," I say. "I'll be ok."

"Yeah, me too," he mutters, glancing over at Lisa. "God, I'm really over being polite with her. We're going to need to find another spot in the woods."

We probably won't come back here ever again.

It will be too hard after Jason is dead.

"Sukhy, how do you put up with this guy?" Lisa says. "He's such an idiot."

"Oh, I manage," Sukhy says flatly.

"I mean, who would want a high school dropout as a boyfriend?" she says.

"It honestly beggars belief," Matt said.

"I didn't drop out," Jason says, ruffling Lisa's hair aggressively.

When did he get so tall?

It's like he looms over us now.

"I was expelled. Big difference there, you know."

"Hardly," she said, pushing him off.

But he just smiles, like he's in on a joke that Lisa isn't.

It's a smile I know well, and it makes me sick.

I know for a fact that he doesn't go out at night anymore. He doesn't use his fake ID. It's all been building for this. He was just going home. He'd done his practice, now it was time for the main event.

I nearly asked her for help, for advice. But what good what that do? She's never trusted anyone enough to make them her...assistant, her partner, her...number two?

She'd never put up with cleaning up the messes and the blood.

What would she even say to me in this situation?

"I wish things were different," I say to Matt.

He glances up from his phone and gives a frustrated shrug.

But I really do wish things were different.

You know, when she found me burying that cat, she rolled her eyes. She rolled her eyes. That was her way of showing me right and wrong?

Did I ever have any control over the kind of person I was going to grow up to be? Or was the only option to turn out like this the second that stick turned blue on her?

"Look who got whisky from his dad's cabinet, whaaat?" Jason says cheerfully, pulling it out of his bag.

"You are so lucky you don't have school tomorrow," Sukhy says sulkiliy.

"Hey, I remember the home-room hangovers," he says. "Come on, babe, piss off my dad with me?" He sits down on the overturned log and pulls her close against him. She nudges him off and opens the bottle, taking a swig.

"I think it's so modern that you drink," Lisa says to Sukhy brightly. "So many women of your culture don't."

"Fucking hell," Matt says a little louder than I think he meant to.

"Oh, I didn't mean it like that," she says. "Matty, come on, Sukhy knows how I mean it."

"Why don't you have a drink, Lisa?" I say, taking the bottle and passing it to her. "Something to think about."

She laughs and sips it daintily before quickly passing it on. "Ergh, I hate whisky!" She shudders and takes a beer from the side of the fire. "I much prefer this sort of thing."

"Beer is good," Sukhy says. "More classic."

"We need some red cups," she says. "That's the proper way to do it."

"No, that's how Riley Sanders does it," Jason said. "And we all know what happened to him."

"Ew, don't be gross," Lisa says.

"Yeah, Jase, come on," Sukhy said.

"It was a tragedy," Matt adds, but the words don't meet his eyes.

Jason snorts and takes another drink.

"Sooo, other than talk about dead classmates, what do you guys do out here?" Lisa asks, rolling her eyes. "You've been so protective about it, I was expecting a little more."

"A little more what?" Jason asks.

"I don't know, excitement."

"You just need to catch us on a good night," he says, "It gets pretty exciting around these parts."

I start scratching at the top of my hand.

I can't even help it.

I watch him, and I see him watching me watch him. He smirks because he knows how trapped I am, he knows how little I can do.

And this hurts because I really liked things as they were. He's so selfish.

"Hey, Fiona, what crawled up your butt?" Jason asks.

Lisa laughs too loudly.

"Just a headache," I say, "What's got you talking shit?"

"You guys are like so mean to each other," Lisa says.

"It just means we're pals," Jason says, "How we know we get along."

"Right, you dumb bastard," I say.

I have my knife in my boot, tucked by my ankle.

I have my spare in my jacket pocket.

"They are as good friends with each other as Matt is with his phone," Sukhy says, nudging Matt with her foot. "Are we boring you?"

"No," Matt says, jumping.

"Who are you texting, Matty?" Lisa says, instantly joining him on the other log, leaning over as he tries to cram his phone into his pocket as quickly as humanly possible. "Is he cute?"

"It's nothing," he said. "I'm texting my mom."

"Oh sure," Jason says, rolling his eyes. "I look just like that when I text my mom."

"No, you look more pissed off," I say, "Because your mom never texts you back."

I see anger flash in his eyes, see his fists tighten up.

Sukhy gasps and laughs out in surprise, "Oh my God, harsh, Fiona!"

I shrug.

"It's a fact."

"At least," he says, "I'm not scared of my mom."

I glare at him. I can see all eyes on me now, including Lisa, who has for once, realised when it's time to be quiet.

"What's that supposed to mean?"

"You're scared of your mom," he says it slowly like he has to spell out each word for me. "It's funny."

"I'm not scared," I say.

He laughs at me, rolling his eyes. "I'm not scared," he repeats in a babyish voice. "You're probably scared of the dark too. Should we get a night light for baby Fiona who's scared of her mommy?"

"Jase, don't be gross," Sukhy says.

"No, it's fine," I say. "It's got to be hard for you, Jason, I mean, you don't have much to compare it with. I feel bad for you."

"Oh, I'm Fiona," he sneers, "Don't go in my mommy's basement or she'll get cwoss."

"I'm Jason, and my mommy would rather take it up the ass for cash than see her kids," I say in a cold flat voice.

He lurches forwards then and nearly knocks Sukhy off the log with the impact. He grabs my collar and pulls me upright to my feet. His fist is shaking, and for a second, I feel my fingers close around the knife in my pocket. But then he just stares at me, I hear Sukhy calling to him, her voice is frantic and far away, Matt is on his feet, hands gripping at Jason's arm, saying something. And there's Lisa shrieking and yelling.

Then Jason smiles and lets me go.

"Buddy," he says, laughing and picks me up in a bear hug, spinning me around. "God, you're mean!"

"It's what I do."

He squeezes too tight, and I feel my ribs start to ache from the pressure. Eventually, he releases me, and I can already tell where I'm going to have bruises.

"God, did Beth knock herself out from stress," Lisa says. "You guys are so scary! I mean, this one time, across the pond-" She interrupts her own story by letting out a high-pitched scream, her hand coming up to point at something behind me.

I turn around and Jason steps out in front of me.

Freddie Hankerson is stood in the clearing, panting and looking slightly uncomfortable now. He smiles and brushes back his hair.

"Erm, sorry, I heard a scream," he says.

"What are you doing here?" Matt snaps.

"Fred-ster," Lisa says cheerfully. "Hi! I'm so glad to see like one more normal person here! Come sit by me and Matty, we have beer."

He laughs and goes to step forward.

"No," Matt says. "We're having a good time here, the four of us and erm, Lisa." He folds his arms. "You should leave."

Jason looks suspiciously between the two of them.

"Matt, can we just talk for five minutes?" he says, "Please? Please?"

He looks so sad.

I remember the look of stupidity and self-pity on his face as he walked past me that night in the woods.

"No," Matt says.

Freddie goes to step closer, but Jason steps out in front of him.

"That's as far as you go, I'm afraid," he says.

"Oh, can you just buzz off?" Freddie says to him. "This has nothing to do with you. This is to do with me being an idiot and Matt."

Lisa is looking like she's just worked something really obvious out.

"Matt knows Freddie Hankerson?" I hear her whisper to Sukhy.

I see the way Jason inches forward, one hand in his pocket. He is smiling that hungry, reptilian smile that I've seen almost every day of my life since I could remember.

I know it doesn't have to be Lisa.

It doesn't have to be Beth.

It could be anyone at all.

Why not another big strong jock, who likes to look down on other people?

But then I think about the look on Matt's face when he dragged me away from Freddie that day at school. I think about the slight smile on his face when he gets those stupid never-ending text messages. This is someone, who despite everything, Matt wants to protect. Someone he wanted to protect from me, because deep down, he knows what I am.

"Jase," I say, so Matt will hear. "Back off, ok? We've got no problem here."

Please, Matt, please, you've known me for eleven years. Please understand when I'm trying to tell you that something's wrong.

I glance back and see his expression change.

Matt gets to his feet and brushes past me and stands between Jason and Freddie. His hands are trembling a little.

"Fine. You get five minutes," he says.

Freddie looks almost tearful. He reaches down and grabs his hand. "Five minutes, you can time me! Can we, erm, go somewhere more private?"

"Whatever, come on," Matt says. "Later, guys." He waves his hand carelessly behind him as he steps out back into the woods. He doesn't look back, but as it grows darker around them, I see him take Freddie Hankerson's hand and hold it tight.

"How do you think they know each other?" Lisa asks cheerfully.

Jason rolls his eyes. "Fucking hell, Lisa. You are dumb."

"Oh, you! Always being mean to me, as usual!" she says. "Pass me another beer, you big weird freak."

· · · ·

As I sit watching Jason watching Lisa from across the fire, I almost want to blame her for this, for ruining our happiness. She invited us to that stupid party, insisted we go along, put us all in harm's way. I wish she'd never come to this country. I wish she'd stayed far away and we'd never gone there that night, we'd never have been out in the woods tonight.

I'd really like to think that if Lisa hadn't come here, then my life would have gone on as usual. I'd be a regular teenage girl who kind of hates her mom, who likes loud music and ditching class and maybe every now and then kills a cat or a dog, but mostly is fine. The kind of girl, who, when they arrest my mom, people would see my photo and feel bad for me. The kind of girl who might go on to never hurt another person in her entire life, not even emotionally or by accident.

I really wish that girl could be me.

Matt doesn't come back to the clearing. He texts me to say that he is going to get coffee at the all-night diner with Freddie, that they've talked it all out. He tells me that he loves me, that he really, really loves me and the others.

I don't know where his teachers get off giving him such bad grades.

I think Matt knows well enough what's coming next.

I mean, the story tells itself. High school drop-out and local delinquent Jason Danvers invites foreign exchange student and local nuisance Lisa Jones out to the woods with us on a Thursday night, to drink whisky and talk and dance. It would get later and later. And say, around the time, his girlfriend, Sukhy starts getting woozy and curling up by the fire, Jason would find an excuse to be alone with Lisa. To cut her again and again and again, then stagger back to the clearing and nice as pie, ask his friends, just like I did, 'Help me get rid of her'.

He watches her across the fire from him with that fucking sick smile on his face.

It isn't fair. He doesn't care about the rest of us.

I never looked at Riley like that.

I'm not like my mother. I cared about what happens to all of us.

It's why I started doing these things alone, even though I know I need to stop. I have boundaries and he has none. He doesn't deserve to do what I do.

I watch what I drink, and I watch her. I follow her when she skips ahead to look at the river. I follow her on her walk back. I listen to her dumb jokes. I let her hug me and tell me what a shame it is that we weren't better friends before. I let her do it and watch Jason watching us.

I'll stick with her all fucking night if I have to.

He'll have to take it up with me later.

If he fucking dares.

If he fucking dares.

Only suddenly it's late, and everyone has gone quiet. Lisa is snoring happily by my side.

"Fiona, come here," Sukhy says.

The campfire was going down, and she nudged me over to her. Jason is lying beside her, flat on his back, expression gentle, star gazing.

"What's up?"

"You look wired," she said. "Is everything ok?"

"I feel fantastic," I say and itch my wrist.

She takes my hand and holds it down onto the log until the urge goes away.

"Do you remember when we were little kids," she says. "And we'd sleep over at your house?"

"Yeah, I do."

I remember feeling so anxious about us being noisy that it felt like my stomach was full of poison. But I also remember whispering spooky stories, watching Disney movies and eating popcorn and not brushing our teeth.

She smiles at me.

"You know, I used to be so scared of your house."

"I know," I say. "You used to try and find polite ways of saying we should do it at your house instead."

She laughs and shakes her head. "Here I thought I was being subtle."

"Nope, not subtle at all."

"I was scared of your basement," she said. "I know you still don't go down there."

"She's scared," Jason grunted sleepily.

"Go to sleep, dip-shit. And yeah, well it's creepy."

He laughs and shrugs at us before lying back down and humming tunelessly to himself, one foot swaying casually.

"I had bad dreams there like all the time."

"Oh, come on, we were little kids. I used to have bad dreams about ice cream."

"Ice cream?"

"It made my teeth fall out."

She chuckled. "That's a surprisingly common one. The whole teeth falling out thing."

"So, was it what Shit-For-Brains said about me being scared of it that brought this up?" I ask. "You're ok to talk about that with me, you know? I'm not five, I won't be offended you don't like my house."

"It's not that," she says. "It was just the creepiest dream."

I nudge her. "Story time, like when we were kids. Go on. Tell me about it."

"We were five, I had this dream where we were hanging out on your sofa, and it was really late. You were asleep and so was I..." She shakes her head, voice slurring. "But I could move and walk around; I was kind of watching me sleep. It was like that for a while, but then, there was someone else. There was someone singing in your basement."

"Creepy," I say.

"And I walked over and opened the red door, and there was this woman sat at the bottom of the stairs. She was singing this nursery rhyme and wearing a red dress and her hair was all wet."

I don't make eye contact with her.

"She was singing really loudly, and it gave me the creeps, it was like she was sleepwalking. I remember that I turned around to try and wake you up. But then she saw me. She crawled up the stairs up to get me, she snarled at me like a cat. And her hands were all red and…" She laughed. "It was a really creepy dream."

"You should make movies," I say. "Seriously."

"Part overhearing my parents' movie night too often probably," she said. "But for some reason, I'd always get so scared of going to sleep when I came over to yours."

"You should have told me," I said.

"Oh, come on, about a gross dream? You'd have laughed at me."

"Maybe," I said.

"Maybe, huh?" she says, nudging me. "A likely story, indeed!"

I laugh and nudge her back.

A dream, huh?

"We should go," Sukhy says, stretching. "Friday means more pop quizzes. I swear to fuck, they are trying to kill us."

I laugh and get to my feet and suddenly realise that Jason's humming and Lisa's snoring has stopped.

I got clumsy.

I got stupid.

All of a sudden I remember Lisa muttering something about wanting to get some shots for Instagram by the river. I remember Jason's humming getting quieter and quieter and then not there at all.

"Holy shit! Holy shit!"

"What's the matter with you?" Sukhy said. "Fiona?"

"Where the fuck did they go?"

"Who?"

"Jason and fucking Lisa!"

She tries to grab my arm as I turn to run. I shake her off and clamber off into the woods. I hear Sukhy running after me, calling my name. I clamber around in the darkness, no time to find my phone, but I see the light of Sukhy's behind me. I stumble and slam against a tree.

"Lisa! LISA!"

Sukhy tries to grab hold of my hand but I shake her off.

"Fiona, what the hell is going on?"

"JASON! JASON, COME HERE!"

I see the sudden fear on her face, and she starts yelling for him too.

"Jason, help! I've hurt my leg!" she calls. "Jason! Help me!"

I dodge past her as she calls, frantic, her hands cupped around her mouth. I make a break for it, hearing her calling my name after me, terrified and hysterical. But I can't let her follow me here.

I duck through the undergrowth and suddenly the light of the moon in the river, still flowing and silent. Then, glinting in the dull lighting, I see Jason's knife.

I clamber through the undergrowth and land out by the river, panting for air and steadying myself. I spot Lisa on the ground. She is quiet and still, there's blood on her forehead, even in the gloomy light I can see that.

"Jason, what have you done?"

"She's still breathing," he says, smiling and waving the knife lazily at me.

I notice at her side is a large rock. I think he's knocked her unconscious, to make it easier. This way, she wouldn't piss herself and fight and become the Beth he loved as a friend.

Ignoring my presence now, he bends down over her, knife raised.

I didn't know I could move this fast, but I break the distance, jumping over the rocks and kicking him hard in the chest. He falls onto his back and slashes uselessly with his knife. I stamp on his chest as hard as I can but leap back, recoiling as he manages to twist his knife up at me. He leaps onto his feet and barrels into me, sending me flat onto my back. We roll down towards the dirty wet ground by the still water. I land on top and try to keep him flat on the ground with my body, but he is so much bigger and stronger than me now.

He scrambles and kicks and throws me off. We stagger to our feet, facing each other by the water. Lisa lies still, away from us, unmoving, her breathing barely audible over the rustle of wind in the trees.

"What the fuck, Fiona?!"

"No! You fucking stupid bastard! No! You don't get to do this!"

"You're a hypocrite," he hisses. "It's different when it's you!"

"I know when to stop!"

"I'm doing this! This little bitch needs to die! I have to!"

"No! You'll get us caught!"

He leaps forward and slashes at me. The knife comes inches from my nose. I duck under him and hit him hard in the chest where his arm meets the socket.

He drops the knife, and I fall to my knees to grab it. His hand tightens in my hair and he yanks me upright before shoving me bodily onto the ground. I kick water and dirt in his eyes as he tries to scramble towards me.

Sukhy is screaming at us from the clearing.

I want to tell her that it's going to be ok, but his hand jolts out and he slaps me hard across the face. It shocks me, and I feel my face burn. Jason lumbers over me, abandoning his fallen knife, his hand raised again.

He thinks he can hurt me with a slap.

Like I'm weak.

I scratch his face and somehow manage to break the skin at his forehead. Jason howls in pain, and I stagger to my feet. He kicks blindly at me, holding his injured eye.

But I am ready for him and punch him in the jaw, sending him staggering back into the water.

"STOP IT! STOP IT NOW! Leave her and let's go."

"I'm not going anywhere," he snarls. "I'm having this!"

His eyes are crazy.

I wonder if I looked like that when I cut Riley. I wonder if someone had tried to get between us, tried to stop me. Say Matt's boyfriend came back and tried to protect his friend from my knife. Would I have stabbed him too?

I think I would.

Jason is on his feet, he leaps out of the water. I hit him in the mouth as his fist slams up into my stomach.

It hurts, oh God, it hurts.

Is this what it's like to really hit someone?

I stumble to my knees and vomit all over myself. I can hear myself gasping desperately for air, on my knees, unable to get up. My head is spinning.

"Jason! Jason, no! Leave her! Jason!"

I am looking up at him as his next blow smashes down on my head. I think he's hit me with a rock. It must be a rock.

And it's all suddenly so strange, so distant. I can't hear. It's like all my hearing has gone...like pop in my brain and my vision swims like he's thrown me under the water. I feel dirt on my face.

I wish I could understand what Jason is yelling.

But the world just keeps spinning.

I feel him pull me upright onto my back and he's on top of me, he is shaking me, slapping me, pulling my hair. I can see the whites of his eyes. He looks fucking crazy.

You're fucking crazy, I tell him, but the words don't come out.

I feel it when he breaks my nose. It's like a dam has burst on my face. I turn my head to the side and feel the blood gushing out of me like a river. I can see his hand scrambling around in the dirt, looking for his knife. He won't take his eyes off of me, but I can see it right there...

And I'm thinking, 'Oh shit, this isn't how I thought it would be'.

That's when I hear another voice. Over Jason panting and me groaning. I hear a voice that's crisp and clear and frantic and scared.

"Detective Brankowski, you need to get here! Please, we're in the woods. We're near the clearing by the river! We're!"

And now, you know, it makes sense.

I mean, that day outside my house, he spoke to her casually, like the two of them had spoken a hundred or so times before. She's always been the smart one, she had to go and remind him right there and then, 'I'm Sukhy Khan and you and I have not met before. Hello. It's good to meet you'.

Of course, if he needed an informant, of course, he used Sukhy as that.

She has always been so much smarter and stronger than the rest of us.

She's known my mother since we were children.

She wasn't asleep that night she saw my mother sitting in her basement covered in blood.

She was wide awake when Mother came at her with a knife.

She knows me. She knows that what's wrong with me came from somewhere.

And she must have always known, must have always been so aware that if we were ever caught, that big bright future she had ahead of her would disappear like a puff of smoke.

I think that I always knew, deep in my heart, that I lost the chance of moving away to the city with her the second I cut Riley into pieces.

Jason is snarling and staggering to his feet. He is calling her ugly words.

I can't move, but when he makes to go and run at her, knife in hand, I feel my hands clasp onto him tight. I grip his leg and dig my nails in, and he drags me partially across the ground with him as he moves to run.

"Sukhy, run," I groan, but my voice has been crushed out of me.

He digs the knife into my arm at first and tries to drag himself forwards. He stabs me in the side, but I won't let him go.

"JASON! Jason, please!" Sukhy is sobbing.

He kicks me in the side of the head. He cuts my hand, and I feel my strength leave me as his body tumbles away from me, and I fall into the dirt on my back. His boot comes down hard on my chest, and it's like the rest of what follows happens with me watching through a watery veil.

I am delirious, helpless, voiceless as he charges at her, screaming and cursing. He calls her names. He says that she betrayed us. He waves the knife around while she holds up her hands, flinching back, trying to reason with him. There is so much fear in her voice.

I hear her crying, telling him to put the knife down, telling him to calm down.

"How could you do this?" He keeps shouting. "How could you do this?"

She tells him she loves him, she loves him so much.

And it's the last thing she will ever say to anyone. It's her last words, and she says them to him.

She is my best friend and I can't protect her. I can't help her when he cut her—the first one is a slash across her cheek that sends her back against the moss, screaming and holding her arms in front of her body.

I can't protect her. I can't drag her away from him as she screams. No, all I can do was lie there and watch and try to get up. My arms and legs are so weak. The blood from my nose is clouding my vision, painting my world and everything in it red.

I can hear my strained voice, weak and pathetic and compressed tight into my chest, sobbing and calling for help.

He wrestles her down to the ground while she sobs, and he keeps stabbing her until she is quiet. He tells her that he loves her, tells her that she's all he ever wanted. He calls her a bitch, a fucking horrible bitch.

And he's crying, and I'm crying, and eventually, I manage to get up onto my feet. My body feels empty, like everything has been squeezed and pumped out of me. I stumble as I walk over to them, where he is leaning over her lifeless body, clinging to her like he has the right to hold her.

I see in her discarded jacket a taser. She was armed with a taser but didn't use it against him. She couldn't even bring herself to hurt him a little bit.

Oh Sukhy, you were supposed to be the smartest among us.

I reach them, and Jason looks up at me, eyes red from crying, spittle on his nose and mouth. He is panting and cradling her head to his heart.

His last words are more satisfying to me.

"Fiona, what are we gonna do?"

You know, I should have killed him when I found him with that dog when we were children.

CHAPTER TWENTY

(Transcript of interview with Miss Sukhy Khan, 15)

Brankowski: This is the fourth interview with Miss Sukhy Khan, who is helping me provide testimony on a suspect in the Red Creek murder case. Sukhy, would you mind introducing yourself for the recording?

Sukhy: Sukhy Khan, erm, age fifteen, I'm a freshman in high school. My favourite colour is purple (laughs). Sorry, I never know what to say.

Brankowski: That's ok. These are only informal. This investigation is completely unofficial.

Sukhy: I know, I know and I am taking this seriously, I promise. I'm just nervous.

Brankowski: There's no need to be. Everything you say is in confidence. So you believe that Ms Taylor was responsible for the recent murder of your classmate Riley Sanders, isn't that correct?

Sukhy: Yes, that is correct.

Brankowski: So, Sukhy, when was the first time you met Ms Sylvia Taylor?

Sukhy: I was in pre-school. She is the mother of my friend, Fiona Taylor.

Brankowski: And how would you describe her? As someone who has grown up knowing this woman?

Sukhy: She's...weird. She's kind of present, but not present. It's like she doesn't have an opinion on anything in particular. Like she's, erm, reading from a different script to the rest of us, I guess.

Brankowski: You mean she is detached?

Sukhy: Yeah, but at other times, she's very clued in. There was this one time, where she told off this pervert guy.

Brankowski: A pervert?

Sukhy: He worked at the swimming baths. He was a cleaner. He would stand by the changing room entrance, and if you were on your own, he'd say something gross, like ask you to help him with the fly of his pants or ask if you'd like to help him clean the back room. He was really weird, but kind of subtle. He knew when he could get away with it. The girls he'd pick on were like us at the time, like ten years old, so we would just feel uncomfortable but ignore it. None of the grown-ups ever noticed. I had no idea how to tell my mom, and she was stood like, looking right at me the first time he harassed me like that. People didn't even have a clue.

Brankowski: But Ms Taylor did?

Sukhy: Yeah, so this one time, he'd been gross to me before. But it was Fiona's first time going swimming there. Ms Taylor was going up to the stands where the parents sat, but suddenly she turned and followed us right to the changing rooms. And she got between us and the pervert cleaner, and she said, 'Get the fuck away from my kid or I'll have you arrested'.

Brankowski: (whistles) And what did he do?

Sukhy: He looked scared, really scared. He tried to apologise, but she kind of swept us all past him. He never bothered me or Fiona ever again. He'd physically move when he saw us coming.

Brankowski: So she was observant too?

Sukhy: Yeah, it was like the whole detached thing was kind of an act.

Brankowski: That's interesting. Right, so Sukhy, last you mentioned a very disturbing incident to me briefly? I was wondering if we could talk more about that.

Sukhy: I was at Fiona's house for a sleepover. We were four. My parents let me stay the night. We were watching The Little Mermaid. We fell asleep, and I woke up in the night to use the bathroom.

Brankowski: And you heard something from the downstairs basement?

Sukhy: I went downstairs to get a glass of water. And I heard someone singing the song 'Humpty Dumpty'. It was creepy, but it sounded like Ms Taylor. So I went and opened the basement door.

Brankowski: What was the first thing you noticed?

Sukhy: You know, it's so long ago, it sometimes feels like a dream, like an out-of-body experience.

Brankowski: You were just a kid. That's normal. Just start with what you can remember. Don't worry about how parts might seem like a bad dream.

Sukhy: She was wearing a red dress...and her hair was wet. Or rather, the dress looked red. It looked...dirty. And it smelled... (pauses) I don't remember, but it scared me. It scared me a lot. I screamed, and she saw me. I remember it was dark, but her eyes turned and looked right at me. We both stared at each other. Then she started rushing up the stairs towards me. She had a big knife.

Brankowski: She had a knife?

Sukhy: Yeah, she slowed down to pick it up. It was at the bottom of the stairs with her. I ran upstairs. I was screaming for Fiona and Ms Taylor. She was chasing me, she was slipping on all the blood. It was definitely blood.

Brankowski: Did she get you?

Sukhy: She grabbed me when I got outside Fiona's bedroom. But all the screaming woke Fiona up.

Brankowski: Did you recognise the woman was Ms Taylor?

Sukhy: Not right away. Not until...the whole thing sank in a little bit more.

Brankowski: So, Fiona woke up?

Sukhy: Ms Taylor was holding my arm and the knife and Fiona came running out. She started screaming and crying, and she put herself over me and pulled us tight against the wall. We were both crying. And Ms Taylor was trying to pull her away, but she bit her. I remember she bit her whenever she got close.

Brankowski: What did she say to her?

Sukhy: I don't remember it well enough. It was like a blur. I saw it like I was about to be eaten by a monster or something like that. Like I said, it didn't make any sense at first.

Brankowski: And what did Ms Taylor do?

Sukhy: I was hiding behind Fiona and we were crying. And Ms Taylor went away. She came back, all cleaned up and showered and in her dressing gown. She'd...made us a hot chocolate and told us that we'd had a bad dream.

Brankowski: A bad dream?

Sukhy: Yeah (laughs). And Fiona acted like that was fine, so it made sense to me to, like that, for a little while. I mean, I thought about it a lot after, like all the time. I feel, scared for Fiona, Detective. Do you really think that this will help her?

Brankowski: Yes, Sukhy. I promise it will.

CHAPTER TWENTY-ONE

He doesn't deserve to lie here with her. He doesn't deserve it. I can hear the sirens, pounding in my ears. I stumble and fall, dragging his body through the undergrowth as the sun starts to rise.

I'm crying, I can hear my heart in my head, pounding like it's going to escape. Every scratch, every cut I have ever made on myself burns. My wounds ache, and I stumble and fall. Jason is limp, still and heavy. We are covered in dirt and blood and vomit, and I kick his head as hard as I can.

"You fucking dumb BASTARD!" I snarl, kicking him again.

Jason says nothing now.

He can't even smile like her.

My body burns as I stagger down at the end of the woods. His head thuds against every step into my back garden. And I'm sobbing because Mr and Mrs Khan will never see their daughter again. I'll never get to go away to college with Sukhy. I won't get to talk to her or laugh with her again.

I'd have fucking let him kill Lisa if it meant I could just—

I am sobbing as I enter my house, trying to drag Jason over the threshold. His hair, matted with dirt and blood gets caught on one of the lower latches. I tear at him, dragging and struggling and fall onto my backside.

I can't breathe.

I can't breathe.

I can't breathe.

And my mother is just…kind of sat there, like I'd just walked in after school. She is drinking tea and watching me from the kitchen counter.

"The police are coming!" I scream at her. "The fucking police are coming!"

"Is that right?" she says as though I've just mentioned some light fucking rain.

"I can't close the fucking door!" I stamp on Jason's body again and again, hysterical. I drop his arm and kick him in the face, my foot crushing against his skull. Why did he have to go and do this? Why did he have to—Why?! Why?!

"I thought that boy was your friend," she says flatly.

"He killed Sukhy," I wail. "He killed her!"

She watches me as I catch my breath. I cover my mouth to stop the crying. I let myself calm down, try and ease my aching head. Then I bend down and pull Jason's head from the lower latch and slam the door shut and lock it as though that will be enough to keep the police out.

"Ah, there we are," she says.

"Didn't you hear me? Didn't you hear me? I said the police are coming!" I scream at her.

"Yes, you mentioned," she said. She moves to get past me, and I grab hold of her. I'm suddenly shocked at how easy it is to cling to her, to push her back. I never imagined I could be this strong.

"*Just fucking help me! Help me! Why don't you ever help me? Good! God!*" I howl. "Help me! Stop fucking thinking about your stupid job! *Help me! Help me! Help me!*"

Again, she just watches until I calm down. I let go of her, leaving bloody handprints on her pale blue shirt. I scratch blunt and broken nails against my cheeks, trying to stop the beating of my heart because it's fucking deafening me! I can't fucking hear myself think! I curl my knees to my chest and wipe the vomit from my chin.

I can hear the sound of sirens in the distance. Sirens, loud and proud, and then they grow distant and faint, and with it, my heart seems to slow back down. And it's just silence between us again.

"You know," she says, breaking it softly, "I stopped for a little while." Her gaze is far away, and her voice strained like she was talking on the phone on a bad connection. "I stopped all of this... what was it you called it, cello practice? Yes, I stopped. For a few years actually."

"What are you talking about?" I snap. "Now isn't the time for any of this!"

"I got pregnant." She interrupts me. "It came as kind of a surprise. A moment of weakness really, but I got pregnant." She wipes her hand across her face. "And despite all the little doubts I had, I decided to just go on and have the kid. I mean, I had savings, a little inheritance money, so I bought this house in this stupid town. It seemed like the right sort of place to raise a child. The kind of place my parents raised me. The kind of place I really hated while I was growing up. Everyone knows everybody. Everyone talks in the same way. Everyone has a role. It always seemed so medieval, so structured, like a tin of sardines."

She laughs to herself, smooths her hands through her hair.

I don't dare make a sound.

"I don't think I ever told you, but did you know that for a while, I claimed to have a husband who worked away from home when we first moved here? People always seemed so shocked by a single parent, especially in a backwater like this. I didn't need questions or judgement, so I wore a ring and when it was suitable, I started telling people my husband and I were getting a divorce. That earned me sympathy from a couple of the local biddies and those strange... nosey people from across the street. I had to sit there, suffering through their empathy and their pity. It was irritating."

"Mother, now isn't the time," I try to tell her.

Her expression is scaring me. A lot more than the crocodile smile ever did.

"So then, I had you and I decided to put my tools in the basement and just stop. I'd try and be...I don't know, a...a real mother. I'd stop killing and focus on keeping you alive instead. And it was hard, but I could do it. For you." She itches at her neck uncomfortably. Her hair parts and exposes old scars, old scratches from an earlier time.

I briefly wonder how many times she thought about shovelling rat poison down my infant throat.

"And, really, Fiona, for a while, that was enough. I remember holding your baby feet in my hands and feeling you kick around. It was better than anything I did at Red Creek. It was just me and you, no interruptions, nothing going on in my head. You were going to fix me."

I try to drag Jason's body past her. "Mother!"

She swats my hand hard, making me drop his arm.

"The one thing I couldn't stop doing was going to the tribute service for the Red Creek victims. I figured that it was the closest I'd get to cutting someone up again, so I hired this old woman to watch you. She worked in the library, and she was clingy and overbearing. She forced me to go to this awful Mommy and Baby class once, truly dreadful. I was gone for two hours. The old woman had a stroke. She collapsed but didn't die. No, I could tell that she was alive when you cut her."

I freeze and stop trying to fight her grip.

"What?"

"She was lying on the floor, not able to move, she may have been trying to tell you to call for help. And you started jabbing her face with her knitting needles. I came home to find you covered in blood, playing with her eyeballs like they were marbles."

"You're sick!"

"No. You are sick, Fiona," she said. She leans down and holds my arms tight to my body, freezing me in place. Her eyes are wild and, I realise for the first time, afraid. "I passed my sickness down to you. I thought I could start again, but the damage was done the moment you were conceived. You were born just like me—just as wrong and violent!"

"I'm not! I hate you!"

"You never smiled until you learned it from the other children. You didn't cry or play. You were like me. You couldn't be like other people."

"I'm nothing like you! Stop lying to me! Stop it!"

She laughs, exasperated.

I've never heard her laugh before.

"I've seen every day of your life! Are you telling me I'm wrong?"

"I wouldn't do any of that stuff! You're a liar!"

"A liar? I dragged her body down to the basement and got rid of her!"

"I wouldn't!"

I would.

"I tried to tell myself that it was just one bad thing, that you were just confused. You got all mixed up. I mean, you were so little. Even

I hadn't…started any of that when I was that young. So, I got rid of her body—" Her hands are really trembling. "But after that, the urge to go out and get another was excruciating for me. It's like…like a former addict finding their teenager's marijuana stash years later, you can't even imagine. But I told myself it was just a mistake, it was an accident, and we could go on like before. I was going to be better—a role model to you…But then you did it again, didn't you? You pushed a little girl down the stairs. You were in pre-school, visiting a farm and you broke her neck with the fall."

No.

"I didn't do that! I DIDN'T, MOTHER! I didn't do that!"

But, of course, I remember, her name was Amber Darlington.

The red thumb tack from the little red box used to belong to her.

I remember her blonde pigtails and missing front tooth.

Mostly, I remember the loud SNAP her neck made when it hit the ground.

I remember my little pink sneakers kicking up in my car seat on the drive home. I remember how all the other parents cried, how the other children cried. But I smiled.

'Snap,' I said to my mother as she drove us back. 'Snap! Snap! Snap!'

My hand clutches my mouth, and I whimper miserably into my palm.

"I couldn't make you better. The damage was done. You were mine. So, I decided to get rid of you. You were sick, and I was helping you. I was going to smother you while you slept."

It's the thing I've been afraid of ever since I was little.

Why go out and bring someone to the basement when I'm her witness, upstairs, waiting.

Kids run away all the time.

Why didn't she just…

Now her grip on my arm tightens, too tight and for a second, just a second, I'm afraid of her.

"But I…I…" She looks up at me with this strange soft expression on her face. "I couldn't do it. It was my fault. Whatever makes you lash out, it comes from me. It's all my fault." Her fingers stroke my arms gently. "I couldn't ever hurt you."

Her voice catches in her throat.

"So I started again. I started hunting and killing and getting rid of corpses in the basement. I got that little incinerator. It was so much easier than stashing the bodies somewhere for fat librarians to crash into. I made it no secret from you. I wanted you to see where your path would lead. I did it so much that it made you sick. It repulsed you."

That feeling of familiar nausea again!

"You would be sick and cry and eventually stopped wanting to come and see Mommy work in the basement." She strokes my cheek with her hand. "One time, I even locked you down there with one of the people I abducted. I'd cut out his tongue, removed his legs and left the two of you down there in the dark. I even left you there with a weapon."

My dream.

That dream of darkness and red and her arms around me, way too tight.

"But you didn't attack him, you just sat there crying for me until I came and let you out. And I was relieved—I was so relieved because I thought that I'd saved you. It was too late for me to stop, but I thought I'd done right by you. You'd grow up normal, go to school, have some friends. Maybe be resentful of me, but you'd go off to college and never come back."

She hugs herself and sighs, "Maybe sometimes, you'd get the urge, but the sight of blood would make you tremble. I tested you all the time, just to be sure. I thought I'd made you better, I really did. But you're just like me, aren't you, Fiona?"

Her hands smell of rot and blood, and I push against her chest.

"You're lying!"

She isn't.

Deep down, I think I've always known.

I think I remember it all.

I remember Amber's neck breaking.

I remember my first set of marbles.

"I'm sorry I didn't do a better job of protecting you," she said. "I really am sorry. But this is who you are."

I cover my face with my hands and sink down to the floor.

"No. No, it's not…"

And I want to blame Beth for being cowardly and weak.

Chapter Twenty-one

I want to blame Riley for being strong and a monster.

I want to blame Jason for being stupid, so stupid.

I want to blame Lisa for coming here.

I want to blame Matt for his poor, poor taste in men.

I want to blame Sukhy for going to the police.

I want to blame Sukhy for not using her taser.

I want to blame my mother for having me, for raising me, for not being able to stop me.

But I can't.

And after all of them are gone, the only person left is me.

This is what I am.

But still, why, why did she have to have me? Why did she have to go and do a thing like that?

I'm sobbing as she stands over me, not looking at me, rather down at Jason's body. She doesn't make a sound as I heave and cry and dig my nails into the sides of my face, swearing and gasping, "FUCK, fuck, fuuuuck!" Before I know it, I'm crying out, just like in my dream, "Mommy, Mommy, what am I going to do?"

The tears are hot and burn as she bends down and holds me in her long and bony arms, stroking my hair. I want to hear some comfort from her, something gentle, anything…

But then she says, "You're going to leave." She says it in that same flat voice. "You'll go far away from here and you won't come back."

"No, don't be crazy. We can't run away from—"

"I am staying right here," she said, "I'll get rid of this." She prods Jason's bloodless face with her foot. "And when the police come, which they will, I'll tell them this is my fault." She smiles, this time without teeth. Her thin lips pull together into a long and lonely smile, and for the first time I want to reach out and hold her.

"This is all my fault after all," she said. "I had to go and give birth to you." She sighs and rubs between her eyes, frowning. "Alright, there are a couple of things you need to do from this point onwards. Don't worry, I'm taking care of all of the hard stuff."

I didn't know what to say.

It was kind of like she'd opened the floor from under me.

"I have a storage vault in Woodbury. Remember, I drove us by there last year. Do you remember?" She waits for me to nod before she goes on. "I keep some cash, credit cards, contact information for some people who can help. You stay in the vault until a week after I'm arrested and my face and name is leaked to the papers." She cuts across me when I go to interrupt her. "Get some of your things, essentials, nothing sentimental, nothing big or electronic. Nothing that might draw suspicion. Then, you're going to need to re-open one of those horrible wounds on your arm on one of my knives. Leave it in your room and feel free to really go to town on it before you leave."

"Mother, no, this is too crazy—"

"Do as I say for once," she said coldly. "Just this once, for God's sake, Fiona. Can't you even do that?" I can see that her hands are shaking.

When I don't respond, she says, "You need to lay low for a while. I'm going to tell the police that I was responsible for all of it. I'm sure that bumbling young man has his theories anyway. I'll be vague about you, let the knife and the mess in your room speak for itself." She gets to her feet and brushes down her skirt. "You're going to get out of here and never come back." She takes my hands and pulls me to my feet. One hand gently brushes my hair behind my ear. "Grow up, try to be careful. Don't cut yourself anymore. Be smart about how you...play the cello, and you'll be just fine." She smiles that lonely smile again.

My legs are shaking as I take one of her knives and walk towards the stairs.

"Fiona," she calls after me. "If I can offer you one piece of advice, it would be to make sure you don't end up having a kid. That's where it all went wrong for me."

CHAPTER TWENTY-TWO

The noodles are stodgy and do not taste like barbecue beef, as the packet would suggest. I slurp them up and lean back against the sofa. The tv is on quiet and the signal is wonky. Is this how people lived before satellite, before Wi-Fi?

I fiddle with the antenna and watch my mother's face flashing across the screen. I enjoy lukewarm noodles that taste like shit while the whole story flashes before my eyes. I watch Sheriff Myerson, who looks way too old for any of this, explain the case.

He talks about two, now suspended police detectives, who were conducting an investigation on a member of the public, and their informant, a yet-to-be-named teenage girl, who was murdered last Thursday night along with her best friend and boyfriend. The two policeman's poor judgement and duty of care is discussed. However, their efforts and the deaths of these young people led to the capture of the notorious serial killer, Red Creek, now identified as Ms Sylvia Taylor, nee White, a local gardener and landscaper.

Lisa was found with a severe head injury but is otherwise unharmed. Well, as long as fucking Lisa is alright.

I wish she'd bothered to keep some beer in her creepy storage facility lair. I think I could use a drink now more than I ever had in my life. I lie back against the uncomfortable sofa and watch them cut to Sukhy's parents, stiff-faced and coldly weeping as they leave the police station, followed by Jason's father, who wears his baseball cap low over his eyes, clutching the hands of the twins, whose expressions are hidden beneath unruly hair.

Sukhy and Jason have not been formally named, but they can't avoid the issue of me.

"The daughter of the killer, is fifteen-year-old Fiona Taylor, she is believed to be one of the victims in the tragedy last Thursday night. Her body is yet to be uncovered."

Mother told you guys that she didn't have a daughter. According to the reports I read, she kept mumbling it over and over again and avoiding the question of my whereabouts whenever it came up.

I heard that the police have been looking for my body, digging up the woods, digging up the backyard, digging up the floorboards all over the house. They won't find me in any of those places, but my absence speaks louder than my bones ever could.

I mean, be realistic. The woman is a complete and utter psychopath, why would she stop short of killing her own child?

So do it.

Go on.

Dig up the woods, dig up the basement, do all the digging you want.

You won't find me there.

. . . .

Her face is everywhere. It's on all the papers. It leaks out at me from every corner. Her cold eyes meet mine on the television screen. In a way, It's comforting as well as creepy. It's like she's still watching over me.

I don't know if she'll get the chair.

She confessed as soon as they caught her. So, it's not like she can get away with it at this point. She confessed to Riley and Jason and Sukhy. She confessed to me. She is quiet and refined and chilling. By all accounts, this was definitely the person the psychiatrists and reporters all said Red Creek was from the start. People want to know how she did it, why she did it.

I heard something about an interview between her and Winnie Gails. I know Mother will be pleased about that.

Woodbury is pretty nice, it's like a classier version of my own shitty town. I sneak out of the lot every now and then, go to the arcade, go to the park or the mall. I mean, at first I was pretty scared—people have always said that the two of us have the same face, that we look like a younger and older version of the same person.

But Mother had accounted for that and so had I.

There were coloured contact lenses in the lair. I cut my hair when I got here, did a pretty bad job, but it passes. Short hair, heavy fringe. I even picked up some clunky looking glasses from the drug store. That and thanks to Jason breaking my nose, my resemblance to her is so slight that if someone asks, I can say something like, 'Oh yeah, we all look alike to you, Mr Progressive' while my heart nearly breaks my ribs.

I won't stay here for long. I borrowed some contact information from my mother and got in touch with a guy who is going to put some documents together for me. Something that says I'm nineteen and from Illinois. I'm going to California. I have some of her money. I'll find a place, get a job, keep my head down. Find something... new to do. I'll be free from her at last.

· · · ·

The man from the phone meets me in a parking lot of a seedy motel. I wear my hood up and smoke aggressively for twenty minutes waiting for him. Some dirty old man makes a pass at me on his way to his room, and I roll my eyes and move to a better lit area. I think fleetingly that he looks like that dirty old man from the woods that night and feel myself going to scratch old wounds.

I imagine Sukhy's hand on my arm and return my hand to its pocket.

There's no point in being scared now.

This is life.

I'm choosing not to be a child anymore.

Then I see my contact coming towards me from his smart red convertible. He looks like his picture, he is fat and in his early twenties or at least he was when Mother knew him. He wears a jacket that seems two sizes too small and waves in greeting when he sees me.

He doesn't talk much. I give him the cash, and he gives me my envelope with my new life all packaged away inside.

"You don't look much like her," he says finally as I turn to walk away. "I kind of thought you would."

"Well, that's probably for the best," I say. "Can I ask how you knew my mother?"

253

"She did right by me once," he says. "Put a bad man in a cell where he belonged, even if it was for the wrong thing. She was a strange woman. Gave me a beautiful garden..." He sighs and offers me a hand. "I don't like mess, kid. So, you best not be like her."

"Oh, I'm not," I say. "Any similarities are only skin deep."

He frowns at me, and I watch him go back to his car and drive off into the night.

· · · ·

In the morning, as my mother sits down to talk to Winnie Gails, I leave Fiona Taylor behind and Sookie King gets a bus to California with a bag full of emergency cash and a few changes of clothes. She ends up sat next to a dorky looking teenage boy who is watching the interview on his phone. His headphones are shit, so Sookie King gets to listen in when she wants to.

"So, when did this all begin for you, Sylvia, do you mind if I call you, Sylvia?"

"Oh, please do," she says. "I suppose it's just a part of myself I was always aware of, a little. But I didn't realise it properly until I was about thirteen. There was a supply teacher at my school who was incredibly rude and incompetent. She helped me, in a way, to put into action, something I suppose, I had always wanted to do."

The dorky teenage boy notices Sookie staring. Nervously, he takes out a headphone and offers it to her.

"Can you believe this?"

"No way," Sookie says and takes it, smiling like Beth did, "It's so weird she's getting like a platform to talk about this stuff. I mean, this is a mass murderer, not celebrity time with Ellen."

"I know, it's so fucked up," he says, laughing.

"So, our topics today are kind of limited while the investigation is still going on," Winnie Gails says, rolling her eyes, "So we are only allowed to talk about the murders at Red Creek."

"A subject you're an expert on now, Winnie."

"You mentioned before that you started killing at age thirteen, but this doesn't account for the death of little Bobbie White. You would have been...five-years-old at the time?"

Mother smiles her crocodile smile.

"I was a month shy of four, actually. We were playing in the woods by Read Creek and Robert—only Mother called him Bobbie—fell into the water. The water was running fast that day, and I watched him get mangled by the rocks. I didn't know how to describe what I had seen to my parents, so I just didn't."

"So, you didn't do it?"

"I am sure plenty of people have formulated their own ideas about what happened to my brother. Yours were particularly…imaginative. That detective from Franberg had a lot of ideas how I, at age three, was able to wrestle my brother, who was so much bigger and stronger than me, into the water and hold him under. That man had a lot of ideas about me. But that's the truth, whether you believe it or not. The damage done to my brother's body was worsened with water damage and age. I had no idea his remains were there, amongst the moss and the rocks where I concealed my victims' bodies."

"And, Sylvia, do you think witnessing such a violent act when you were so young may have influenced your…actions in later life?"

"It would be nice if that were true," she said. "But no. One of my earliest memories was, as you alluded in your first Red Creek novel, torturing insects. I would watch a line of ants and crush one in the middle with my thumb. By the time I was four, I had moved onto small animals, then larger ones, and then finally, at thirteen, I had found my purpose."

"Your purpose? So you have always felt a drive to hurt others?"

"Yes. It's something I gained more control over as I moved out of adolescence, but could never quite break the habit. It was nice to have the whole country in a frenzy from a tired little town like Franberg. It was exciting to outsmart the police and set up someone who really deserved to go to prison."

"Randall Kayne, of course. So, his story about how he nearly bested the killer in the woods, that was…"

"Oh, very much true," Mother says. "But I let him take the knife from me. I needed his prints all over it."

"And you knew about Mr Kayne, I hate to be probing, but did he ever…"

"No, Randall Kayne preferred little boys. It was completely distasteful. I had observed him with a classmate of mine when I was nine. We were on a school trip and the bus broke down. A few of us were hanging around a gas station, waiting for our parents to collect us. Myself and my classmate were the only two remaining. I disliked the company of others so had retreated to sit in the broken-down bus while the other child played outside. Randall Kayne had stopped to fill up his truck, and on seeing a little boy, all alone, he approached him. He bought him ice cream and kept finding ways to touch him, seemingly innocent, but it unsettled me. Fortunately, the boy's mother came for him soon after and Randall very quickly left. I knew what he was then."

"You knew?"

"One monster can always spot another."

"That's interesting. So, Sylvia, you said you enjoyed the attention you achieved as Red Creek?"

"Yes, it was a rush. Some kids have extra-curriculars like football or tennis, others have music or drugs. I had this. I had always thought of myself and others as insignificant, but I had made the whole country stop and look at me. I even had my favourite columnist write not one, but three books about me."

"Oh, you are too much," she says, laughing and shaking her head, tapping the glass between them as though it was my mother's shoulder. "So, I know I'm not allowed, and to reiterate, I am not asking about new victims or the new case, or anything like that. I'm just curious because I wrote a lot, well, you read them, a lot of psychological profiles about you. And in all that, I never expected you to be the maternal type."

I feel my heart sink.

Mother's face shows no reaction.

"I know, you can't talk about her here," Winnie Gails says, "But, I am surprised, I mean, fifteen years is a long time to be a mother. Heck, I passed my little bundles of joy along to Carly, my nanny before they could crawl. But not, you, you raised yours. You lived together for over a decade. Can I ask about your daughter? Her name was Fiona, right?"

Mother pauses. I see her hands wring together.

"I named her Fiona, after my grandmother."

"Your grandmother White?"

"Yes. She was the only person who tried to understand me when I was small."

"Were you close?"

"My grandmother and I? Not especially, she died when I was very young."

"No, you and your Fiona. Your daughter."

"Well, you know what teenagers can be like."

"I am being told we can't discuss this matter further," Winnie Gails says, looking noticeably irritated at somebody off-screen.

"I can tell you this," Mother says, "Fiona was my only weakness. And now she is gone."

· · · ·

Sookie's life, or rather, my life, is pretty decent. Sookie lives, or rather, I live in a loft apartment with two other girls, Letitia and Gabbie, just twenty minutes from the beach. The two of them are nice, kind of loud and chatty, one a college drop-out, the other a runaway with what I suspect is a fake ID, just like me. The landlord lives downstairs and has a lame obsession with superheroes. His walls are decked out in memorabilia, and he's too innocent to be a perv, so I sometimes head down there with Gabbie to watch movies.

I have a job as a waitress in a fake Hawaiian restaurant a few blocks away. The boss is nice, her name is Carmella, and she's pretty protective of me. She saw my old scars and broken nose and thinks I must have run away from some abusive relationship or whatever. It's nice to have someone watching my back, particularly as it took a few weeks for me to get used to waiting on tables.

It's hard work, but I get to wear a flower-crown while I'm taking orders and busing tables.

I think I'm getting used to my new home. It's a lot bigger and better than what I'm used to. I know a good place to get Chinese. I know pretty places to sit and chill out in the evening when the apartment gets too noisy or I want a moment to myself. I know all the shortcuts home. And now it's like I've never been anywhere else.

But, I sometimes check out how the others are doing.

It's not incriminating. It's the library computers downtown. One click onto my old high school's website and I can see that Beth went back to school and won her tennis competition at regionals this year.

She went to the prom with Jesse Macinera. The two of them look like a pair of baby politicians in the photos on the school website. Matt's secret Twitter account that he thought none of us knew about implies things worked out with Freddie Hankerson. I hope things stay that way.

He won't have me around to protect him anymore.

Sookie King looks out for Number One.

It's what Mother would have wanted.

Sookie is even getting better at responding to Sookie. Or rather, I am getting better at responding to Sookie.

I'm even finding it easier to let go of all of that crap from home. All of that panic, all of that rage. All of those nasty little urges.

. . . .

"Sookie, we are good for the rest of the shift now," Carmella says. "You should head home."

"You sure? I don't mind closing." I put down the empty plates and wipe ketchup from my thumb where it clung to the edge of the plate.

"No, we got this. You take care of yourself now."

Flower-crown comes off my head and into my backpack. Cigarette lit and I'm walking home. It's a nice clear night, you can see so many stars. I wonder what Sukhy would have made of them. I sometimes like to imagine she's here too. Like if Gabbie has gotten up and gone to work early, I see her empty bed and imagine Sukhy sleeping in it. I like to imagine we're both here, she's studying at college, and we meet up by the beach and skim rocks off the surface or lie down on the sand.

Guess you can take the girl out of a backwater, but she'll still have a part of it, that she'll miss.

"Young Fiona."

I freeze and turn to see beautiful Detective Brankowski stood staring at me, Clark Kent glasses off, mouth wide open.

"Fiona. Fiona, that's you, isn't it?"

And I can't find my voice.

Like it's stuck underneath me.

He reaches out and takes my hand, staring at me through my gas station glasses and clunky bangs.

"It is you."

Somehow, and I don't know how, I manage to make myself talk.
"Yes."

"What are you doing here?"

"I can't say. Look, you have to come with me. I know somewhere we can talk."

"Fiona, no, tell me what's going on."

"Please?" I say, squeezing his arm. "Please, I'll tell you everything. It's just around the corner."

He is reluctant, but he follows me. He doesn't let go of my arm. He holds on tight like he's afraid I'm going to disappear. But I won't. It seems almost funny when I think about all the times I kind of fantasised about him holding me like this. But that was another time, that was Fiona Taylor's thing.

I climb over a fence, and he follows with ease. I know all the nice quiet places to come when I want a moment to myself.

We step through the back door of the abandoned house on 23rd street. I can't actually believe my luck. I mean, I knew he was kicked off the force for involving a minor in his illegal investigation, but I didn't know he'd come to my new town to await the outcome of his tribunal. I didn't expect to just wander into him on my way home from work. And despite my best efforts, of course, of course, he recognised me. We have the same face, me and her. He stalked her for years, wrote notebook after notebook as he watched her carry that fucking cello case into the house, knowing what was in there—as if he wouldn't recognise her or me after a little dressing up.

"Fiona, what the hell is going on—"

He doesn't get to say much more before I jab Sukhy's taser into his throat.

．．．．

He is waking up, delirious and muttering, but he's back with us.

"You knew her better than that, better than any of them," I say. "I read your little notebook, I can't believe you're still carrying it around with you. God."

He groans and tries to get up.

"So, you know better than anyone that she wouldn't have kept me around for fifteen years if she'd ever intended to hurt me. You've seen us together, seen me act up and her just smile and put up with it. You know she couldn't have cut me up even if she'd wanted to."

He sways uncomfortably in his chair and tugs uselessly at his zip-tied hands.

"I wouldn't pull too hard if I were you."

He flinches when I lift his gun and point it at him.

"Figured they'd have taken this off you when you got kicked out of the force. I've never held one of these before, you know? Don't think I'd be a good shot."

"Fiona," he manages to say, the feeling coming back to his mouth. "Why are you doing this?"

"Oh come off it. Do you know how hard I had to work to set up shop here?" I say. "That's the thing about big, tough guys like you and Riley and Jason and I suppose that old man when he was young —you think that your physical presence is enough to protect you from coming into harm's way and you barge into people's lives without a second thought. You stalk around in the dark, calling me, 'Fiona, Fiona, it's alright, I'm here' and think that making yourself known to me was smart."

Don't look at me like that.

You were smart until you came to get me.

"Fiona."

"You knew she was a dangerous killer and you enlisted Sukhy to help you put her away. Did you even think there was a chance she could get hurt?"

He looks ashamed, and I'm glad for that at least.

"No, you didn't. Why are all adults so fucking stupid? You know, Detective, my mother used to be smart before she had me. Having people depend on you only holds you back. She did just fine before I was born. She never should have had me. We'd both have been better off." I take the safety off his gun. "As you're obsessed, I'm sure you know that she's going to prison for Sukhy and Jason and Riley and that old man, and those girls and all the rest. She's going down for her crimes as well. She's making news and history and everything. And she would never have been caught if it wasn't for me. I did a better job than you, really, didn't I? Fantasising about catching her and being a hero. It was a nice dream, sure, but you never acted on it. All you did was watch her and make little notes about when she moved her cello case back and forth. Look where that got you."

He struggles against the zip-ties.

"Let me go."

"Are you fucking serious?" I hold the gun against his head and make him go still. "How many people died while you waited and watched? Not very heroic of you, was it? I'll bet you had enough evidence to get a search warrant ages ago."

"I was just trying to stop her."

"You did a lousy job," I hiss at him. "Some detective. I mean, you didn't even notice that I killed Riley Sanders. You think she'd have ditched her cello that easily? You didn't even notice the people Jason killed and he was really fucking clumsy about it."

I hit him in the jaw with the gun as hard as I can to make him look at me.

"You..."

"Yes, me. I was always going to hurt someone, so it might as well have been a scum bag like Riley Sanders."

"Fiona, your mom is sacrificing her freedom for you," he says.

"What? You think that means anything to me?" I say, trying to hide my smirk. "I mean, sure, she did kill some of those people, but what, I'm supposed to feel bad that she's finally getting locked up for it?" I start to laugh, "What do I care? I'm just some dumb fifteen-year-old who hates her mother. Remember?"

He looks so miserable, it's like the world has opened underneath him.

"It really was stupid of you to call out to me," I said. "You should have just called in the police or something. I mean, ever since Sukhy died, I've had this really heavy heart, like a part of me is gone. I thought getting rid of Jason would fix it, but no, it wasn't enough. And really, it's because of you. I think I'll be able to let go of this whole mess, once you're gone."

I hold the gun against his head.

"Don't worry, I'll make it quick. I mean, it'd be pretty dumb of me to kill you Red Creek style, it's practically patented and y'know, now she's gone and taken the rap for all of my confirmed kills, it would be monumentally dumb of me to hack you into pieces like the others.

Hell, it could work too well and get the case against her thrown out completely. So, no, I won't hack you up. I'll make it gentle like you intended for it to happen. You even did me the favour of bringing your own murder weapon. Guns are heavy, aren't they? I know I said I haven't used one before, but at this range, I can't exactly miss."

"My partner will know I was killed."

"Maybe that would have been the case while you were investigating my mother, but now, I'm not so sure. I mean, why wouldn't you want to kill yourself?"

He looks like he's going to cry.

"You're a disgrace. You used a teenage informant in an investigation, and because of you, she died. I suspect her parents will be heartbroken. She had a bright future, you know. She was going to make something with herself. I wonder how much trouble you're in. Conscience wise, I'm doing you a favour by killing you."

"You don't know what you're talking about!"

"And besides," I interrupt him, "What would you have done? Gone to work? Found another case? Please. The Red Creek killer is in jail. What are you going to do with yourself now? You watched me, but you forget I watched you. You stood outside my house every day. Every day. Just doing your job, my ass. You were obsessed. Obsessed with catching the killer. Obsessed with my mother. I was kind of jealous, to be honest."

"You're going to end up just like her!" he says frantically.

"I might. But you won't be here for that, Red Creek was your life, and you wanted it to be perfect. As if your colleagues, your family, won't find those notebooks and think, 'Poor obsessed bastard, gone and lost his purpose in life. Boo hoo, so sad, too bad'."

He is muttering something under his breath.

I don't care what it is at this point.

"Sooo, sit back, settle in, maybe close your eyes. You know, I really did enjoy our little talks, Detective. I'm going to miss those. Don't take this too hard. You should think of it as some time off from perving on houses and taking fake walks around the neighbourhood."

"No! No!"

"Feel honoured, you'll be the last person I ever hurt," I tell him, finger twitching on the trigger. "I mean, probably."

Acknowledgements

I'd originally written Down Red Creek as two short stories, and though I was happy with both, I didn't feel finished with Fiona. I felt like she had more to say. So in November, 2018, I challenged myself to National Novel Writing Month (NaNoWriMo) and that's how Down Red Creek the novel came to be. First as bullet points, then as 45,000 words, then as a first proper draft.

Writing a novel has been my dream ever since I was six years old, so I have quite a few people to thank.

George, who sat with me every day during NaNoWriMo, to write after work. You read every draft—every one—even the one that was terrible! I count my lucky stars every day I have you in my life. I'm blown away by your work ethic and your creativity. You keep me sane. You encourage me. You always know how to me laugh. Thank you!

Amanda and Emily, who read the original short story. You kept reading, which made me want to keep writing. Meg, who listened to me rant every lunch break for three years. Your love of books made me want to write one you could enjoy. And thank you for letting me borrow your name for our handsome young detective.

Joy, who made me believe that my gory little book could be a very good gory little book. Ian, who wanted to see what Fiona did next and helped me get serious about getting published. Mark from Sulis International Press, for sending me the most exciting email of my life (so far), thank you for taking a chance on me.

My brother, Ieuan, for always making the time to talk through ideas with me—I could tell when I had your attention with this one, because you insisted 'no spoilers'. My sister, Charlotte, who made me want to write a book that you couldn't put down.

Kate, who got so excited reading this book you had me wanting to go back and read it all over again. You continue to be very tall and brilliant and inspiring to me. You've always pushed me to follow my dreams instead of just sticking to an 8-5.

And finally, to my incredible parents, Paul and Lesley Llewellyn. You've encouraged me to write ever since I could hold a pen. My first fans, you've always read every scrap of paper I've passed over to you, even when it's been a bit on the gory side. I wouldn't be where I am today without you. Thank you for everything.

About the Author

Rachael Llewellyn is an English writer living in Wales, where is is about to start her PhD exploring memory and folklore in the novel. Her work aims to challenge its readers in its uncomfortable social and moral themes. 'Down Red Creek' is her debut novel.

Impulse Control, **Book Two of the Red Creek Series** coming soon.

Read an excerpt at the end of this book. Join the Sulis Newsletter for preorder and publication dates. https://sulisinternational.com/subscribe/

If you enjoyed this book, please consider leaving an online review. The author would appreciate reading your thoughts.

Visit the author's website at

Subscribe to thee author's newsletter at

You can also follow the author on Twitter at @FumigatedSpace

About the Publisher

Sulis International Press publishes fine fiction and nonfiction in a variety of genres. For more, visit the website at
https://sulisinternational.com

Subscribe to the newsletter at
https://sulisinternational.com/subscribe/

Follow on social media
https://www.facebook.com/SulisInternational
https://twitter.com/Sulis_Intl
https://www.pinterest.com/Sulis_Intl/
https://www.instagram.com/sulis_international/

IMPULSE CONTROL

An Excerpt from
Book Two of the Red Creek Series

On my lunch break, I find out that they are making a movie about her.

A movie.

I mean, she's probably never going to see it. If they have movie nights in prison, I doubt it'd be anything with even the suggestion of violence. I bet it's just a lot of Disney movies on repeat forever. I suppose that's kind of like torture?

But she'll know it's out there. Her movie.

I dread to think what it will do for her ego.

Maybe she'll find out from one of those trashy magazines, or through her secret cell phone, or maybe her gal-pal (total hack journalist/author Winnie Gails) told her months ago.

But yes, my mother is the inspiration for a three-hour Hollywood feature about her life choices.

And yes, the film has already accumulated a fair chunk of controversy. For one, the victims' families are all still out there, protesting that it's in very poor taste to make a movie about Red Creek. Particularly as the director leading the project is known for movies that stylise gore and violence. I doubt that this movie is going to deal with the way 59 people died with dignity, sensitivity or caution.

Additionally, there has been criticism that making a film about a serial killer – particularly a living one – glamorises the things that they did. That this film is in particularly poor taste as the killer known as Red Creek was only caught six years ago.

One online search and you can find people all over the internet saying that the final victims' families deserve longer to grieve – that it's morally wrong to force these people to face a heavily stylised version of their loved one's death up on the big screen. But as usual, for every one of the protestors, you can find ten more people saying 'Well, they don't have to go and see the movie though'.

The element that has caused the most controversy, however, is the fact that they cast Scarlett Johannson to play Sarah White / Sylvia Taylor as an adult.

I wonder who will get to play me. Probably someone hot and, like in their early thirties and barely able to pass for a high-schooler. I have never been the type to dwell on who would play me in the movie version of my life.

So I'm pretty much on board with the people in the comments saying that the movie shouldn't be made at all.

Winnie Gails is a creative consultant.

Oh, fuck me.

· · · ·

At some point in your life, someone will tell you to try to find a career where you can do what you love. It's why they force those dumb career aptitude tests on you in middle school. It's why they started going loco about college credit on your first day of high school.

You go to school, you do the whole college thing, you do some jobs along the way, something in retail or bussing tables, but then you find your *forever* job. The job that you love and you love going to work for. Maybe you start your own business, or you get to play Captain America at Disney World, or you become a professional athlete or... Well, nobody thinks of their forever career, their best life, sat around in an office, surrounded by dull paperwork, getting calls from dull people with complaints or an inability to process basic information.

They tell you to do something you love, sure, but you're a kid then. One day you grow up, you realise that the whole 'Do what you love thing' is horseshit.

As I look around my office, the bright Santa Cruz sun blaring offensively in through the back windows, I try to imagine that anyone here would have imagined *this* as their forever career. Behind me is Tanya, playing Fantasy Football and trying to sell her Ikea coffee table on Facebook, using one of the student applications as a makeshift fan. Rajish is by the printer, low-key on his phone. Kiko is doing her lipstick using the black mirror of her computer screen.

I watch Claudia from her seat across from me. She is subtly giving herself a manicure and at a guess, possibly googling holidays because she mentioned the prices of hotels in Peru ten minutes ago. Behind her, I can see Jack, our *amazing* boss, rolling himself a cigarette and humming loudly.

In the desk next to me, there is Donnie, who has been looking at the same Excel spreadsheet for twenty minutes – this is a cover of course, for the fact that he's on Tinder on his phone, under the table.

I bet none of them imagined that their lives would turn out this way.

"Claudia, coffee?" Jack says as he heaves himself upright and breezes past the rest of us to the front door.

"You'd like a coffee?" she asks, shoving her nail file under the keyboard.

"That's what I said, isn't it?"

He slams the door behind him, and Claudia flips him the bird once his back is turned, before getting up to her desk, muttering under her breath as she makes her way over to the kettle.

"Sonova bitch, he should shove his coffee," she mutters. "Can you believe him?" she asks when she notices me watching. "He never asks anyone else to make him his fucking coffee."

"Hey, you forget that I'm his cigarette mule," I say. "The man hasn't brought his own cigarettes in months. His wife gives him three in the morning, he smokes them on the drive to work, and by 10, it's 'Oh, Sookie, can I nick a smoke?'"

"You should tell his wife, man," Donnie says.

"Oh, right, sure, I'll tell his wife."

"You should, you're like his cigarette woman, it's basically cheating," he says, shaking his head. "It's sordid."

"Why don't you tell his wife, Donnie?" Claudia asks. "Since you're such a good friend of theirs."

"I saw them at the hardware store once," he corrects. "That doesn't make us friends."

"Woah, that's cold," she says. "At last year's Christmas party, you basically went home with them."

"Excuse me, nobody needs that particular image in their heads," Rajish calls from the far side of the room.

"Sorry, Rajish." Claudia puts down a mug of coffee onto Jack's desk before flopping back into her own and letting out a heavy sigh. The nail file comes back out from under her keyboard, and she leans back before going at her nails with a newfound ferocity.

The door opens, and Jack strolls back inside, reeking of *my* cigarettes and takes a sip of his brand-new coffee without thanking Claudia. After a moment of leaning back into his chair, he spots Kiko applying a second coating of bright red lipstick and moves to loudly berate her in front of everyone.

Of Jack's management style, we are kind of dead inside.

I don't think anyone planned their forever job to be like this.

I would be depressed that this is how I'm spending my life. Only I'm not. It could be worse.

I have a fake name, a fake high school diploma, in real terms, I don't even have one full year of high school education, so getting a job like this is actually a relief. It would be too risky to apply for college with fraudulent paperwork. There are too many facts to check, too many questions that could be raised. I didn't really mind.

My desire to go to college died a long time ago.

I think the whole 'What are you doing with your life' thing is only on my mind because today is actually my birthday. I'm twenty-one, despite what it says on my ID.

Twenty-one. I know, big birthday.

The last big birthday before society dictates that I get snippy about my age. So yeah, it's my birthday, but nobody knows. Not because I'm prone to early self-consciousness about my age or I'm ridiculously private or whatever – it's because technically all the documentation that exists around me states that I'm twenty-five years old and that my birthday was four months ago.

To be more accurate, and accuracy is important - *Sookie King*, had her twenty-fifth birthday four months ago. However, *Fiona Taylor*, soon to appear in a major motion picture about the Red Creek Killer (played by some white girl presumably), believed to have been murdered over five years ago, turns twenty-one today.

I'm not celebrating for obvious reasons.

Though, as I do every year, I'll buy a doughnut on my way home as a makeshift-just-for-me birthday cake. Why not embrace the two birthday's thing a little, like the Queen of England or one of those girls from *My Super Sweet Sixteen* who spread their birthday out over six months?

Work finishes for the day. I end up staying late because the mother of a student will not get off the phone. Jack turns out the light on his way out even though he can see me still sat there. So, I sit in near darkness, tapping my pen on the desk.

It's not the first time this has happened, not even with this particular woman. She wants to know her daughter's grades, she doesn't have permission to check these, but every few months tries, anyway. She doesn't trust her child to be honest with her about how she's doing in school, and if I was her daughter, I wouldn't want her to know that I'm failing either.

Eventually, I get bored, so I pretend the connection is bad so I can hang up.

The hallway outside is empty, except Greta, the cleaner, who is scrubbing away at a blood stain on the floor.

"Kid came out of Chem 1 with a nosebleed," she says to me. "Pretty gory stuff."

"Ew, not nice. Hope it doesn't keep you late, Greta."

She won't get it out like that.

But this is information that I keep to myself.

· · · ·

Part of what pushed me to apply for work at this college – other than their policy of hiring people with nothing further than a high school education – was its proximity to my apartment. It's always a short walk home, so staying late never pisses me off that much. I stop off at the shitty supermarket at the end of my road to buy a jelly doughnut and some beers for the fridge. I'm planning on spending this birthday night in, possibly watching a bad movie. Nothing by a certain director and nothing with any slashers.

Tickle me put off.

The cashier asks me for ID and says, "Twenty-five, really?"

I got that for a while. Always the moment of panic at the beginning, age fifteen, terrified that the person behind the counter would call out my ID for what it was. F-A-K-E.

But no, I paid good money to become Sookie King. So, the most I get is a disbelieving roll of the eyes or a 'Seriously?' but otherwise, leave unexposed.

"Yeah, twenty-five," I say. "Haven't lost my baby face yet." I pinch my own cheek and he laughs, shaking his head.

"Man, I don't remember the last time someone asked to see my ID."

"Blessing and a curse," I say, "Have a nice night."

I take my brown bag of birthday treats and stroll home. There are a couple fighting outside a café, a drunk old guy wandering around, muttering to himself. My apartment is across the street. My flatmate Leda is out, but I can hear the TV is on.

Believe it or not, I actually hate the idea of living alone. I've never been able to do it. I lived with my mother, and then I lived with room-mates. I met Leda through my friend Gabbie. Leda is nice and very beautiful, but a complete scatter-brain. With very little prompting, I can make her think that we were hanging out all night – you know, if anyone asks.

Often, there's also Leda's ex-girlfriend, Tammy, the worst person in the world, so more frequently than not, there are actually three of us. Tammy is kind of a sponge, she sits around the apartment when nobody's home like a really greedy burglar alarm. She watches our Netflix and eats all the toast. They have been off/on for the last two years. Personally, I wouldn't mind if they were permanently 'off', but on this matter, I get zero say.

So when I come home to the TV on and the smell of popcorn, I know that Leda and Tammy are 10/10 back on.

I climb the stairs from the front door to the living room and find Tammy sprawled out on the couch, wearing the big blanket and eating an enormous bowl of popcorn. She looks up when she sees me and waves, leaning back on the couch.

"Hey, Sookie, did you know you guys are out of milk?"

"Woah, seriously," I say.

Tammy never contributes anything but is quick to point out when the apartment is missing something.

I kick off my sneakers and leave them on the rack.

"Oh yeah, I texted Leda about it earlier. She should be home in an hour. Hey, have you seen this documentary? It's about people who get their pets to enter talent contests and stuff. It's totally wild."

"No, what?"

I glance up from the fridge and spot a Persian cat sat in the middle of a red carpet, glaring at a wild-haired old man, trying to lure it along the literal cat-walk with a plush fish on a stick to little effect.

"This is the weirdest fucking thing I've ever seen," Tammy says, laughing. "Want to watch with me?"

"Thanks, Tammy, but it's been a long day, and cat-walk pets are a tad too weird for me right now."

"Suit yourself," she says, leaning back into the sofa. "But on a less long day, you should totally check this out. There are like twelve episodes, and I literally cannot see how."

I leave her chuckling to herself as I take my beer and my doughnut to my room and kick the door shut behind me, drowning out the rustling of popcorn and displeased meows of the contestants.

. . . .

In TV and movies and stuff, serial killers keep their bedroom two possible ways. Either, it's like a cliché, there's photos of victims and actual murders pinned up like wallpaper, or the murderer is a complete minimalist. You know, like you go into their room and there's like a bed, plain white sheets, blinds, a really organised desk and a wardrobe with like a variant of the same outfit. Maybe there's a handful of books about Satan or Nazis or Japanese prison camps or something else super unpleasant. The books are usually tucked away so that later on when the police come and do a really thorough scouring of the room, they find them and get like, 'Oh, yeah, here's our sicko alright'.

My room fits neither stereotype. For one, what kind of idiot would keep evidence in their damn bedroom? For two, I have always found the whole minimalist thing to be difficult and pretentious. Also for the record, why would a serial killer own white bed sheets? It's almost like owning a white car and then getting pissed when it gets dirty, which it will, every time you drive *anywhere*. My desk is a kind of organised chaos, my tablet is propped against a pile of books – notably not books about Satan or prisoner of war camps, you know, normal books, about coming of age losers or inventors or lonely women going on holiday and finding love with a hunky barman/waiter.

My wardrobe looks like a bloated holidaymaker, bright flashes of blouses and skirts popping through the doors and spilling across the desk chair and the bed. I relocate the ones on the bed to the chair and flop down on my bed, readjusting the cushions and leaning down.

"Happy Birthday, Taylor," I say to myself, taking out the doughnut and carefully biting in to avoid getting jelly all over me.

My second phone buzzes.

Only one person has the number, of course, so I know who it's from.

I take it out of my bag and glance at the screen.

From M:
Happy Birthday.
I hope you are staying out of trouble.

I smile, despite myself, and text her a picture of my birthday doughnut and beer to which she responds with a thumb's up emoji.

From M:
Goodnight

I lean back against the pillows and close my eyes as I finish my doughnut, fishing for my tablet to put something rubbish to watch. As birthday's go, this one has been ok. Minimal annoyance at work. Minimal annoyance at home. The most birthday card a mother can send her allegedly dead child.

I don't mind no presents or anything fancy.

She's done more than enough for me.